I wanted my sister Gerry *not* to fall in love with the first man who was different from her own kith and kin—different from the lean, sun-browned men of Australia and the soft-tongued amusing men of Ireland who occasionally came our way. She would meet lots of other men and I didn't want her to lose her heart to a sailor for fear he had a girl on every ship. I was filled with pity and care for Gerry—until the dance was over.

When the dance was over, Gerry sported not a broken heart but a large cigarette burn in my beautiful blue dress—the one I didn't really want to lend her. The scene that followed could hardly be called mild and Sam went up on deck and disowned us both. So I went to bed and cried. Not because my blue dress was spoiled but because Sam had left me.

I was certain that life would never be the same again. . . .

NOBODY READS JUST *ONE* LUCY WALKER!

THE BELL BRANCH

Lucy Walker

BEAGLE BOOKS • NEW YORK
An Intext Publisher

TO THE MEMORY OF
HELEN AND MAY CREETH

AUTHOR'S NOTE

The adventures of the Montgomery family abroad are the kind of adventure that might have happened . . . but did not. They are written in the first person to give a verisimilitude that is, in fact, a fiction in itself. There were never any such persons as Gerry, Reggie, the three teachers of St. Hilda's, or the Vicar. There was never any St. Hilda's at all. I feel sorry about that myself.

ACKNOWLEDGMENTS

The author wishes to thank Messrs. Faber & Faber Limited for permission to use the lines from James Joyce's *A Flower Given to My Daughter* (published in *Pomes Penyeach*).

Published by arrangement with the author and the author's agent, Paul R. Reynolds, Inc.

First printing: July 1972

Printed in the United States of America

BEAGLE BOOKS, INC.
101 Fifth Avenue, New York, NY 10003

CHAPTER ONE

The Montgomery family was lining the wharf and looking up at the deck of the ship. They were looking for Gerry. The expressions on their faces changed gradually from eagerness to query. Where was Gerry? It wasn't like Gerry to hide her light behind a bushel of passengers nor her wit in flashes of silence. Gerry, of all the Montgomeries, was the one most likely to be hanging from the funnel in her eagerness to be the first to see home and where the river flowed down from the hills, through Pepper Tree Bay, into the vast illimitable distances of the Indian Ocean.

Gerry wasn't with us, and Sam and I couldn't shout the whole story over the lessening space of oily harbour water as the ship slowly heaved itself towards the wharf.

Sam wasn't the shouting kind, anyway.

Sam and I had been married on a morning in September two years earlier. In our part of the world, down under, September is spring. There had been a shine on the river when we came outside, so that the brilliance dazzled my eyes and I couldn't see Sam for seeing the sun, and seeing my unexpected wisdom in marrying him.

We had had our wedding reception. That was at my sister Vicky's house because Vicky had more money than the rest of us and moreover she had good taste in decorations and food. Both mattered to the Montgomeries. Mama had a new gold lace dress with a little lace jacket to make it fit for a day wedding. For years afterwards, after Sam and I came back from England, we were, several of us, destined to take it in turns to wear Mama's gold dress for evening wear—without the jacket, of course.

After the wedding reception Sam and I went back to 'Forty-five' to get my cases. The house was empty because everyone was at Vicky's. I remember that I came out on the veranda and pulled the door behind me. It shut with a little slam. I remember thinking:

'Thank God that life's over. The scramble . . . the noise . . .'
I wanted to say to Sam, 'Thank you for rescuing me.' But

somehow I couldn't. I was just a little ashamed that I needed rescuing.

All that was on a Saturday. On the Monday Sam and I were going to England so that he could take a research degree at London University. We had our fares, Sam's fees and very little more. It never occurred to us to be afraid. We had ourselves. Being a Montgomery, it never occurred to me that all would not be well in the best of possible worlds.

What we didn't bargain for was the general evacuation from Pepper Tree Bay of the Montgomery family. Well, nearly all of them . . . to England. There had been bland talk of Mama following us. Mama would 'get a job' too. We knew that Vicky and her husband David were going on the 'grand tour' in any event. We didn't know about Gerry until we reached Fremantle on the Monday of our departure. Mama and Vicky and Denney were waiting for us at a little café for our last afternoon tea together.

'Go on, Mama, you tell her,' said Denney. There was a look of mischievous triumph about Denney's great violet eyes.

'What is she up to?' I thought.

'Tell me what?' I demanded. Sam and I kept touching one another under the table until Mary said, 'For Heaven's sake . . .' and Denney said, 'Can't I go somewhere else and have tea by myself? I can't stand broody people.'

'What are you going to tell me?' I asked haughtily. I had visions of the ship cancelling its sailing, or of the University cancelling Sam's leave.

'Gerry is going to England, too,' Mary said matter-of-factly.

Nothing about Gerry ever surprised me. If someone in the family had been taking off for the moon, Gerry would have essayed to deflect the limelight momentarily to herself. She would have announced her intention of circumnavigating the globe in a submarine.

'What on?' I asked laconically, meaning, of course, on what money.

'On the *Moreton Bay* . . . same as you,' Denney said with wicked anticipation of my indignation.

'*Mama!*' I burst out. 'She's *not*. You're not to let her.'

Mama undid one's indignation by looking defeated and a little tragic.

'I can't stop her,' she said sadly. 'David lent her the money.

6

A hundred pounds!'

I looked at Vicky accusingly.

'*David lent her a hundred pounds*!'

Vicky shook her head haughtily.

'Why not? David thinks Gerry is the pick of the whole bunch. He thinks she should have her chance . . .'

'He didn't know she was going to book on the *Moreton Bay*,' Mary said in that small voice that meant the pouring of oil on troubled waters. 'She didn't mean it herself. It was a cancellation . . . and there's not another berth to be had for six months.'

'When did she do this?' I demanded.

'This morning.'

'This morning! Good heavens. What is she going to look like? She won't have any clothes.'

'There's always yours,' said Denney. 'It wouldn't be the first time . . .'

'*Mama* . . .' I implored.

'You've got Sam now,' said Denney. 'Why don't you appeal to him!' But Sam was laughing quietly to himself as if the whole thing were a joke.

'Don't you *mind*?' I said.

'Not very much,' he said. 'I don't think you will either . . . once you've got used to the idea. Gerry's amusing . . .'

I'd wanted to be alone with Sam on the ship . . . in the kind of a way that didn't matter. It would matter with a member of the family on board. Why did they spoil everything?

'You ought to have more control over Gerry,' I said to Mama, accusingly.

'I never had any control over any of you,' she said. 'You're all wilful and stubborn . . . except perhaps . . .'

She was going to say 'Mary' but remembered in time that it didn't help Mary with the family to be singled out for praise.

Gerry did not come near us as the ship pulled out of harbour. Maybe she was waiting for the fires of my wrath to set with the sinking sun.

When Sam and I had fixed our table with the dining saloon steward we went below to our cabin . . . and there was Gerry sitting cross-kneed on the bunk; a cigarette in her hand. She looked like a dark Helen half reclining there, the white oval of her face showing nothing of her wit but everything of her

7

Irish handsomeness. She looked so like our cousin Laura, the real dark Helen of our family, that she quite smote my heart for a minute. I softened.

'We've booked in the second sitting. You can come if you want,' I said.

'The other side of the dining saloon, thank you,' she said coldly. 'The prospect of you and Sam honeymooning does not enchant.'

'Then what did you come for?' I sat down and lit a cigarette, too.

'Hullo, Gerry!' Sam said in his kind voice that said he bore ill-will to no one: if anything he was a little fond of Gerry.

'Lo, Sam!' she said. 'Hope I'm not a niusance, and all that . . .'

'Not yet, anyway,' said Sam. 'One never knows with you, Gerry.'

'You don't have to own me,' Gerry said brightly. 'After all, we haven't even got the same name, have we? Theodora! What is she? Mrs Sam Richardson! Who is to confuse that name with anything as illustrious and ear-shattering as Geraldine Rory Montgomery?'

I blew smoke rings in silence while Sam started to unstrap a portmanteau. This was altogether too peaceable for Gerry.

'Richardson . . . !' she said. Richardson! Theodora Richardson! You know I ever only knew two people called Richardson. One was a policeman and the other was a butler,' said Gerry.

I looked at Gerry with concentrated venom but said nothing. I don't think Sam heard.

The next day *mal de mer* kept me imprisoned in a deck chair where the wind off the sea would touch my face but not penetrate the rugs Sam dug in around me. Gerry had come lurching along the heaving deck but stopped short of my chair to lean over the rails and look out over the deep Prussian blue of the sea.

Someone, another passenger, came our way and looked first at me and then at Gerry. She leaned over the rails and spoke to Gerry.

'Would you be sisters?' she asked. 'There seems a likeness . . .' Gerry turned round and glanced at me coolly.

'My name is Montgomery. Geraldine Rory Montgomery,' she said. 'You could perhaps find out the other lady's name from the back of her deck chair.'

Mal de mer was the only thing in the world that mattered to me. I didn't mind about names or that Peter's sister must also have heard the cock crow thrice. I didn't even mind very much if the ship turned turtle and we all drowned,

CHAPTER TWO

Pepper Tree Bay is so remote. It isn't really in the big world. It is another little world all of its own. A thousand miles of desert to the north and east. The Antarctic to the south and the rolling Indian Ocean to the west.

Leaving it, sailing through that dense blueness in ever-increasing heat towards the lands of one's reading was so much a dream one could hardly believe in it all. One certainly didn't believe a war would some years hence devastate it. So far the world was rosy and inviting.

Asia! Europe! They were dream lands to be discovered only in print. To marvel and wonder at. And here were Sam and I, and Gerry Montgomery, doing that incredible thing . . . sailing into them. We were leaving behind the Bay and the river and the yellow sands; the sun-beaten stockmen of the north; the gold diggers, the well-sinkers and the laughter-loving, easy-going children of Pepper Tree Bay.

Life on the ship was static. Impossible there would come a day when the doctor's pretty wife would be a nobody walking down the Strand; or the masses of Trafalgar Square not part their lanes for Jimmy Renderruth to pass between. It was outside the realms of possibility that people would not know that Jimmy Renderruth had even passed that way. He stood for thirteen million acres of sheep and cattle land.

On the other side of the bar lounge another group had taken possession. They were the young unmarrieds. Some were husband-hunting and some were fun-hunting. It was to this circle the ship's officers drifted in their immaculate whites and it was here, within forty-eight hours, that Gerry had taken command.

Sam and I didn't quite belong. We were shy of attaining the married status and being married were of no interest to the unmarrieds, who were so exclusively occupied in the eternal game played with bold eyes and swishing skirts that once was played behind a fan; and from around the corners of the ample bosoms of chaperones.

I longed for Saturday. On Saturday I would have been married a week. I would emerge from the shyness and embarrassment of having to say 'four days' when asked. It seemed terrifically important really to get a firm footing on the married status. It seemed to me that it would be a wonderful thing to have been married two months. I'd be a veteran then. That was a long time away.

Gerry, true to her word, disowned us. When anyone commented on the likeness she said laconically:

'How quaint! Must be something to do with the air around Pepper Tree Bay.'

Or:

'Possibly we're all descended from the same emigré Irish.'

Or worse:

'Must be the convict streak!'

This I received with ire. I had had to go abroad to discover the old world thought we were all black fellows or descended from convicts.

'What will I do about Gerry?' I wailed to Sam. 'Sooner or later they'll all know we're sisters. They'll wonder what sort of a family we are.'

'They won't be able to say you're not imaginative,' he said with a grin. 'And nobody will be left in any doubt as to the wonders of Pepper Tree Bay.'

This brought home to me the fact that I talked too much about Pepper Tree Bay . . . so I stopped.

'What would you do if Gerry was your sister?' I asked.

'Leave her alone. That's only Gerry's way of showing she is embarrassed by our existence too.'

I smoked two cigarettes in succession and thought about that. It was hard to believe Gerry was embarrassed about anything, but Sam insisted he was right. Sam was nearly always right and I hardly ever was, so I gave in to him. In the meantime Gerry had lassoed the Third Officer.

He was a nice tall naval type with fair hair, clear-cut features, a firm chin and a way of being amused at Gerry that didn't give her too much licence.

'Seems to me the Third dances with Gerry more often than with anyone else,' I said to Sam.

'They look so well together.'

'But they can't see that. They don't look at themselves.'

'Well, I'll ask them why they do it, shall I?'

'Sam, don't be an ass!'

'Well, stop worrying about Gerry. She's disowned you—that relieves you of worrying.'

'I'm not worrying, only wondering.'

'Same thing with you, dear.'

I began to see Gerry's point about disowning the family. I couldn't keep my eyes off her. If I thought the drinks steward went too often to the table where Gerry sat at the centre of a galaxy of seamen and pretty girls I found myself craning my neck to see how often he set a glass in front of her.

'Gerry, you won't have any money left . . . you shouldn't drink often . . . or much. You're only twenty . . .'

'I'm thirsty,' Gerry said.

She was sitting on Sam's bunk and we were eating sandwiches left by the steward last thing at night. This was the only time of the day Gerry came near us.

'Anyhow,' she added. 'It's not my money. It's the Third's.'

'Don't lose your heart to a ship's officer,' I said. 'Every girl does that. He'll have a girl on every voyage.'

'Think so?'

Gerry lifted dark, inscrutable eyes to me. Something in them smote my heart.

'She couldn't be serious about him . . .' I groaned to Sam after Gerry had gone.

'You can see Gerry's point in not wanting an elder sister hanging over her,' Sam said.

'Why doesn't he do any work?'

'He does. You just don't notice when he works. You only notice when he's in the bar lounge.'

I reflected that that was probably so. It was clear that Sam was on Gerry's side in this matter of independence. I lay on my back and thought about it.

If I had been Gerry I wouldn't have wanted an elder sister watching over me. I had sudden visions of Vicky playing the chaperon to me. I gurgled with laughter. The thought was ludicrous. I always felt superior to Vicky. Perhaps Gerry felt that way towards me . . . Perhaps all sisters feel superior to one another.

'Do you know what Gerry has in that glass every time the steward sets it down?' Sam asked.

'God knows,' I said. My reply was a mixture of anxiety and despair.

'Dry ginger-ale. The Third sees to it.'

'My love to the Third,' I said with relief. 'He can stick around as much as he likes, if he looks after Gerry that way.'

At Colombo I was torn between the excitement and wonder of being in the real East and irritation with Mama. The mail boat brought out a terse cabled command:

'*Look after Gerry. Love to you all.*'

'She might as well ask me to look after a rattlesnake,' I said to Sam.

I was feeling that way.

The night before had been the ship's dance before landfall. Gerry had come to my cabin and quietly leafed through my brief wardrobe.

'You don't need the blue dress,' she said. 'Blue is a bait for catching a man and you've got yours.'

It was a special dress and I was waiting a special occasion to wear it. It was a sweet soft dress, draped across the bosom Grecian fashion, with long trailing tulles and a spangled belt.

'Not *that* one,' I said, already resigned to lending her one of my frocks, and since we were officially unrelated, of not being able to wear it on a subsequent occasion.

Gerry had taken it down from the hanger and was holding it against herself.

'I'll have to try it on here,' she said. 'I can't be seen leaving your cabin too often.'

'You won't try it on anywhere,' I said tersely.

But Gerry had already pulled off her white linen dress and begun to slip the blue chiffon over her head. It fitted perfectly, as I knew it would. She kicked off her shoes and put on my silver ones and stood in front of the mirror combing back her hair.

Gerry had the beauty of youth, and the dress gave her a faint faraway-ness that suddenly brought home to me the old heart-burning days of loves that were gone and not quite forgotten. In Gerry's face reflected in the mirror I saw my own as it had once been, eager, but with a haunting doubt at the back of the blue eyes. So often we look at love in other people with nothing more than a sly interest; or at the best a whimsical humour. But love isn't funny to those in love and shouldn't be funny to the onlookers.

I gave in.

'If it weren't for Mama . . . I wouldn't,' I said with a bad grace.

Gerry had looked lovely in the blue dress. Better than I would have done. She was tall and swayed a little when she walked. The dress lent grace to gracefulness, and silhouetted against the immaculate 'whites' of the Third it was a beautiful colour.

There were coloured lights and the fantastic mystery of the tropic night. The ship glided over the Indian Ocean which was as flat and still as a land-locked pond. Other ships passed us now, their lights a necklace of dancing diamonds hung under the dark, star-ridden sky. There was music and laughter and the clink of glasses. There was the Captain asking me for a dance and Sam taking a turn at the piano to play his own version of Chopin.

It was a night one had waited for all one's life.

Then we went to the Purser's cabin for drinks.

'What is the Third Officer's real name?' I asked. It hadn't occurred to me to ask before.

'Arbuthnot. Reggie Arbuthnot.'

I looked beseechingly over my glass top at Sam. My eyes meant to tell him that a name like that wouldn't suit a Montgomery. Look at Laura! Laura had turned down one suitor after another because if she couldn't marry his eyes or the way he took his meals, she couldn't marry his name.

Sam grinned.

'Is he a lady's man?' I asked the Purser.

'That's not a fair question to ask at sea,' he countered as he lit a cigarette for me. 'But he seems to have got this one rather badly.'

I couldn't excuse the bad taste of my question because I couldn't tell him that Gerry was my sister. I caught a hint of a smile in the Captain's eyes and I wondered if he guessed. Much later in my life I discovered that Captains of ships, especially small ships, knew all about their passengers, and probably the Captain and the Purser knew all about Gerry and me. It probably served as quite a diversion to watch the little family play we enacted for them from Fremantle to Southampton.

In the mellowness of this night, however, I only wanted Gerry not to fall in love with the first man who was different from her own kith and kin; different from the lean, sun-browned men of Australia and the soft-tongued amusing men of Ireland who occasionally came our way. She would meet lots and lots of others like Reggie Arbuthnot from now on. I

13

didn't want her to lose her heart to a sailor for fear he had a girl on every ship. I didn't want her to lose her heart and be hurt at all. I was filled with pity and care for Gerry. That is, until the dance was over.

When the dance was over Gerry sported not a broken heart but a large cigarette burn in the skirt of my beautiful blue dress.

The scene that followed could hardly be called mild and Sam went up on deck and disowned us both. So I went to bed and cried. Not because my blue dress was spoiled but because Sam had left me.

I was quite certain that life would never be the same again.

In the morning I thought of Gerry as a rattlesnake. And meant it. Sam and I were sufficiently reconciled to want to go off on a rickshaw instead of with a Cooks Tour of Lavinia and Kandy.

The affair of Gerry and the Third, like all the other affairs on board settled down to a seriousness that made one think that either the ship must keep on sailing for ever or that life on land must subsequently become a continuation of it. The loves on ship-board were passionate and indestructible and to the people concerned it was unthinkable there should be a period to them.

One day we were sitting on the deck near the officers' quarters when the Third came out of the gangway and sat in a deck chair looking for-ard. He hadn't turned his head and did not see that Gerry was in a deck chair a little aft of him. Gerry did not stir but sat watching him. From where she sat she could only have seen the back of his neck and head above the chair. I sat idly watching Gerry, wondering why she did not speak to him. Presently I saw a look almost of sorrow on Gerry's face. I knew she was just letting herself sit and love the back of Reggie Arbuthnot's head in the kind of way that was so heartfelt it was almost sad.

Presently Gerry got up and went away, without the Third even knowing she had been there.

I moved my chair back a little behind Sam and examined the back of his neck as his head bent forward over the book he was reading. I examined the creases in his neck and the carefulness of his immaculate hair-cut. I looked at the back of his ears and the shaven look at the edge of his cheek. I waited to feel the way I knew Gerry had been feeling, but I didn't feel anything at all except irritation that I would have

14

to feel my own pulse to know if my heart was beating any quicker.

'Sam,' I said. 'Have you ever loved the back of anybody's neck . . . or the line of an arm . . . or an ankle , , , or something?'

Sam shook his head.

'No,' he said without looking up.

'Well I have . . .' I said after a minute or two. 'But I don't feel that way about you. Why don't I?'

Sam came up from the depths of the intellectual tome he was reading.

'What did you say?' he said.

'Why don't I love the back of your neck?'

'Because it's not worth looking at I suppose.'

He bent back to his book.

That wasn't any answer and there was no way of telling Sam what I meant, or what I felt. Sam would be puzzled and not-understanding. My silence more than my questions must have disturbed him, for after a little while he looked up at me. I remained staring out to sea.

Sam put his book down beside his chair and walked away. I felt desolate because he could not understand me. Here was I, troubled in spirit, and all he did was get up and walk away.

Five minutes later he came back and put something on my lap.

'The shop's open,' he said with a smile. He'd brought me a box of chocolates, one of the luxuries barred on account of our impecunious state.

I knew he did understand after all.

CHAPTER THREE

Thus it was all the way across the world. Gerry and the Third were seen less and less as their 'affair' deepened and they chose their own company rather than that of others. Occasionally they emerged to play deck croquet. The Third was probably the champion player and Gerry always looked so striking and wind-swept on the fore-deck and was so obviously putty in the hands of the Third's proficient captaining of the game that they both attracted interest and a gallery. Not quite such a gallery, perhaps, as a match between the Third and the Chief Engineer whose flashing strokes always won a gasp of admiration.

Then Gerry and her man would disappear again to some remote place on the ship where they could tell one another in private whatever it was they had to say. It was endless.

At Aden there was a momentary cessation of their friendship when the Third went ashore on some errand of the ship's company and did not come aboard again until Port Said.

Sam and I were leaning over the side watching the bumboats below with their population of itinerant salesmen . . . the smell of the Orient wafting across the foreshore and the cries of the Egyptians, thin, sweet and musical like reed-pipes, filling our ears with astonishment at the things new and with pleasure at things pleasant. We saw a naval cutter breaking through the water to the *Moreton Bay* with the Third standing alone in the stern sheets.

Where Reggie had been or on what business I did not know and he did not vouchsafe but it was a Royal Navy cutter that brought him back to his ship. It had all the simple discipline and pristine beauty of the perfect instrument of a great Navy. Reggie standing upright, was the personification of the 'naval look'. With magnificent simplicity . . . in spotless whites . . . he left the cutter, took the salute from the ratings, saluted his own superior officer and rejoined the ship's company of the *Moreton Bay*.

'He'll do,' I said to Sam. There was a suggestion of a lump in my throat. I heard another passenger say—

'Makes you proud to be British, doesn't it?'

I hoped Gerry had seen that return. To her, the mystery of this journey through the East and the charm of Reggie Arbuthnot must have made at this time of her life one of the great wonders of romance.

We barely saw them as the ship moved west then north.

I don't know what kind of a parting they effected at Southampton. After all, this was our first glimpse of England, too. Only fleetingly did I have time to think of Gerry.

The chalk cliffs of Southern England were just what all the books had said they were, nothing but a strip of white along a grey skyline, but they were journey's end. England!

On the morning that we disembarked we were still a shipload of Australians faintly sprinkled with returning English,

England a thing yet to grasp with our understanding, until breakfast drew to a close. Then unexpectedly the ship's internal loud-speaker system gave a loud crackle.

Big Ben tolled nine o'clock and the bells of Westminster chimed through a silent dining saloon.

With the usual traditional reserve not an Englishman batted an eye, but there was moisture in those of the Australians. It had not yet occurred to them that they were Colonials and very nearly 'outsiders'.

In the boat-train to Waterloo, Gerry was silent. We asked no questions. If she had something to tell us she would tell us in good time. In the meantime we, ourselves, were too enraptured and too astonished with the countryside, and Gerry perhaps too deep in her own joys or sorrows for us to reach one another.

'Sam,' I said in an awed whisper, for fear that others in the compartment were English and might think I meant criticism in my comment. 'They're so tiny . . . like pocket handkerchiefs!' I meant the fields, of course.

'Imagine how rich the land is compared with ours,' said Sam, making sure that I didn't allow size to obscure my appreciation of worth. 'Look at those cattle! Look at the sheep, lying down already. They're full!'

I understood now what was meant when English people said of Australia:

'It's so vast . . . everything's so vast!'

No wonder they called our country the 'brown land'. No wonder my father used to say, 'People in this country have never seen green grass!'

Then came Waterloo and the long twilight.

It was September and even so the twilight was longer than we had ever known. In Australia night comes on like the drawing down of a blind.

There were porters to be tipped.

'How much do you give them?' I whispered to Sam.

'God knows,' he said. 'I wish there was someone I could ask.'

All around us were Australians in the same quandary. They came from a tip-less country and couldn't afford to tip too much and didn't want to make the mistake of under-tipping. Men in England didn't get a legal basic wage we knew and were dependent on their tips.

Sam tried going to the expert for information.

'How much do I give you?' he asked the porter.

'Just what you like, Sir.'

'What do you usually get?'

'It's up to you, Sir!'

That wasn't helpful so Sam gave him ten shillings. The porter turned it over in his hand and looked at it ruefully. We both felt dreadful and wished we'd given him a pound. But later an Englishman sympathized with us.

'For four cases that was over-tipping.'

We foresaw dreadful complications with the taxi driver and the hotel porter. We over-tipped in a despair of ignorance and a little sadly. We could so ill-afford it.

Gerry came with us to our hotel until she could find accommodation for herself. She flatly refused to think of sharing ours, when we got it.

'You've had me all the way from Australia,' she said. 'That's fair enough. Besides, you'll have Mama and Vicky and David before many months.'

I went to Gerry's room alone as soon as we had settled in.

'Gerry . . . about the Third . . . I don't want to pry . . .'

'You're not,' she said as she brushed her hair. 'Call it a matter of relative interest. He goes with the ship round to the London docks and will be free on Sunday. He has some weeks ashore. I'll be seeing him.'

That, for the time being, had to be enough. They hadn't finished with love when they had finished the voyage. Perhaps neither of them knew what being landlubbers would do to them. It was wiser to leave things so. Clearly Gerry wanted to be left alone now so I went back to our room, sat on my bed and looked at Sam.

'We're here. We're really here!'

There was a knock at the door and the bell-boy came in with a bouquet of flowers. I had seen flowers on a stall in the entrance of the hotel. There was a card from Gerry.

'*Thanks for everything on the journey. Don't thank me for the flowers. I couldn't bear it! Gerry.*'

Sam was as touched as I was.

'She means that about not thanking her,' I said. 'Gerry doesn't like 'feelings' on display between relatives. We'll just wear a carnation in our lapels . . . they can speak for themselves.'

Sam and I found a home in a 'double-bed-sit., all cons.' at Lancaster Gate. I never succeeded in passing Marble Arch without the awed feeling that I was passing the ghosts of Tyburn Tree. If there was an hour of the night when traffic ceased in London I would have been afraid of the wind that might blow that way and rattle the chains and the hanging legs of England's past.

Our 'double-bed-sit.' was cheap but not cheap enough for Sam and me. We didn't know where to look or how to look for something cheaper yet clean. We had not yet discovered Dalton's weekly paper and none of London's millions thought to enlighten us. How did they know what we wanted to know anyway? Incredible though it may seem now, we looked in *The Times* for advertised accommodation. As if *The Times* even wotted of the thousands of itinerant students carrying home their swedes, bread rolls and sausages under brown gaberdine coats to the hives of 'bed-sits.' in Bloomsbury, and South of the Thames!

But at least we had Alice.

Alice lived in the basement, did our fires for us every day and gave us a Sunday dinner of roast beef, brussels sprouts, roast potatoes, all swimming in a sea of fatty gravy. It filled us but upset our livers and we didn't like to hurt Alice's feelings by declining 'Sunday dinner' which was part of her perks of the job and which she was so certain was the mainstay of our lives.

Alice was big, red-faced, kind, garrulous and she had only one tooth in the front of her head. But she told us what to do, where to go, how to do our shopping; who lived in the houses opposite and what was wrong with the Empire. It was an Empire in those days and everyone born under the British flag outside the United Kingdom was a 'Colonial'.

After we had explained to Alice, at great length, what was a 'Dominion' she ruminated, letting the wind in her stomach speak authoritatively to her for quite a minute, before she shook her head, sucked her one large brown tooth, then said—

'Seems like the same thing under another name.'

And she was enthralled with Gerry.

Gerry, whenever she called on us, went straight to the basement with a small gift for Alice, brewed tea with her and sat, her feet almost in the coal fire, and talked. Sometimes when we'd been out we returned to find Alice clumping up the stairs from the basement.

'Heard you coming, Sir. Miss Gerry was here. We had tea,

19

she didn't wait. My, she's a oner that one, she is!' Alice would grin her single-toothed grin and looked reproachfully at Sam because clearly he had married the wrong one.

'She'd get his head out of them books,' she would say to me, sagely. 'There'd be no reading while that one's around!'

As if it was desirable for Sam to have his head out of books!

Gerry, as much to impress Mrs Arbuthnot with her 'virtu-ousness' as for safety's sake, had hied herself to the Girls' Friendly Society Hostel. Here she was fed, kept clean and was able to sound respectable. It had been clear on Gerry's first meeting with Mrs Arbuthnot that Reggie's mother had the greatest doubt about the propriety of young girls travelling around the world, more or less alone.

True to his word Reggie Arbuthnot had arrived at our hotel in Bloomsbury on the Sunday after our arrival in London—this was before our move to Lancaster Gate. He had only grinned when Gerry produced Sam and me. He had known long since of our relationship and had been amused at Gerry's insistence on independence.

He had just left the ship so was still in uniform, the dark blues of winter. He knew a pal who had a car and was taking Gerry to meet him. Then they'd 'take a run' to High Wycombe, the home of the Arbuthnots.

When Gerry came in late that night we were still waiting up, Sam and I, nearly as nervous as Gerry must have been at being confronted with Reggie's family.

'It was more like that they were confronted with me,' Gerry said, with a rather rueful twist to her mouth. 'I don't think they'd seen anyone like me before—I felt like an animal out of a zoo—but they were much too well-bred to show it.'

'Were they *nice*?' I begged.

'Utterly charming,' said Gerry without enthusiasm. 'You must meet them sometime.'

So there was going to be a 'sometime'!

'What was their house like?'

'You know those sort of two-storey houses we saw from the train? Like that, only buried in bushes covered in yellow and brown leaves; it was beautiful. Everything inside is good, and comfortable, and chintzy, with Dresden china figurines all over the place. We sat in the drawing-room and had tea. The worst mistake I made was offering to take the tea cups outside when the maid didn't seem to be coming back. Reggie explained to me that in England people don't go out into the kitchen the way they do in Australia.'

'What did they say when you offered?'

'There was a sort of chill-ful silence and Mr Arbuthnot rang for the maid.'

'Nice to have a maid,' I said wistfully.

'They have four,' said Gerry. 'Not all maids, but four servants. A housemaid, a cook, a chauffeur and a gardener.'

'Only Mr and Mrs Arbuthnot?'

'And Reggie, when his ship's in?'

'Not even Reggie. He has "rooms in town".'

'Four servants to two people. My, oh my! That's the way to live.' I turned to Sam.

'If you get your Ph.D., Sam, maybe some day we'll earn a thousand a year, and have servants, too.'

'A thousand a year won't get you four servants in Australia,' said Sam.

'My father said they used to have ten, in the old home in Ireland,' I said.

'Reggie said those sort of people aren't real servants. They're half servants and half hangers on,' Gerry said. 'Also, he said that in Ireland one can go into the kitchen, that's where the Australians got their free-and-easy habits from.'

Gerry was looking at me with that long dark look that meant she was thinking deeply and making a private reservation of her own.

'So it wasn't altogether . . . wasn't quite . . .?' I floundered.

'It was all right,' said Gerry. 'I stacked on the charm, too!' Gerry could do that with a vengeance.

'And only Reggie knew what you were up to?'

'Reggie was amused. That's the most that can be expected on a first visit.'

I made a mental reservation that Gerry had said 'first visit'. Then she anticipated a 'second'. Perhaps all might turn out well. I knew from my own heart-searing past what mothers of sons could do to the girl who first came to lay claim to a son.

'What else did you put your foot in?' I asked. 'Besides offering to go to the kitchen?'

Gerry got up and yawned.

'I didn't put my foot in it. They did.' She went to the door. She looked over her shoulder as she turned the handle. She mimicked the absent Mrs Arbuthnot.

'We are always glad to welcome the girls Reggie meets on his voyages. You're the first Australian—last time it was a Ceylonese. A most charming girl. Very well bred, and quite beautiful.'

CHAPTER FOUR

On Monday morning Sam went to the University and I went to find the 'bed-sit.' at Lancaster Gate. In the years since then I have learned in many travels that we always arrived at a place on a Saturday and that on Monday Sam 'went to the University'. Therefter he disclaimed all responsibility for the domestic side of life.

If we took a journey to Mars, Sam would have an appointment at the University at nine o'clock on Monday morning and thereafter he would only be seen again to eat and sleep, except when things were so busy at the University he had to stay home to get his work done.

Alice introduced me to Woolworths and crockery at three-pence and sixpence a piece. Knives, forks, and spoons at two-pence each, and the basement of Selfridges where I could buy Australian apricot jam at half the price I could buy it in Australia.

In spite of Woolworths and Selfridges I couldn't keep my house-keeping within the budget we had laid down as the 'safety budget' until such time as the Teaching Profession of Great Britain had discovered a female Daniel had come amongst them and so offer me employment.

I couldn't pass a bookstall with the English *Woman's Journal* offering itself to me at half the price I paid in my homeland. I couldn't pass the Needlewoman in Regent Street without buying a piece of linen, and embroidery threads. I couldn't pass a cigarette counter without replenishing my store. And as my humble house-keeping allowance didn't allow for such extravagances I stealthily whittled down a nest-egg of thirty pounds that had been given to me as a parting present from an old family friend.

I cut Sam sandwiches each morning for his lunch and at the University Refectory he was supposed to buy himself a glass of milk. As the cold of winter closed frighteningly around us

I realized the food was not enough for Sam. Then I learned that he hadn't been buying his glass of milk. He, too, could not pass 'my lady nicotine' without making a ritual pause.

So I confessed that my thirty pounds was now twenty-five pounds and what would I do about it?

With great shame and reluctance we had to tell Alice we no longer would take her Sunday dinner.

'We're not used to eating in the middle of the day,' we said. 'It doesn't really agree with us.'

Alice looked at us with understanding eyes. The next day she offered to do my buying at the butcher for me and she came home with twice as much steak at an almost negligible cost.

'But Alice, *how* . . .?'

She put her finger on her nose and winked at me. She grinned her big one-tooth grin.

'We cockney's 've got ways an' means,' she said. 'Them prices in the shops is for the likes of you. Behind the scenes-like, there's summick else fer us kind, an' not so bad either is it, duck?'

It was a nice piece of steak. I only hoped that Alice came by it and all her subsequent purchases from the butcher honestly.

Meantime after the sternest deliberations, Sam and I decided that the best way to get a job was to send out a greater number of applications. We needed a typewriter. We took ourselves to Selfridges and bought one for nine pounds. Thereafter I spent my afternoons and evenings typing out all the qualifications and letters of reference I had.

I received the most charmingly worded acknowledgments. But not a job. I pored over the *London Gazette* and applied for every kind of post. If they wanted physical training, then I would teach physical training. If they wanted a sewing-mistress, then I was the world's champion seamstress. If they wanted plain arithmetic and spelling and geography, then I had all the tricks of teaching the skills at my fingertips. As for geography, hadn't I travelled half-way round the world?

The Board of Education informed me they were impressed with my qualifications and accorded me recognition to teach in their primary schools. But I only had permission, I didn't have a job. The London County Council sent for me and accorded me the same recognition. They demanded that I be medically examined and the medical officer said flattering things about the straightness of my back. But that didn't get me a job. I had to get one in open competition against hundreds of unemployed English teachers. There were one or two schools who would have taken me on their staff 'if I hadn't been a Colonial.'

At first I thought it was the low social status of 'the Colonial' until I found that for one post for which I had applied there were sixty English applicants. Why should they give the appointment to an outsider? Why, indeed! In the meantime I got a cold. The cold worsened and I kept Sam awake at night with my coughing.

We were both anxious, but neither would tell the other. I began to lose my confidence and thought about trying Woolworths for a job behind the counter. I knew a West Australian graduate, a girl with first-class honours in Modern Greats, who kept the wolf from the door by selling ribbons in Woolworths.

I lay awake at night, not only on account of the coughing, but on account of worry. Three months had slipped by and Sam had lightly suggested it might be a wiser thing if he took an M.A. degree of London instead of the Ph. D. That would take a year less to complete. I was so horrified at the suggestion that for once I was bereft of speech.

The weighing machines on the platforms of underground railways had a morbid fascination for me. I couldn't resist getting on one but knew in anticipation that I would have lost another pound or two.

Meanwhile Gerry had got herself a job typing pamphlets for a church organization in Westminster. It didn't pay much, but it kept hunger at bay in between meals out with Reggie and sorties on the Arbuthnots of Arbuthnot.

'How are you getting on with them, Gerry?' I asked.

'I'm getting on with them famously. I'm too hungry to despise their overloaded table.'

'But apart from that?'

'They're all right,' she said. 'They're fighting for their son. So am I.'

'What's wrong with you anyway?' I asked belligerently.

'My accent. But mostly the possibility of being a future daughter-in-law.'

'It's come to that has it?'

'Not quite,' said Gerry. 'But you never can tell.'

She sat musing into the fire.

'When Reggie makes the next trip, I'll go over to Laura in Ireland,' she said.

'That might be a good idea. Can you get a job in Ireland?'

'I shall live with Laura and learn to speak with an Irish accent,' Gerry said.

My heart went out to her. Gerry, as a matter of temperament and of principle, never gave ground to anyone, on any point. Her feeling for Reggie Arbuthnot must be both deep and sincere, if she would go to this trouble about her accent. In ordinary circumstances her reaction would have been to be defiant.

When Gerry had gone I asked Sam did he think that Reggie would be a suitable kind of husband for Gerry. Sam looked at me with a twinkle in his eyes.

'What's wrong with him?'

'Nothing. He's a nice young man, but just so different. His background is different. His outlook is bound to be different.'

'That's just what the Arbuthnots think about Gerry. No more and no less. They're anxious for their son, just as you are anxious for your sister.'

I was grateful to Sam for putting the thing in its right perspective and thereafter felt more kindly disposed to Reggie's family. In the meantime Laura had written from Ireland pressing us all to go there. I consulted a doctor about my cold but he forbade Ireland in mid-winter. It was damper than England, he said, and recommended we leave Lancaster Gate and move to the outskirts of London, preferably Hampstead Heath.

'It's the fog and the damp,' he said. 'You're just not used to them.'

The finances of the Richardsons would impel us to move from Lancaster Gate and our warm 'bed-sit.' and the faintly grog-smelling Alice with her heart of gold . . . but whither to go?

We had discovered Dalton's paper and the millions of 'bed-sits.' all over London, but what would be the sense of moving if I got a job south, if and when I did get a job?

I renewed my job-hunting with feverish activity just about the time my cold decided to extend its activities to my stomach. I would go by Underground to some County or Borough Education Authority and wonder when I left the safety of the Underground 'Women's Rooms' whether I would get to the County Hall in time before the next vomiting attack overwhelmed me.

One day I went to Harrow. As I sat in the hall outside the Director's room waiting for an interview I became overwhelmed with one of these attacks. The minute for interview was at hand, the prospect of appointment I thought was good. I dared not be *in absentia* when the door was opened. And I could not vomit all over the Director's carpet.

I clenched my hands and closed my eyes. The perspiration streamed over me. It poured down my forehead and into my eyes. It streamed in rivulets into the corners of my mouth. But I sat it out.

The Director was charming to me but obviously perplexed by my appearance. When the interview was over I fled to the nearest Lyons Tea Rooms and precipitated myself into the retiring room where I remained for what seemed hours. I didn't get the post at Harrow.

When Sam came home—book-weary from the University—I was in bed and shivering with a temperature. Alice sent for the doctor and he said I would have to go to the south of France or back to Australia.

Sam remained thoughtful and silent all evening. I wallowed, not only in stomach sickness but in despair of spirit. I, the over-whelming over-confident, was the one who had thrown in the sponge.

I knew what was in Sam's mind though he did not put it into words. Could he send me home alone while he switched to an M.A. course and rejoin me in a year's time?

Gerry brought Reggie to see me that evening and he brought the first ray of hope.

'Rubbish,' he said. 'You're not going to stay this way once you get used to the climate. All Australians get this way if they land here in the beginning of winter. It's nothing to what the English suffer when they hit the Australian summer in their first weeks. What they can endure in Australia you can weather in England.'

I looked at Reggie through different eyes.

He grinned at me.

'Bet you half the passengers who came over on the *Moreton Bay* are just where you are. On the flats of their backs. It's only oak trees like Gerry and bamboo trees like Sam, who

26

really weather the storm. As long as you don't come up by the roots, Theodora, you'll be all right. And when spring comes, you can go home to Ireland.'

Oh, the magic of those words.

Home to Ireland! The land of my fathers!

When Reggie had gone I lay thinking about these words. I turned my head away from Sam's anxious face and the great pile of books he had already accumulated on the table, chairs and every available space in the 'bed-sit.' even the floor.

Sam and his books!

Half of me wanted, more than anything else in the world, Sam and his books. But deep inside me there had come some irrefutable knowledge. They would never be mine. Half of my sickness was nervous. Sam belonged in some other spirit world I could not attain and I belonged in some spirit world he could not understand.

When he had gone, on the Monday morning, to the University, he had set the whole pattern of our life. Always he would be 'at the University', even when he was sitting by my side.

I had been standing on the edge of a void for weeks, and suddenly Reggie Arbuthnot, the sailor Englishman, had said the words that threw out the life-line.

Home to Ireland!

Everyone in Ireland was mad, like my father and all his friends in Pepper Tree Bay. Like Denney, and a little bit like Gerry. Like Theodora would always be. Yes, when spring came I would go home to Ireland.

I had a vision of Laura's lovely sultry face and her Irish temper. I had a vision of Danny Montgomery, the Irishman she had married. The man with the soft voice, and the riding-whip and the spoiled fair-headed beauty of him. I laughed.

It was the first time for weeks.

In the morning I was better and on the day after I had a letter from the Surrey Education Authority asking me if I would go as a temporary teacher to St Margaret's Church of England School at Wimbledon. There was a vacancy for one week.

Would I go!

I flew there on wings of song.

It was pitch dark on a December morning when I sallied forth

27

to Waterloo to catch my train to Wimbledon. Great delivery trucks with headlights gleaming were edging their way through the fog and there was a busyness about London quite different from that which would meet the eyes of those who emerged with the light. This was the world of London's workers. And I was one of them.

In Wimbledon I asked a policeman the way to St Margaret's. He looked down from a height that must have been well over six feet and cogitated a minute.

'First to the left, second to the right; second to the left . . . and you're there. Can you repeat that?'

I repeated it safely.

'Well, keep on saying it all the way, madam. It'll take you there.' He beamed down on me with the fatherly care of all English policemen.

Away I went down the street muttering 'First to the left, second to the right; second to the left . . .'

It was a beautiful school. A new building set in good playing-fields. I was not to see its like again for many a long day.

The Headmistress was tall, handsome, gracious and very firm. She shook hands with me, asked me where I came from and took me to the classroom. There were forty little boys and girls who could read beautifully and sing like nightingales.

That is all I remember about St Margaret's except that I was so eager to impress I was over-nervous and must have appeared very strung up to the staff.

I was only there three days when I received a letter, in the early post before I left Lancaster Gate, asking me to call on the Chairman of the Board of Managers at St Hilda's near Denmark Hill. I showed my letter to the Headmistress of St Margaret's and she most kindly said—

'You must go at once. This might mean a permanent appointment while we can only offer you a week at St Margaret's at the most.'

So I put on my raincoat, my brown woollen cap and set off from Wimbledon to Denmark Hill.

Somehow I knew I was going to get the job. My luck had changed and all the Irish in me believed in luck.

But how to get to the Chairman of the Board of Managers? He was the Vicar and he and the school lived in an ancient cluster of buildings that showed to the world a great massive wall broken only by ecclesiastical windows high up; two big nail-studded doors and one small green-painted wooden one.

I walked round and round the block, for the buildings consisting of Church, School and Vicarage were all immured behind the walls. While I pondered my predicament a black-cowled figure emerged from the little green door, unlocked the biggest of the nail-studded doors, and disappeared inside.

I peeped in after him. This was the Church. It was dim, with a dark ecclesiastical beauty. From the belfry above came the sound of the Angelus. Several minutes later the priest emerged again from the church door. He was of medium height, plump, and had the map of Ireland written all over his face.

'Were you waiting to see me?' he asked.

I don't know whether it was his face or whether it was his voice but I felt a smile of sheer joy spread all over my face.

'You are the Vicar, Sir?'

'I am that.'

I began to fumble in the pocket of my raincoat for the envelope that had brought his command to me. He recognized it before I spoke.

'So it's the School you want to see, is it? Well, come and look at the Church first.'

He opened the church door again and led the way in. He made the sign of the cross as he faced the altar and began immediately to tell me about the architecture and the decorations. Even in the gloom it was profoundly beautiful. This was what was called a 'High Church', something I had never seen in the environs of Pepper Tree Bay. I wasn't even certain what a 'High Church' was, though I vaguely remembered some parishioners taking a cross view of my father having lighted candles on the altar of his Church on the corner of the Highway that wound its way from the sea to the river city of Perth.

The Vicar perhaps read my thoughts.

'I suppose you're "low Church," ' he said. 'Though why they should use the term "low" with anything that's got to do with God is beyond me.'

'I don't know what I am,' I said doubtfully. 'My father was an Irishman from County Meath and I was educated by the Anglican Sisters who have schools in Australia.'

'The Anglican Sisters!' he positively whooped with joy, gathered up his skirts and settled his little black cap on his head. 'Come with me. I will show you something.'

He led me into the transept where along the wall were the beautifully modelled and painted 'Stations of the Cross'.

I, too, gave a cry of joy.

'Why, they're the same, the very same. They hang around our Chapel walls at school. One of the Sisters did them, and sent them out to Australia.'

'Of course. The very same Sister. She is a great artist. An A.R.A.'

A wave of homesickness swept over me, and again the Vicar read my thoughts.

'It'll be a pleasure for you to be coming to Church. I can see it all. It's a grand day that brought you here. It's a hard thing to get the teachers to come to Church, but with yourself now, it's the Anglican Sisters that'll be bringing you, if it's not God Almighty Himself.'

I nodded.

'Come, we'll look at the School.'

There was more locking and unlocking of great nail-studded doors and I found myself in a tiny quadrangle.

'The playground,' said the Vicar. He had let his skirts fall and they swished behind him as he moved rapidly across the tiny square.

We went into the school with its stone floors, stone staircase, worn and grooved with age, and more great heavy timeless doors, and then we found ourselves in the schoolroom. Suddenly gloom had given way to something brave and light. A fire roared in the grate, all around the walls were gay paintings, coloured lanterns swung on a paper chains from one side of the room to the other, and a Christmas tree stood on the lockers at the back of the room. It shone with silver tassels and golden balls.

A tall, thin, angular woman came towards us. Her face was serious, pale, and very good.

'Good morning, Father,' she said. She did not look at me, but rather at him. Her lips were pursed in the tiniest *moue* of disapproval. The children had risen in their seats.

' 'Morning, Miss Anderson. 'Morning, children!'

'Good morning, Father Reilly.'

And they bobbed a curtsey.

'This young lady has come from Australia,' the Vicar said. Miss Anderson shook hands with me and then turned to tell the children they might sit down again. The Vicar lifted his hand to his mouth and whispered:

'That's rocked her!' His eyes twinkled.

'From Australia,' he said to the children, waving a hand towards me. 'All the way from Australia. Right across the world.'

He folded his hands under the cape of his black gown, rocked gently back on his heels and watched to see that take effect on the children. They sat mute and round-eyed.

'Is Mrs Richardson an applicant for the post?' Miss Anderson asked. Clearly she didn't approve of the Vicar. Did she approve of my being an Australian?

'She is, to be sure,' said the Vicar. 'She was educated by the Anglican Sisters. Now what do you think of that, Miss Anderson? And her chief reference is from a Bishop. And what do you think of that?'

Miss Anderson melted and took an interest in me.

'I'll get Mrs Illington-Wharton,' she said hastily and disappeared through another great door. It shut noiselessly behind her.

'She's gone to confer with Mrs Illington-Etc.' The Vicar was always to refer to that lady by that name. 'They won't approve of you if I like you,' he said conspiratorially. 'But they'll approve of the Bishop. Not to mention the Sisters . . .'

Miss Anderson returned with an enormous lady of such scrubbed cleanliness and such intimidating dignity that I wondered that any man had ever wanted to be near enough to her to present her with his name. She had big, white, prominent teeth.

We shook hands all round again, and the Vicar walked away from me pretending faintly to disapprove. The ladies asked me about Australia, about teaching, about my health, about my husband. Then they really settled down to business. They asked me about the Bishop. They bent their heads and listened intently. They then asked to see my references, shook hands around again and quite literally thrust the Vicar and me through the door.

'You see what I mean?' said the Vicar.

I didn't see what he meant because he had said very little. His shrewd twinkling eyes had conveyed that there were under-currents but what was their nature or in which direction they flowed I was completely ignorant.

'You'll get the post,' he said to me blithely. 'Come to the Vicarage tonight at seven. I'll have the rest of the Managers there.' Then suddenly and without ceremony he raised his little

31

black cap, nodded sharply to me and disappeared into the little door in the wall. That, I thought, must be the Vicarage.

So it turned out to be. That evening I saw the Vicar again. I began to suspect the reasons for Miss Anderson's disapproval She was almost grimly tidy and orderly. The study of the Vicarage was incredibly the opposite. The Vicar, still in his black gown and little black cap, sat in a sea of screwed-up papers, pamphlets, ecclesiastical magazines and addressed envelopes. His children, two of them, sat on the floor throughout the proceedings folding circulars and inserting them into envelopes.

The Board of Managers were two elderly spinsterish ladies with high collars and a pathetic deference to the Vicar, the local butcher who spoke with a strong Cockney accent, and Miss Anderson.

Miss Anderson sat in dignified silence, defeated before even the meeting began. I never knew, then or at any time later, whether I would have been her choice for the post or not, but it was clear that the numerical strength lay with the Vicar; and his choice lay with me.

I wondered who had been the other applicants, and why I had been chosen by him. I didn't think the Anglican Sisters, or the Bishop, had anything to do with his choice. He played them as trump cards with his Board but there was a wicked look in his eye when he glanced at me.

No, his reasons were ulterior and hidden from me.

On Friday I had a letter from the Vicar.

'You're appointed to the post of primary teacher to St Hilda's. What is your handwriting like? Everything you've sent me is typed.'

'Sam,' I begged. 'You write the reply for me.'

Sam had a beautiful, clear, firm calligraphy while mine was shocking. Once the Principal of the Teachers' College had stood in the back of a lecture room when I was practising blackboard writing.

'That's the worst writing I've ever seen,' was his comment.

Sam, of course, was too honest to write my letter for me but Gerry was as dishonourable as I was anxious. She did it.

'We have to eat,' I said to Sam.

His disapproval weighed on me, as did all the disappointed applicants who hadn't got the post.

'The economy of the country is based on private enterprise,'

32

said Gerry quoting Reggie Arbuthnot. 'It's every man for himself.'

'But there's always luck in these things,' I said. 'Somewhere along the line I was lucky, and they were not.'

'Luck be damned!' said Reggie. 'That's another excuse for ignorant superstition. You've got something the Vicar wants. What it is you'll find out in due course.'

CHAPTER FIVE

The following week we bade Alice a sentimental farewell and moved to Clapham Common. Mama wrote us frantic letters from Pepper Tree Bay.

'Do you have to live in Clapham Common? Once I had a maid from Clapham Common. She was *awful*. So ignorant!'

We wrote back and assured her that we were living in a charming house, a nice middle-class boarding house run by a Scotsman and so spotlessly clean it was cold. There was the church on the common and ice on the pond, and the South Side, still bearing some of the faded glories of the past, was thick with doctors, dentists, lawyers and other professional potentates.

The boarding-house gave us two meals a day and as Sam didn't come in till nine o'clock at night his dinner was always put in the oven for him. For midday I bought bread rolls and buttered them behind the wardrobe door. We weren't supposed to have food in our rooms at all. The Scotsman was adamant about this.

On Saturdays we had high tea at five in the afternoon. It consisted of one poached egg on one slice of toast; two slices of bread and butter and jam each, and a cake. We could have a second cup of tea.

Reggie and Gerry came to high tea one Saturday and they went away afterwards and got themselves a good hearty meal at the Plough.

Sam didn't have enough to eat, I knew. But I didn't worry until afterwards. I always had a tendency to worry in retrospect. I had given up cigarettes and was getting fat, so with me it didn't matter about food.

Reggie's ship sailed again for Australia and Gerry went to

Ireland. She wrote that milk, eggs, cream and poultry were thick on the tables of Magillicuddy. So was the dust. Laura had one servant and Danny had six grooms. Nobody did any work unless Laura made them, and nobody wanted to work.

Sam went to earth at the University and I entered a new life at St Hilda's.

To begin with there was some kind of conspiracy between me and the Vicar. And only he knew what it was. My conscience about all the English teachers who hadn't got the post because I had got it made me work with a kind of feverish activity that irritated even Sam.

'You're getting an anxiety complex,' he said. 'You want to accept the situation rationally. If only you'd stop believing in luck you'd stop working to appease all the jinxes you think are going to frighten it away.'

'As a moral person you ought to believe in moral responsibility in other people,' I said, aggrieved.

'I accept the situation realistically,' he said. 'Worrying won't make any difference to the quality of your work, except to interfere with it.'

Did it interfere with it?

I was so anxious to win Miss Anderson from her frigid courtesy and Mrs Illington-Etc. from her implacable remoteness that, of course, I over-did everything. If I was asked to do anything, I fell over my feet doing it. If I was asked to teach more landscape painting than still life I plastered the schoolroom walls with desert scenes and polar ice-packs till someone suggested I tried still life again. If it was suggested the spelling in my class might be improved I taught spelling till everyone's head buzzed with the 'hundred demons'.

When asked why I did this I told them that spelling improved my back. They looked at me in cold bewilderment. I told them the story of my back.

Once, when I was very young, and growing too fast, I had developed rounded shoulders. I'd had to wear shoulder straps, the bane of my own life and the irritation of my family. The shoulder straps made me shrug until everyone would cry:

'Theodora, for heaven's sake sit still!'

In my first days of teaching I had come under a physical training instructor who used to thrust me out of the homeward-bound tram that passed along the foot of the Mount which toppled over one side of the river not far from the Bay.

'Walk up Jacob's Ladder on the ball of your foot,' he would command. 'It will straighten your back.'

Since I wanted to straighten my back I took notice of him and all through that summer I climbed the three hundred and fifty steps of the ladder on my toes.

The physical training teacher was pleased with my perseverance. 'When you get into the school-room,' he said, 'always dictate your spelling from the wall.'

'The wall?'

'Yes. Stand against a wall. Put your heels against it, then your backside, then your shoulders and then the back of your head. Now give your spelling lesson, and ten minutes of that every day will be good for you. Tell the children what you're doing. It's a good example.'

So for all my teaching life I gave spelling from this position.

The staff of St Hilda's looked at me in odd silence when I told them about it.

'*But*,' said Miss Bernard, a little frail, anxious, bespectacled woman who rarely ever spoke, 'do you teach *spelling* three times a day just for the good of your back?'

'No,' I said. 'But if I *do* teach spelling three times a day I get philosophic about it. It teaches the children to spell, I exercise my back!'

When they remained silent I burst out defensively:

'The Medical Officer at County Hall said I had a straight back. She wouldn't ever have said that if it hadn't been for Jacob's Ladder, and spelling.'

Quite clearly they all thought I talked too much. Everybody had always thought that, wherever I'd been. Even Sam. So I didn't take offence.

'You ought to hear Gerry and Denney,' I said. 'With them I don't get a word in edgeways.'

They shook their heads again and Miss Anderson suggested that someone ring the bell.

Yes, I had to admit. There were more at home like me.

With the Vicar, now, it was a different matter altogether. He also derived from the land of thinkers. One afternoon I went to see him, just a courtesy call I thought it behoved me to perform. True to my word, I had been going to church

35

every Sunday morning, to the children's service, but I couldn't bring myself to go to Confession. It was something I did not understand. Though I liked calling the Vicar 'Father Reilly' as everyone else did it didn't fit into the pattern of the Church of England as I had been brought up in it. I wanted to explain my defection to the Vicar, if an explanation were necessary. In the meantime I would just 'call'.

He was coming out of the church door when I stopped him.

'Are you busy, Father? May I come and see you?'

'I'm always busy, and you may always come and see me. Come along out of this cold and we'll have a cup of tea.'

We entered the Vicarage and his study. I was quite sure not a piece of screwed-up paper had been removed since my last visit. Not a magazine nor a pamphlet had stirred. If the addressed envelopes and circulars had been sent out then there was a fresh batch waiting on the carpet by his chair.

'Well, now, a cup of tea first!'

He put a kettle on the iron bars of the cage that kept the coal fire confined and gave the coals a poke with the poker from underneath. Clouds of coal dust wafted amiably about the room. The Vicar removed his black cap and put it on his desk.

'Sit there,' he said, pointing to a low, worn and tattered leather chair. 'You can put the circulars in the envelopes while we talk.'

'I know all about this,' I said as I tackled the pile on the floor. 'I spent my childhood folding paper and putting it into envelopes.'

'Now for the tea,' he said, ignoring this. I wasn't going to be let off work. 'Hot, black and strong as befits an Irishman.'

'Yes, please,' I said. 'Where are the children, Father?'

'Out with their mother somewhere. I don't ask where. Nobody in the house attends to me, and nobody tells me anything.'

'Like Soames in *The Forsyte Saga*.'

'Ha! The man of property! But they had a reason for not telling him anything, the cold, irascible rascal. Now, with me, it's only because I forget. I'm bound to forget, they argue. So they don't tell me. Saves a lot of trouble. How's the school getting on? How's Miss Anderson, and how, God bless us, is Mrs Illington-Etc.?'

'Why don't you ask after Miss Bernard, Father? You seem to forget her.'

36

'Don't have to remember her. She's safe with God. A good Christian woman.'

'Aren't the others?'

His eyes twinkled over his cup of tea.

'Sometimes I think God needs a hand with his children.'

I dared not probe any further. What was going on between the Vicar and his Headmistress? I would never learn it from the incommunicable Miss Anderson, or the impenetrable Mrs Illington-Etc.

'And how is the school suffering the impact of *you*?' the Vicar asked, as he audibly smacked his lips over the tea.

'That's just what I don't know, Father. I don't understand them, and they don't understand me.'

'What's not understandable?'

'Well, when I told them about a tarantula dropping off the wall at home and rattling over the floor like a marble they didn't believe me. When I said it was as big as the palm of my hand they looked as if they were going to pray for me.'

'Did they say they didn't believe you?'

'Oh no. They're much too well-bred. They just look at me, and their eyes seem to say, "If she *must* tell stories why doesn't she tell ones we're likely to believe".'

'Um hum!'

He poured himself another cup of tea and filled my cup for me.

'Do you have tarantulas as big as the palm of your hand?'

'We have hundreds of tarantulas, and once there was one as big as the palm of my hand.'

'That's just it. Generalizing from the particular. A bad Irish habit. Some people call it making a good story.'

He smiled happily into his tea.

'I do it myself,' he said. 'The Lord God will forgive me, as long as there was a particular from which to generalize.'

'I see your point, Father,' I said contritely.

'And what is it you don't understand about them?'

'Well, for instance . . .'

I paused.

'Well, for instance . . .' he prodded me.

'You know the soldier in the helmet and things who sits on the horse in Whitehall.'

'Outside the Horse Guards. Go on.'

'Well, the first time Sam and I went down Whitehall I saw him and we waited for him to do something. We waited and waited but he just sat there. So I said to Sam, "Why *does* he sit there?" Sam knows everything, so he said, "He's on guard." So I said, "What is he guarding? The people are all walking in and out and not taking any notice of him?" '

'And what did Sam reply to that?'

'Sam said it was traditional so I said why don't they put a statue there, like Charles the First farther up the road, instead of a live man? Every time I go past the statue of Charles the First I think of him stepping out of a window in Whitehall to be beheaded, and my heart really goes out to him.'

'What did Sam say to all that?'

'He just said, "Don't be so damn logical, Magillicuddy".'

'And why does he call you Magillicuddy?'

'It's the home of my father in Ireland. And I'm going there in the spring. Sam teases me about it.'

The Vicar poked the coal fire and threw another bundle of pamphlets off his overcrowded desk on to the floor in order to gather up the envelopes I had been filling, and begin to address them.

'You told this story to Mesdames Anderson, Bernard and Illington-Etc.?'

'Yes, I did,' I said a little shamefacedly.

'What did they say?'

'Well, it always seems I'm talking just when the dinner-hour is over, and they always just sit and look at me, and Miss Anderson says: "Ring the bell, someone. It's time for school!" '

The Vicar roared with laughter. The tears came into his eyes and he wiped them away with the corner of his cassock.

'And that's why you don't understand them?'

'They're always ringing bells,' I said. 'Just when the conversation gets most interesting, someone gets up and rings the bell.'

The Vicar laughed so much he spilled the tea down his robe. When he'd finished he made the sign of the Cross over me.

'Go in peace, my child,' he said. 'In two years' time you'll know why a Guard sits in Whitehall. Come and tell me when you do.'

When the Vicar let me out into the bitter dark of the January night I remembered I had not spoken to him about things like

High Mass and Confession. Perhaps if they had mattered he would have mentioned them to me. Instead we had spent the rest of the tea hour telling one another about Ireland—what he knew from his own boyhood, and what I knew from my father's stories.

'I've let a stormy petrel into the dove-cote,' he said as he unlatched his door. 'Well, well, that's just how I thought it would be.'

What, I asked myself, did he mean by that?

In spring I didn't go to Ireland. Instead, Mama came to England.

There is something about Mama that when she makes up her mind to do a thing she does it. She didn't have any money, yet somehow she got herself to England.

It all fell out this way.

When we had lived in the Rectory in Pepper Tree Bay, Mama had always kept a cow. After several cows Mama got to know all about them. She could tell a good cow when she saw one. She could always tell other people about their cows, too.

One day, when she was in the legitimate pursuit of her occupation as a Schools' Nurse for the Medical Department, after my father had gone and we were very poor, she had occasion to call on the family of a dairyman who lived by the Swamp on the sea side of Pepper Tree Bay. Something about a child needing its tonsils removed.

The dairyman was too busy to see Mama and as his wife was cluttered up with a whole bevy of adenoidal children Mama went in pursuit of the dairyman. He was herding his cows through a race in preparation for a sale. Either he was indignant with Mama or she was indignant with him, but between their arguing a little Jersey cow got kicked. The dairyman all but wept and this rendered Mama more angry and more voluble.

'You care more for the cow than for your child,' she said.

'Look here, Madam,' he said. 'The cows are the bread and butter of my children. You tell me how I can get that child to the Children's Hospital, wait for three hours in the Outpatients till some god-damned doctor obliges to see her, and my wife mind the rest of the kids and me mind the cows at the same time?'

Mama was silenced for she saw his point. It wasn't the first

39

time she had come across a family that couldn't get medical attention for a child because there was no one to take the child to hospital.

She stumped back to the house, sent word to old Williams the carrier whom she had known in the old days when my father was Rector of Pepper Tree Bay, and demanded that he transport her and the sick child forthwith to the Children's Hospital. After many hours' delay she managed to get the child admitted to hospital. The following day she attended while the offending tonsils were removed and later that evening, again with the help of her old friend the carrier, who also had a cab, was able to return the child to its fold.

'Tell you what, Madam,' said the dairyman. 'I'll give you that cow what was kicked. When she went up for sale this morning she was lame. I told 'em what had happened but no one believed me. I couldn't get a bid for her.'

'But she was a good cow,' Mama said, indignant on his behalf. 'I saw her kicked myself.'

'But you weren't there to tell the ruddy auctioneer that, Ma'am.'

'And you've got to get rid of her?'

'Selling out, Ma'am. You can take her, and God bless you. You've done a good day's work for my wife and me this day.'

'Then I'll take it and be thankful,' said Mama. 'That's what you call casting your bread upon the waters and getting milk in return.'

Again Williams the carrier was sent for. The little Jersey was tied to the back of an old cab. Mama rode inside the cab and the cow behind and thus she rode home through Pepper Tree Bay round the long bends of the river to Forty-five.

History does not record the reception Mama got at Forty-five when she returned with a cow in tow. Opposite was the Observatory with several acres of unmown grass. Here Mama took the little cow each day and left her tied to a banksia. In two months the limp was cured and the cow had presented the family with a calf.

Mama sold them both for fifty pounds.

In the meantime Mama had been making inquiries about how people got to England. She found out that shareholders in some of the Wheat and Pastoralist companies could travel as passengers on the wheat ships—being shareholders they could travel very cheaply.

The family was instructed that between them they buy her

a ten-pound share in one of these companies, per medium of David's business acquaintances. This, in due course, was done, and Mama, a legitimate shareholder, was able to travel as a passenger on a wheat ship leaving Fremantle in January.

The Schools' Nursing Service gave her six months' leave and the kind of reference that made her blush to mention. Armed with this, her passage and twenty pounds, Mama set out on the long way round the Cape to Tilbury, and Gerry and Sam and me.

'How are you going to get back?' we cried almost in unison when we at last got her ensconced in the flat on the top of a house in Lessar Avenue, for which we had abandoned the Scotsman and his boarding-house on the other side of the Common. Mama's coming had altered all our plans. In a cheap little flat, we argued, three could live as cheaply as two. What's more, we wouldn't have to cut bread rolls in the privacy of the wardrobe and creep about on our knees picking up tell-tale crumbs afterwards.

Oh! the joy of being able to hack at whole loaves of bread in a place as public as a kitchen or a living-room!

'I'll have to earn my passage back,' said Mama.

'But you're fifty and have got grown-up children. You're not a chicken any more.'

'We'll see,' said Mama blithely. 'There's always ways and means.'

And we believed her. Mama had found a way out of worse difficulties than these before.

To begin with, she got herself a job with the London County Council Schools' Nursing Service without any difficulty at all.

'It's hardly fair,' I said to Sam. 'She hasn't had to worry at all. Look what I went through before I got a job.'

'You haven't got your mother's aplomb,' said Sam. 'She doesn't give in. She doesn't lie down and die.'

'She doesn't know when she's dead,' I said. 'Like Lazarus she rises up and asks for more.'

Mama's post—of a temporary relieving nature—had one embarrassment for me. I couldn't tell Miss Anderson or Miss Bernard or Mrs Illington-Etc. about her. The Bishop complicated things. When he had written a letter commending me to God and the care of the teaching profession in England he had reported rapturous things about my father's church work, about the Grammar School on the corner of Highway which

41

my father had founded and to which, he said, my mother had also dedicated her life. But he said not a word about the later years of our life, of our near poverty and our struggle to keep the family head above water. Of mother being reduced from the status of a prominent Churchman's wife to that of bread-winner and chatelaine of a middling-good boarding-house which gradually over the years had risen to a 'Flats-to-let' dizziness of social eminence.

And I hadn't enlightened anybody, not even the Vicar.

Whenever I was more than usually brash, or talkative, or tactless for my ability to say the wrong thing was always in the realm of genius, I remembered the Bishop's letter, and in the privacy of the schoolroom tossed my head.

Here was Mama come to ruin it all.

How could anyone as dear to and cherished by a Bishop be tramping the streets of London in a blue gaberdine raincoat, checking children's medical histories?

In England a Bishop is a peer of the realm, in Australia, in my time, he was just a nice clerical gent who used to come and stay with us when he visited Pepper Tree Bay.

I was always in a fever for fear Mama's superior officer would find occasion to send her to St Hilda's, for St Hilda's was one of the hundred schools in Mama's district.

'On the day you get sent to St Hilda's, Mama, you're to have a fever and go to bed. Then they'll send someone else.'

Mama promised.

'I'm not ashamed of you, Mama. I'm proud of you. But the Bishop's letter is my lifeline, and he didn't say anything about what happened when father went. From the sound of his letter you'd think the Bishop still came to stay with us.'

'They didn't any of them come to stay with us any more,' Mama said, shaking her head. 'When your father went they all went.'

'Well,' said Sam cheerfully, 'the Bishop's made amends now.'

'Look at the embarrassing position he's got us into now!' I said indignantly.

'I call that visiting your own sins on other people,' said Sam with a twinkle in his eye.

'Well, what would you do?' I demanded.

'Just what you're doing, Magillicuddy,' he said. 'And what your mother's doing, only not half so well!'

For which Mother and I between us made him a cup of tea,

hot, strong and Irish.

In the meantime Gerry came back from Ireland, but still refused to take up residence with us.

'You can share Mama's room,' I argued.

'She snores,' said Gerry.

Mama went pink with embarrassment and annoyance.

'I do nothing of the kind,' she said.

'You're not awake to hear yourself,' said Gerry. 'Besides, if you only knew, it's an asset. When you go on to one of these Cooks tours to Europe each time you get to a hotel you tell the Cooks man you snore . . . and you'll get a room to yourself.'

It was harder work, living in a flat, but we were all better fed and warmer. It was only now that I began to worry because Sam hadn't had enough to eat when we were on the other side of the Common.

'Good heavens,' he said. 'That's past.'

'I should have realized,' I said. In penance I began to wait on him, and spoil him, in a manner that set the whole pattern for our future life. The more I did to save Sam and free him for his work the more he worked; the more it became the thing of paramount importance in our daily life. I wanted to gain him, but I lost him. I made it possible for him to disappear for ever within the portals of a University.

Years later when I realized what I had done it was too late. Spiritually he was in another world. And could never be reclaimed.

I told Mama nothing of my deferred trip to Ireland. It could wait. The promise of it had helped me to regain my health. I was well enough now to live on hope instead of despair.

Gerry hadn't acquired enough of the Irish accent to impress the Arbuthnots and she had joined a voice production class somewhere in Bloomsbury. Poor Gerry! How she was eating humble-pie! She must be very much in love with Reggie Arbuthnot.

We didn't tell Mama anything about Reggie Arbuthnot just then.

'It saves such an awful lot of talking,' I said to Sam.

'It leaves only one prospective mother-in-law worrying instead of two,' said Sam.

Gerry, too, remained silent. If it hadn't been for the voice production class in Bloomsbury and occasional flights to High Wycombe we wouldn't have known how she felt.

Of the Arbuthnots themselves she said nothing, but one morning like a bolt from the blue, Sam and I received a card from them. The Master of King's College was dining with them on such and such a night—would we join them. The address was Cadogan Square.

'Oh yes,' Gerry said carelessly. 'They've taken a house there for the season. Belongs to a sister of Mrs Arbuthnot.'

First of all we were in a state of mind as to what to wear. The card was formal so that meant formal dress. There would be ladies present, so that meant a white tie and tails.

To accept a dinner invitation at a friend's house in Australia and appear in a white tie and tails would have been bordering on the ludicrous. But in London we didn't dare to do otherwise. It meant a sleeveless dress for me, too. I thought of sitting out an icy evening in an evening dress and promptly cut down a woollen vest to fit under the dress.

When we got there the house was centrally heated and I sweltered.

The canopy over the outside steps, and the carpet, not to mention the footman with an umbrella who received us from the taxi, were impressive. The servants, all in spectacular livery, who received us and passed us from one to another till I found myself in a ladies' boudoir—and Sam, I supposed, in the masculine equivalent—were positively intimidating. I felt sick about my floating draperies and Sam's white tie and tails. When, oh when, would we meet our hosts and know finally and irrevocably if what we had worn was right?

The maid in the boudoir was frigid. When I said I felt hot and wished I had not worn a woollen vest she advanced on me as if to undress me.

'Perhaps Madam had better take it off,' she said.

I reared back like a frightened pony from her outstretched hand. Have someone else undress me? And, worse, leave my poor cut-down woolly with the raw edges still unstitched to grace the beautiful quilted bed and be the object of her disaproving eyes! I was much too frightened of the maid to take off my vest. I preferred to perspire all night.

As I turned to leave the room I had another moment of agonizing doubt. If we had worn the wrong things, if we did

44

the wrong things, we would have irrevocably damaged Gerry in the eyes of the Arbuthnots.

Then the shades of bishops, and even an Archbishop or two, came to my aid. They were peers and yet how simply had they sat at our table in the old Rectory at Pepper Tree Bay! I had not been afraid of them. My father used as his watchwords 'Courage and Courtesy'. 'If you have courage,' he used to say, 'you will not be afraid to be honest. If you have courtesy you will honour your neighbour as yourself. That just about covers the whole ten commandments.'

I sallied forth from the bedroom with my head in the air, down the beautiful marble and gilt balustraded staircase to the drawing-room below.

Across acres of Aubusson carpet a beautiful, polished gentleman, in white tie and tails, and an equally beautiful shining lady in a low-cut white satin evening dress, detached themselves from a group round the Adam fireplace and came across the room to greet us. They shook hands warmly and led us back to the fireplace where we were presented to the Master of King's, and his wife.

I could almost feel waves of relief emanating from Sam. Except for my woollen vest we were satisfactorily attired.

Sam and the Master of King's, and his wife, were immediately and joyously at ease with one another. For an Australian Sam had the unusual quality of being interested in academic women, and of having a wholesome respect for their minds. The wife of the Master of King's was quite as academic as her husband. She was a medieval historian with a formidable array of research publications behind her. Sam found her engrossing.

Mr and Mrs Arbuthnot, on the other hand, devoted the few pre-dinner minutes to me.

In her soft feminine way, Mrs Arbuthnot was an attractive woman. She was as tall as I was . . . but bigger. As I gazed at her with admiring eyes I thought I would never again mind height. She carried hers superbly, wearing everything that emphasized it. She had on a glorious white satin gown—very *décolleté*—and a string of diamonds like the Himalayas. A giant arctic fox fur stole hung precariously across her shoulders. Her hair was black, soft and shining. Her skin was white and her lips like red apples. Her eyes were a pale blue and only in them did I find the hint of reserves, of the matriarch at bay.

45

Her husband was tall, immaculate, courteous, silent. He led the wife of the Master of King's to the dining-room where we dined beautifully, luxuriously and accompanied by as many servants as there were guests, by candlelight.

Mrs Arbuthnot had left her fur stole in the drawing-room and I wished I had left my woollen vest with the maid. Only the servants were intimidating and presently, when the goodness of the dinner and the excellence of the conversation had taken my mind off them I stopped worrying about them and gave myself up to the pleasures of food, wine and company.

The company discussed the grouse shooting and we had to confess that the only thing we'd ever shot in Australia was an occasional cockatoo, and that was to spare the apple trees and not as a sport.

'But the dingoes?' said Mrs Arbuthnot in her quick clipped voice. 'Reggie says he has been dingo shooting.'

'You've got to go out-back to shoot dingoes,' Sam said, 'and I'm afraid a University man, unless he's a geologist or an anthropologist, rarely has time to go out-back.'

We discussed the relative merits of the English countryside compared with the Australian out-back. We were each polite about the other's country and Mrs Arbuthnot said we must visit them in their house at High Wycombe.

At the back of my mind I was wondering why Gerry hadn't told us Reggie's people were such as they really were; and at the same time I understood the pathos of her 'fight for Reggie'.

I looked across the table at Sam. There was nothing uneasy about him. He was engrossed in a conversation with the medieval historian. I began to notice he was talking and not eating. The course had come to an end and Mrs Arbuthnot was literally toying with a pea on her plate. Sam wasn't even half-way through his course.

I tried to listen attentively to the Master of King's as he recounted some anecdote of the Common-Room but one eye and three-quarters of my mind were on Sam. Why wouldn't he get on with his dinner?

I tried to catch his eye. But Sam, so often silent, for once was launched on a stream of words. He had forgotten everything, except what he was talking about.

At long last the butler came to everyone's rescue. Sam had put down his knife and fork and the butler simply took his plate away. Sam didn't notice.

I sighed with relief and unexpectedly caught the eye of the

Master of King's. He gave me a conspiratorial smile.

'I predict that young man will go far in the Senior Common-Room,' he said.

I smiled at him gratefully, and somehow the next course didn't last quite as long. Moreover, Mrs Arbuthnot drew Sam's attention to herself and he had perforce to put a period to his medieval discussions with the lady of King's.

Mrs Arbuthnot caught the lady's eye and together they rose. I'd read about this art of leaving the wine to the men but I'd never seen it done. Had Mrs Arbuthnot caught my eye I would have thought she was signalling that I'd spilt the dessert down my dress or something. But it was simple to do what the others were doing. The men rose and bowed and we simply departed, first to the boudoir, where again the maid advanced on me, this time with a huge powder bowl and a little silver tray of cosmetics. I was too clumsy to accept her offers of ministration and much too frightened of her to let her near me. She might see down the front of my gown and detect the unsewn edges of my vest! Oh, that shameful vest! Never again, as long as I lived, would I go out without sewing my things properly!

Brusquely headed off by me, she now paid her attentions to the lady of King's. I halted my fussy hunt in my evening bag for my own powder-puff and lipstick to watch spellbound the ministrations going on before the great mirror on the other side of the room. The lady of King's had seated herself, the maid pushed back the shoulder straps of her gown, exposing the top half of the lady's neck, shoulders and bosom, and began to powder her with the big swansdown puff. How narrowly I had escaped the revelations concerning my vest!

Then delicately the maid powdered and rouged my lady's face and applied lipstick with a paint-brush. She touched her hair with her fingers and then retrieved the shoulder straps back to their proper place. The result was a work of art.

Somehow, in my agitation, I had got the rouge on my own face in heavy daubs and was busy trying to rub it off. Of course, I was only rubbing it in and making matters worse.

'Excuse me, Madam,' said the maid.

With quick hands she had produced cold cream and was applying it to my face.

'If Madam would sit down. Just here please . . .'

I was propelled on to the little chintz period stool but I clutched my dress up round my neck.

'Never mind my neck,' I said. 'I never like anything on my neck.'

'But, Madam . . .'

'It gives me a rash,' I said feverishly. 'Please leave my neck alone.'

I looked imploringly at the lady of King's.

'Just make up her face, Smithers,' she said easily. She stood looking at me with a faint interest. I felt very small.

After the ministrations in the boudoir we joined our hostess in a drawing-room, smaller and more intimate, on the same floor, as the bedroom. Here we had coffee, and again talked about small things.

'Does the climate agree with you?' asked the lady of King's.

'No,' I said. 'Not yet. Everybody tells me it is a matter of time. And our climate in Australia, except in Tasmania, is very hard on people coming from Europe too.'

I looked quickly in Mrs Arbuthnot's direction.

'Gerry hasn't suffered from cold,' I said. 'Gerry is more resilient than I am.'

This, I thought, must surely bring the conversation to the reason for our being present. Gerry's name had not been mentioned.

'Oh, yes! really!'

This neither invited me to go on or cease. There was a momentary silence.

'We find that is the case with the students,' said the lady of King's. 'Some take the whole of the first term to acclimatize, others don't appear to suffer any inconvenience.'

Then the men came in. Sam had a faintly replete look. He was benign, affable and still talkative.

I began to feel angry with him because he did not suffer the difficulties I suffered. And I wished he weren't so affable. It wasn't like him and I began to be afraid it might have been as a result of the passing of the port. I hoped he had remembered to pass the port clockwise.

When I wasn't worrying about doing my best for Gerry I was worrying about Sam showing unexpected traits of personality when he had looked on the wine while it was red.

We had more coffee and more polite conversation. After about an hour the Master of King's rose to leave and Sam and I followed. There was more intimate embarrassment with the maid and I didn't know whether she should be tipped. I didn't understand the practice of tipping other people's servants, and besides they were so dignified and awe-inspiring. One felt a tip was an insult. Rather unhappily I left without making a gesture.

We shook hands with our hosts in the upstairs drawing-room and were escorted by a footman to the door.

'Your car, Sir?'

'No, we haven't a car,' Sam said, looking with surprise at the man. He was sufficiently vague to be wondering if somewhere along the line we did have a car and he'd forgotten it.

'We haven't got a car, have we, Magillicuddy?' he said, looking at me as if it were an effort to remember.

Through the open door I could see two taxis drawn up on the other side of the road. The canopy and carpet had been the signal to them to 'stick around'.

'We'll take a taxi, thank you,' I said.

The footman held up a finger and the taxi swung round below the steps. The footman opened the door and put us in. Should we tip him? Sam had blithely forgotten everything except that he'd had a good evening and his mind was still on the theme of medieval history.

'Where to, Madam?' the footman asked.

Sam stirred. In a minute he would say the dreadful, socially damning words, 'Clapham Common'. Moreover, we couldn't afford to go by taxi all the way to Clapham Common.

'Sloane Square Underground,' I said. I had a moment of pleasure at my presence of mind, rapidly followed by one of dismay that I hadn't said one stop further afield. Sloane Square was just around the corner. It gave our financial position away to the footman, an indignity I couldn't bear. In the meantime Sam's thinking processes had caught up with mine.

'Sloane Square, my man!' he said with an air of one who has just dined well and with the great.

The taxi moved reluctantly away from the aristocratic carpet.

'Sam, should we have tipped the footman?'

'Blowed if I know. I didn't think of it.' And he dismissed it from his mind. Oh, to be Sam!

When I got undressed for bed I took the offending vest and threw it in a corner. I was half tempted to tell my troubles to Sam but somehow I knew he would be puzzled as to why I had to cut a vest down to fit my dress, and, if I had had to do it, why I hadn't stitched it.

I crept into bed beside Sam.

'That was a good dinner,' said Sam. 'Nice people. I'm glad I met the Master of King's.' His voice was happy and replete like his face when he had come into the dining-room after dinner.

I began to think I was lucky in having met Sam in my own country, of having married him with so little fuss and bother from parents or in-laws. I began to feel thankful, and even grateful to God, that my matrimonial troubles were over. And that I'd got Sam. I began to feel sorry that I had been angry with him when he wouldn't finish his dinner, when he would persist in a conversation with one person instead of with all, when he was so carefree instead of anxious as I was. I began to feel glad that Sam had enjoyed himself. How seraphically happy he had looked, how simply and naïvely happy he had really been!

My heart warmed to him and the little dull ache of anxiety ebbed and eased itself away.

'Sam!' I whispered. I put out my hand and touched him. But Sam was sound asleep.

CHAPTER SIX

Gerry remained uncommunicative about the Arbuthnots.

'Why didn't you tell us they lived like that?'

'They don't, most of the time. That is Lady Angell's house and her servants. They do that sort of thing—rent, or lease, or borrow one another's houses for the season.'

'But they belong . . .'

'Oh well. So do we. Only we're poor and they're not. It's easier in Ireland. It's not formal.'

'Well, I liked them,' I conceded. 'Immensely. Only there's a barrier. I couldn't tell you what or why because they were charming. Perhaps because the conversation never got around to *why* we were there. I mean it never got around to you or Reggie.'

'But it never does,' Gerry said. 'You don't talk about personal things at dinners. Besides, you were there because of Sam and the Master of King's.'

I gave up in despair and repaired that afternoon after school to the Vicar. In between drinking black tea and folding pamphlets I told him about the vest, and about not tipping when perhaps we should have done.

'My child, never despise to give a servant a tip in England. When they go below stairs and take off that grand uniform they take off that grand manner, and are very poor indeed.'

On the subject of the vest he looked at me with twinkling eyes.

'I always have a bad time with the Bishop's valet when I stay at the Palace,' he said. 'But I remind myself that Jesus Christ did not despise hunger or even rags. And there's no valet I can put on the same plane as Jesus Christ.'

'It seems to me I always have to come to you when my pride needs comforting,' I said.

'And that, besides a vest, is something Jesus Christ didn't have either.'

I drank more tea, feeling rebuked, and folded more pamphlets.

'On the subject of pride,' said the Vicar with a sheepish smile. 'Don't tell Miss Anderson or Mrs Illington-Etc. about my struggles with the Bishop's valet, will you?'

Miss Anderson and Mrs Illington-Etc. remained cool and distant and somehow I guessed they thought I was 'in with the Vicar' and therefore guilty of consorting with company of which they did not approve. Apart from these faintly repercussive atmospherics we got on very well in the school. To begin with, I had developed a tremendous admiration for them as teachers. It seemed to me as if in teaching, in spite of the ancient, shabby, and almost unhygienic buildings, these women were elevated by a greater vision and social duty than I had encountered before. It mattered that children should get their sums right, but nothing like as much as it mattered that they were well, that they understood social conscience, that the important thing was not the getting of a sum right but in the character forces that were involved in the business of working and playing together.

Sometimes it was all so serious I wanted to laugh, but I never laughed so that I forgot that here, in the hands of these people, was the daily moulding of the British character. They were good women and their goodness shone forth in every deed and word. It had to leave its imprint somewhere on the children.

To begin with there was the mastering of the morning Milk Register. This was so involved it was like keeping in operation a giant jig-saw puzzle. There were the free milks for the very poor; the 'doctor's milks'—some free for the very poor but some to be paid for at a halfpenny a bottle and some to be paid for at a penny a bottle, according to the ability of the parents to pay. There were the voluntary milks to be paid for at a penny a bottle, and there were the 'teacher's milks' to be paid for at a penny a bottle. This register had to be made up by ten minutes after prayers for the milkman might call shortly afterwards. Sometimes a 'doctor's milk', which meant a child had compulsorily to take the milk, would be unpaid for and I would slip the penny or the halfpenny in, to save time and struggle. When I was caught out doing this I was sternly reproved. Those who had to pay must pay. When I made a mistake tallying the bottles in my room with the halfpennies, pennies and 'frees', I would put the extra penny or halfpenny as the case may be, in the box, just for peace of mind and to balance the budget. One day I was found out in this, too. There was one too many bottles of milk in my room, yet I had made my balance according to the number of children present and the amount of money needed to account for the milk in my room. When the bottle was retrieved and sent to its proper place there was, of course, a halfpenny too much in the kitty.

The milk registers and the attendance registers were sent for by Miss Anderson and she devoted the morning to going through them. Of course I was found out. Where had the extra halfpenny come from since there were only so many children present? I had to confess I had put the halfpenny in to tally with the milks and not the children. If I had been caught stealing the halfpenny instead of putting it in I couldn't have felt worse. The entire staff sent me to Coventry for the week.

When I did make a genuine mistake in the registers, which was occasionally, until the pain of the disgrace that I suffered subsequently taught me that better death than a mistake, I was doubted and the whole school would be turned upside down tracing the mistake. I would be so nervous that the more I tallied my register, the more I made the same mistake, and therefore could not trace it. When eventually it was sheeted home it would be pointed out that the entire dislocation of the school routine and timetable had been the result of my carelessness.

Of course it was the best possible way of teaching me to be accurate. My disgrace and the cold disapproval of the school was more than I could face with equanimity. I learned to keep my registers with infallible accuracy.

Did I say infallible? One day I fell from grace, and never as long as I live do I hope to suffer again the mental torment I then suffered over one bottle of milk worth a halfpenny.

On the milk front there had been peace for many months. Nobody had made any mistakes for so long a time that I had forgotten the ignominy of such an error. It seemed now trivial that I had ever worried, even had nightmares about registers. I was at peace, and forgot to be wary.

One day, when the children rose for lunch at twelve o'clock, there was a bottle of milk left in the crate. To whom did the milk belong? I checked all the children. Yes, each had had his milk. Impossible that it could be one extra—the registers would have shown a mistake when tallied with the day's attendance. I dragged out the attendance register—it tallied with the milks in my room. Then I remembered that Billy Sugden had been called for by the district nurse and had gone without taking his milk. A heinous offence in itself. In a minute Miss Anderson would come around and there would the bottle greet her. What to do with it? I could not hide it. There had to be the same number of 'empties' as fulls that had come in. The children were already out of the door. I was alone in the world with a bottle of milk and Miss Anderson's tread in the next room. I poured the milk into a vase in the cupboard and put the 'empty' amongst its brothers.

Miss Anderson knocked and came in.

'I just want to check your milks,' she said. 'There's been a mistake.'

She counted the empties and looked at the total of children present.

'That seems to tally,' she said thoughtfully.

Now was the time to tell her the truth, but I was born a coward. If only I'd left the milk in its bottle, confessed to letting Billy Sugden go home without his milk and promised to see that he drank it that afternoon. That was my only offence: I had let Billy go home without his milk.

My mind raced furiously. There couldn't be a mistake in the registers, everything tallied except that Billy was without milk; and he wasn't here to tell on me.

And I couldn't say that Billy's milk was in a vase hidden behind some books in the cupboard. Milk was the life's blood to these children. That was why the staff were so stern about it. I stood looking at Miss Anderson knowing she would have gone without all her meals for a week rather than deprive a child of its milk. Yet I had done so out of moral cowardice.

Minutes ticked by as Miss Anderson looked around my room. My guilt must have shown in my face because she did not stir. And after the long silence it was too late to tell the truth.

I put on my coat and hat and gloves, and still Miss Anderson remained in the room. Something was amiss but she couldn't put her finger on it.

'You're going out in the park for lunch?' she asked.

'Yes. I thought I would today.'

With relief I remembered it was not only the practice but also the principle to lock up cupboards and drawers. I locked them up. The cupboard would keep its secret behind locked doors.

'Leave your keys with me will you, Mrs Richardson?' she asked. 'I want to look through those old boxes of counters you have in stock. We might get them written off. They take up space and are never used.'

With a hand that visibly trembled I handed her over the keys.

'Well, have a pleasant lunch hour,' she said bleakly. 'Are you taking something to read?'

'No, I usually buy the *Telegraph*,' I said. 'I take it home to my husband.'

'Well, off you go now. Don't stand about, time is precious.'

I let myself out of the door that led into the playground while she disappeared slowly through the door into the main school.

My feet were like lead as they led over the road into the park. I bought the *Telegraph* without knowing I was doing it. I opened my packet of sandwiches and only crumbled them.

She suspected from my manner there was something wrong. When she went to the cupboard to check the counters, would she see the vase of milk? Had I hidden it well from view? Did, perhaps, some telltale edge of milk-filled vase protrude around the corner of the books?

Miss Anderson had picked up the milk register and the attendance register from my table; she was obviously going to check them. But they would be all right. It would only be the milk in the vase or, if she came in to check with the children in the afternoon, Billy Sugden, if he came back, might confess to have foregone his milk.

What was the mistake of which she complained? It had nothing to do with the offence in my room. Its inquiry would, however, discover my own delinquency!

At last I stood up, folded the unread paper and threw my uneaten sandwiches in the bin. Slowly I went back to St Hilda's. Would the milk in the vase have revealed itself in my absence?

As I turned in the school gate I could see Miss Anderson in grave conclave with Mr Bellew, the Headmaster from the Upstairs school. Whenever Miss Anderson was in conclave she was grave. Once when I had gone to her room to ask some advice she had been in grave conclave with Mrs Illington-Etc. and her niece who taught in the Upstairs school. They had been sitting round her table, their faces gloomy with seriousness, an almost pregnant silence filling the air with portents of direful things to come. I had crept away. Even if it were not some error of mine over which they thus sat in conference it was obviously something not to be intruded upon.

I waited ten minutes, quarter of an hour, twenty minutes. My errand had some importance, so I went back to Miss Anderson's room. They sat as before. I dared not intrude. Perhaps it was a death, a funeral, a discharge from office! Some vital personal thing held them in the thrall. I crept away again.

At last I must needs complete my errand, in a few minutes the bell would ring and the results of seeming neglect on my part would be disastrous.

'Miss Anderson, excuse me please . . .'

'Come in Mrs Richardson. What is it?'

She looked at me as if bringing her thoughts back a hundred miles. Mrs Illington-Etc., and the niece, also looked at me. I felt I ought to report nothing short of an earthquake thus to impinge myself upon their privacy.

'I'm so very sorry, I did come before. I could see you were occupied—I've left it rather late.'

'Why didn't you come in? We're only discussing a choice

55

between two pieces of material at Liberty's. My niece is going to make herself a dress!'

I blinked and swallowed.

And so it was now on this day of the undrunk milk. Miss Anderson stood in solemn conclave with the Headmaster from Upstairs and the air was heavy with portent. She had found the milk! She had reported my infamy and disgrace. I could not live and work with them. If I had stolen the Church plate, or thrashed a child, or come in drunken I could have brazened out my crime as bad, bold, and worthy a criminal of my stature. But the awful littleness, the poky meanness of hiding a bottle of milk behind a pile of books, was something against which I could not hold up my head.

I would have to resign. I would have to work behind the counter of Woolworths and, estimable and honourable job though it might be, it would not feed and keep a roof over our heads.

'Oh, there you are, Mrs Richardson,' Miss Anderson said, looking up. 'I've just been telling Mr Bellew about the milk.'

I forced a hollow laugh. Sam couldn't get his Ph.D. now. And all on account of a halfpenny bottle of milk!

'I don't believe a word of what Miss Anderson has been telling me,' said Mr Bellew with a guffaw of laughter. 'I believe she drank it all herself.'

'You will have your little joke, Mr Bellew,' Miss Anderson said with a faint smile. She turned to me.

'It was all the milkman's fault, Mrs Richardson. We were four milks short. I couldn't trace them anywhere. When he came just a little while ago he confessed he had broken four bottles before school. I'm afraid I had to speak very sharply to him. He should have left a note. The routine of the school has been upset for the whole morning.'

'Oh!'

'I don't believe a word of it,' said Mr Bellew persisting in his little joke. 'Miss Anderson drank them all herself and she's frightened to confess. What do you think, Mrs Richardson?'

'I don't think Miss Anderson has the capacity,' I said, not knowing where the words came from or who framed them. Certainly not trying to be funny.

Mr Bellew laughed heartily. 'A very good counsel for the defence. Very good indeed.'

It took me a long time to do the household shopping that afternoon. I was tired. My feet dragged and I could find little

56

that was interesting, of suitable price and that would cook quickly. I walked the long way up Abbeville Road to Lessar Avenue and the nearer I got home the more weary I felt. I was too tired. It was all too hard. I didn't want to work any more. I didn't want to stay in England any longer.

Sam would be sitting at the table buried in mathematics. The tea tray would be set as it always was, waiting for me to come home. Sam would get up and poke the coal fire together and say:

'Oh, there you are! The kettle's on the boil.' Then he would go back to his books while I made the tea. He would drink his tea with one eye on the sheet of figures before him and unless I watched out he would drink it too hot and burn himself, or drink it without sugar and wonder why he hadn't enjoyed it.

At five minutes past five Mama would come in and say: 'I lost my way again. Why doesn't somebody make the maps of London intelligible to people of average intelligence. I don't claim to be anything more.'

Mama was always getting lost!

So it all fell out, only Mama did not come in till six o'clock. She had been well and truly lost this time.

'Mama,' I said in a desperation of weariness. 'A *child* can understand those maps . . .'

'No they can't. In any event they don't have to. Have you ever seen a child walking round London with a map?'

'They *live* here. They know their way.'

'If they don't know their way, they ask. The same as I do.'

'Mama, if you ask, you will get lost nine times out of ten. With the best intentions in the world people misdirect you. And even if they don't you don't know how to find your way back to the main thoroughfare afterwards because you never know what was the main thoroughfare you were on.'

'Well, I've been asked to go to St Michael's in Camberwell tomorrow. Will you find out where it is and draw it on a map for me?'

'No, Mama, I won't. I'm tired of drawing streets on bits of paper for you. Look it up in the guide map, a fool can understand a guide map.'

'Then I'll get lost again . . . and be late. How am I to report back to headquarters and explain why I've been a whole morning at one school when it would only have taken a London nurse an hour?'

Suddenly Mama's eyes filled with tears, too.

'Oh, you are a selfish girl, Theodora!'

Sam got up and turned on the light so he could see his figures better. He turned a leaf of his book. Suddenly I sat down in the arm-chair and wept. Sam looked up puzzled and perturbed.

'Why! What is the matter with you both?'

I couldn't tell him. How could I tell him that it was too hard a way for Mama to work her way round the world? That I had done something so incredibly foolish he would be horrified at its meanness.

Only the Vicar gave me comfort.

I sat in his study this time making paper baskets for the sweet stall at the church fete. I told him about the bottle of milk.

'Father, how could I do anything so stupid? And will I ever look Miss Anderson in the eye again?'

Father Reilly applied his scissors to the crepe paper with a flourish.

'Love,' he said happily, 'is mostly pity. Pity for the little things of life. The rabbit in the snare; the human heart craven before the little giant. There's no doubt in the mind of myself that God would have more pity for you, my child, and therefore more love for you than for Miss Anderson.'

This surely was heresy. He sighed deeply.

'I once hid in the Chapel of Mary from Miss Anderson,' he said. 'I'd come in to ring the angelus in my carpet slippers. I only remembered them when I heard her come into the church with Mrs Illington-Etc. There was only one thing to do in a crisis like that, and that was pray to Our Lady for protection. I did it at length and in the face of such devotion even Miss Anderson was put to the rout.' His eyes shone mischievously over the rolls of coloured paper.

'When are you going to Ireland?' he asked.

'In the summer holidays. When Mama comes back from Germany. She's going on a Cook's Tour in July.' I'd told him about Mama, after all.

'Why don't you bring your mother to see me?'

I looked at him solemnly.

'Father, she wouldn't approve the candles, or Confession.'

'Or the bedroom slippers?'

'Oh yes. She'd know all about them. She was married to an Irishman.'

58

CHAPTER SEVEN

Mama continued to get lost.

'I've no bump of locality,' she would say. This infuriated me, though after our tearful duet I never again was without sympathy for her. I spent hours drilling her in the use of the guide-book. But it was fruitless. She had made up her mind they were not understandable and she wouldn't really try.

The Underground was just as bad.

'Mama, the notice says—'Follow the blue light to Piccadilly.' All you've got to do is follow the lights.'

'I do—but I don't come out at Piccadilly.'

One day we had a holiday. Some ancient of the Church had obligingly died and we were disbanded for the day. It was a day on which the district School Nurse could find no work for Mama either.

'Let's go to the West End,' she said.

Mama's idea of heaven was to promenade Oxford Street. So we took the Underground to Tottenham Court Road. Always when we left Waterloo Station I would sit back and think of two things. One got out at Waterloo to go to the Old Vic. Of all the things I loved most, the Old Vic and Sadler's Wells took first place. I never felt a moment so grand as when I arrived at the Underground ticket office and said 'One to the Angel, please.' These words were the open sesame that took me to opera. To Mimi and Rudolph, to Tosca and Carmen. 'One to Waterloo, please' meant one seat for the *Green Table,* or *Hamlet*, or *Pygmalion*. It follows that there was always a request for 'one', for Mama rarely went out at night and Sam never. Sam worked day *and* night.

That was one thing I thought about when the train was at Waterloo. The other thing I thought about was that now we would go under the Thames. Always between Waterloo and Charing Cross I thought: 'Now we are under the Thames.' This seemed to me so wonderful a thought that I would savour every minute of that three-minute ride.

If Mama was with me, or even Sam, I never failed to say those magic words: 'Just think of it. Now, *this very minute*, we are under the Thames.'

Sam, too, thought there was something to wonder at in that. He would look pleased and happy and speculative. I never knew whether he was weighing up the volume of water above us in his mathematical head or whether he, too, pondered on the meaning of wonder.

Mama sat in silence. It did not occur to me that she did anything else but marvel on the strangeness of a fate that had brought us right across the world to travel several times a week under the fabulous Thames. But on this day of our holiday she disabused me. As usual I sat in silence until the train had pulled out of Waterloo.

'Now, Mama. Now!' I said, touching her arm. 'Imagine it! We are under the Thames!'

Once again the unexpected and frightening tears sprang into her eyes. She slapped my hand away.

'You always do it! You are a selfish girl! You do it to torment me!'

'Torment you?' I asked in astonishment.

'You know I'm frightened. You know I'm terrified. You rub it in.'

I was so astonished I nearly fell off the seat. Mama, who had not been too frightened to face a hostile world and bring up five children alone! who had not been frightened of a tumour in her breast; who had not been frightened by the death of Denney's husband; who had not been frightened by the Archbishop; or by smallpox; or by poverty; or by crossing the world in a wheat ship with only twenty pounds to her name—was actually frightened when she travelled in the world's wonder train under the Thames!

And worse, she didn't know that it made me exultant with joy. She only thought I said it to torment her! Would we ever understand one another?

I promised never to mention it again and recommended the bus route into the West End.

'You can see the Towers of Westminster if you go over Vauxhall Bridge, Mama,' I said. 'All London laid before you.'

'I always thought "Vauxhall" was a make of car.'

We emerged into daylight at Tottenham Court Road and Mama regained her gaiety. She loved the shops.

'Now where are we now?' she said, as we emerged from one shop.

'We're in Oxford Street again. Mama, if you don't recognize the landmarks can't you recognize the bus numbers?'

'I don't recognize anything. It's these bi-focal glasses.'

We went into Bourne and Hollingsworth. We prowled round counters looking at bric-à-brac, at cosmetics, at fancy evening bags. We drooped over the needlework counter for we both loved needlework, done by others if not by ourselves.

'Let's go down to the Needlewoman in Regent Street,' said Mama suddenly. Without looking round she hastened towards the nearest door which led into a side street. Out through the great glass doors she hurried, turned abruptly left and literally charged off in the direction opposite to that we must take if we were heading for Regent Street.

'For goodness' sake, Mama,' I said. 'Look where you're going.'

'There's nothing in my way,' she said aggrieved, as if I had meant she might bump into something. Mama always walked at a terrific rate. She said it was because all her life she had had to fit three lives into one and Providence hadn't seen fit to lengthen the day for her. So she had to *hurry*.

'Mama's passage through life is meteoric,' Denney once said. 'Look, here she comes, there she goes. This is Mama, that was!'

Now in the side street of London my detaining hand would not stay Mama's progress—in the wrong direction.

'Mama! What street are you in?'

That halted her. She stopped and looked around.

'This is Oxford Street, isn't it? We're always in Oxford Street when we come out of Bourne and Hollingsworth, aren't we?'

'How can you be in Oxford Street? Look, there aren't any buses. And it's a *little* street. There's the end of it, and behind us is a T junction.'

Mama deflated.

'Oh,' she said. 'I must have gone the wrong way again.'

'Why don't you look where you are when you come out of a door?'

'How am I to know there is more than one door to the shop?'

'It's a *big* shop. Even Boans way back home in Pepper Tree Bay has more than one entrance.'

Mama turned round and accompanied me back towards Oxford Street.

'I told you I didn't have any bump of locality. Now, you've got a gift for it, Theodora. You should be sorry for people like me. It's a gift, like being born with red hair like Laura.'

'Gerry said Laura's hair isn't red any more. She's gone black. It's more aristocratic to be black, in Ireland, than red.'

I thought longingly of Ireland.

Whenever Mama or London or Sam or St Hilda's got too much for me my heart took flight to Ireland. One day I'd get there. It would be like going home.

We walked up Oxford Street and down Regent Street. My feet ached because I didn't walk as much as Mama, and my left arm ached from being prodded. Every time Mama saw something interesting or pretty she prodded me.

'Look, Theodora, isn't that lovely? Wouldn't that look beautiful on Vicky? When Vicky comes we must bring her here. She'll be able to afford these things.'

'Yes,' I said wearily and rubbed my arm.

By mid-day I was tired of Mama and tired of London. Suddenly and inexplicably I wanted Sam. Instead of seeing lovely furs and shining diamonds and brilliant glassware I was seeing his head bent relentlessly over the books spread out on the dining-room table. I thought of the loneliness of that great task he had set himself. Not really quite enough food either!

'Now let's take a bus to Richmond and have maids of honour for lunch,' said the indefatigable Mama.

'No,' I said. 'I'm going home. Sam has a cold and I want to get something hot for him.'

Mama looked at me aghast.

'You didn't come all the way to England to get hot drinks for Sam,' she said. 'Besides he wouldn't even notice you were there.'

'Maybe not, but I want to go home. Look, Mama, here's a bus that will take you to Putney. You'll get one to Richmond from there.' I propelled her on to the step of the bus.

'Tell her where to catch a bus for Richmond,' I implored the conductor.

'Right ducks! Inside with you now, ma'am, and mind that brolly.' He tipped his cap knowingly at me. 'The sun never sets,' he said. 'And sooner or later all roads lead to Richmond.'

'The accent again,' I thought. 'The bus conductors can always pick us.'

I dived into the Piccadilly Underground and headed for home and Sam. He looked up at me surprised when I came in.

'I thought you were having a day out,' he said. 'You feeling all right?'

'I thought I'd like to come home and have lunch with you.'

He went on working for a minute and then, as always with Sam, what I had said sank in about two minutes after the event. He put his pen down and stood up.

'I'll put the kettle on,' he said. On his way to the door he stopped.

'Poor old Magillicuddy,' he said. 'Get out that book of yours, the one you've never finished. We'll work together. When I've finished this so-and-so thesis I'll edit it for you. Who knows? You might be in print before I am.'

It seemed very sweet and peaceful to be sitting there together, drinking tea, and each of us leafing through our creative efforts. Perhaps writing my book would be more profitable than sight-seeing. At least, my feet wouldn't ache so much.

In July Mama went to Germany. She had her Cook's Tour ticket and five pounds.

'I hope she doesn't get lost.'

'People like Mrs Monty never get lost,' Sam said. 'Not for long—you couldn't miss her in a crowd, you know.'

'So little money . . .' I said sadly.

'Cooks will look after her,' he said. 'Some of the students at the University travel all over Europe, through the youth hostels on a shilling a day.'

'Mama is not a student. And she's over fifty.'

'It isn't age that matters. Magillicuddy. It's courage and resourcefulness, and Mrs Monty has got more than her fair share of that.'

I thought for a long time about that.

'You never can tell,' I said at length. 'When Mama sets out on a thing, somehow it comes out differently.'

How right I was.

Gerry had come to stay with us in Mama's room. Reggie's ship was due home again shortly and Gerry was making herself a summer wardrobe. Laboriously we were making up pretty voiles and flowing silks by hand. Then our landlady told us about Singer's sewing-room where one could use a machine for two shillings an hour. After that we merely tacked and fitted things and Gerry repaired to Singers to sew.

'I have a grand time down there in their basement,' she said. 'There are about a dozen machines and a dozen nationalities using them.'

'I guess you do as much talking as sewing,' I said.

'Certainly,' said Gerry. 'I make it my business to acquaint people with Australia.'

'And isn't there any competition from the other nationalities?'

'It's a bit of a struggle with the Americans, but I've got a louder voice. If you speak quietly you might as well keep quiet when I'm around,' said Gerry.

Meanwhile, released from hand-sewing I got on with my book. It wasn't as hard as I thought it would be. I'd written it once and now I took each chapter and worked on it polishing it and, under Sam's direction, cutting it.

'It's a temptation to leave in the bits of fine writing,' he said, 'just because it is fine writing. If you don't cut it out the editors will. Better to be your own executioner.'

Ten days passed by and we hadn't heard from Mama.

'Cooks are in charge of her,' Gerry consoled. 'If anything happened to her they'd let us know. Anyhow, she's due back home in three days.'

It was the following day, however, that we heard from Mama. The landlady called us to the telephone downstairs. It was Mama speaking.

'For goodness sake, Mama, where are you?'

'Croydon. I've just landed.'

'*Landed.* What are you talking about? Why aren't you in Germany?'

'I haven't been to Germany. I had to get off at Paris with a sick man. He died yesterday. Cooks have flown me home.'

'Mama! For crying out loud! An aeroplane! Not been to Germany?'

'Listen, don't stand there arguing, Theodora. Get some food if the shops are open. I've only got enough money to get me up to London and I haven't eaten all day.'

'Oh, Mama!' I could have cried. 'Do you know how to get here?'

'I'll find out, Theodora, *get something to eat.*'

We were aghast. The shops were shut but there were two sausages in the flat and a pound of tomatoes. There was bread and butter, and tea. We borrowed a tin of pineapple and a carton of cream from the landlady.

'We can't cook the sausages till she comes,' Gerry said. 'She might be hours getting from Croydon.'

We sat and stood about listening for steps in Lessar Avenue: peering out of the window into the endless twilight of a summer evening. At last she came.

Poor Mama. She was shabby and just a little untidy. Her face was grey with fatigue.

'Have you got something to eat?'

'Fly, Gerry,' I said, 'and put the sausages on.'

'Isn't it cooked yet?' said Mama, nearly in tears. 'I haven't eaten all day.'

'But, Mama, why haven't you? What's it all about? Haven't you any money at all?'

Mama pushed everyone before her into the tiny kitchen. 'I'll talk while you cook.'

Sam took off Mama's hat and coat and placed a chair for her. He brought her a glass of water.

'Take it away, take it away,' she implored. 'I want tea. Gallons of it. Hot, strong and Irish!'

Gerry was madly slicing tomatoes.

'Put the kettle on again,' I implored Sam. 'We couldn't cook it till you came, Mama; it would have been spoiled.'

'As if I cared . . .'

'What happened, Mama?'

'He was sick—the man. Thorndyke his name was. He had a heart attack when we got to Paris. I offered to stay behind with him till they got in touch with his people.'

'But that must have been nine days ago.'

'I know. Cooks couldn't trace him, he doesn't seem to have any people. Cooks paid my hotel for me but I had to special him at the hospital—he was dying. Gerry, will you stop looking at me and put that sausage in the pan. Cut it in half, it won't take so long to cook. Sam isn't that kettle boiling yet?'

'Coming right now, Mrs Monty.'

'Go on, Mama, go on. What happened next?'

'Nothing. He died. Yesterday. Cooks got the aeroplane passage for me.'

'But why an aeroplane? Why not a train and a boat?'

'I didn't have any money, and Cooks are only philanthropists up to a point. They could get an aeroplane passage probably for good-will. A train and a boat would cost money.

Put more milk in the tea, Sam, it's too hot.'

The sausages frizzled and spat fat while we stood in a circle round Mama while she drank her tea as if she hadn't had a drink all day either.

'Mama, why haven't you eaten all day?'

'I thought there'd be a buffet out at the aerodrome. There was but it was shut. You don't eat breakfast in Paris and I thought I'd get lunch at the aerodrome, or on the plane. I didn't.'

'And your money, Mama? Your five pounds?'

'Oh, I've got a shilling or two left. I could have bought a snack if there'd been anywhere to buy one.'

'And the five pounds?'

'I spent it all in Paris. Gerry, isn't that sausage done yet?'

'Coming, Mama.' Gerry's hands were shaking with haste as she dished up the sausages and tomatoes.

'Never mind the gravy—give it to me just as it is.'

Mama fell on her meal. We stood in silence and watched it going down in lumps.

'What is Paris like?' Sam asked, trying to lighten the atmosphere. Clearly, he was afraid that at any moment Gerry and I would wring our hands and burst into tears.

'I don't know. I didn't see it. I didn't even see the hotel, except twice. I stayed in the hospital.'

Mama's mouth was full. She looked up at us.

'I told you I had to "special" him.'

'You mean you had to stay day and night with him?'

'Yes.' Mama put even more in her mouth.

'Then how did you spend the five pounds?'

'He had to have things . . . oh, have some sense, Theodora! He wasn't unconscious. He was *alone* . . .'

'And afraid . . .?'

There was a pause.

'Yes,' she said, 'very afraid.'

Sam began to pour us all tea. We sat down. Gerry on the coal-box, me on the table and Sam on the floor.

'Didn't he have any money on him, Mama?' I asked gently.

'I don't know,' Mama said. 'The hospital took his things, they handed everything over to the authorities.'

We drank our tea and gulped.

'It must have been very sad,' I said.

Mama had cleaned the plate of the last tomato seed. It was as clean as if it had been washed.

'I bought a wreath,' she said.

We all bent our heads. That poor, lonely dying man, and no one, no one but Mama to send a wreath!

'Well,' said Sam thoughtfully. 'We all have our guardian angel. You were his, Mrs Monty. And if I had been in his place I couldn't have wanted for better.'

Sam, so uncommunicative, had said something very nice. I looked at him gratefully.

That night the moonlight streamed through our open window making a pattern of silver across the counterpane. Reflected in the mirror was the tracery of the tree outside.

Sam stirred and touched my arm.

'Theodora,' he whispered. 'Listen!'

I turned over on my side. In my half-sleep there had been coming to me a sound so sweet and pure it was, I thought, a dream. But it wasn't, it was a bird singing.

'Listen,' Sam said. 'It's a nightingale!'

I crept up the three stairs to Mama's room where Gerry and she were sleeping.

'Mama,' I said, shaking her. 'Listen to the nightingale!'

She sat up and rubbed her eyes. The garden, the street, the little room was flooded with a sound so delicate and piercingly sweet it seemed to come straight from heaven.

'A nightingale? In London?'

Sam was at the door in his pyjamas.

'Shall I put the kettle on?' he said.

'There was never a moment of crisis in the Montgomeries' lives,' Gerry said, 'when they failed to put on the kettle.'

I kissed Mama.

'I think the nightingale is singing for you, Mama,' I said.

CHAPTER EIGHT

In early August Vicky and David arrived from Australia. Also Reggie's ship came in and he didn't bring home a different girl, as predicted by the Arbuthnots of Arbuthnot. These events did not set the Thames on fire but they deprived me of my trip to Ireland which, as far as I was concerned, was equally catastrophic.

St Hilda's had its fete and I dutifully helped the Vicar's

wife serve afternoon teas to the parishioners. She was a shadow of a woman, as delicate and silent as the Vicar was robust and discursive. There was something strange and unequal about them though I didn't know what it was. Moreover, Miss Anderson and Mrs Illington-Etc. did not dissemble their disapproval of the Vicar's wife. They quite palpably ignored her existence. Somewhere there was a mystery. Perhaps one day I would penetrate it.

After the last counting of the last coin the Vicar took me home to take supper with him. The two children were in bed and Mrs Reilly sat silently in a corner doing *petit-point* on a frame.

'School's out for a month,' said the Vicar. 'And now for Ireland, I suppose.'

I shook my head dolefully.

'No,' I said. 'Too much family. They're here in droves. Besides, Sam can't spare the time. There's no holiday for him. If I leave him alone I leave him to the mercy of the Montgomeries. They don't think he should work all the time. So they'd stop him.'

The Vicar shook his head.

'So you won't be seeing the fairies this year.'

'Do all Irishmen believe in the fairies?' I asked. 'Even a godly Churchman?'

He shook his head.

'But you thought I might be after seeing them?'

'Everybody who goes to Ireland sees fairies. At least they look for them. And sometimes they nearly find them.'

'Then you don't believe in them?'

'I didn't say I don't believe in them either. It's not wise to cross the Little People. They might be listening at the half-door.'

'Sometimes, Father, I think you're incorrigible. I begin to see why . . .'

I bit my lip and broke off.

'You begin to see why Miss Anderson disapproves of me? Is that what you were going to say?'

He failed to shake the ash from his cigarette in time and it toppled down in front of his cassock. He lifted his skirts and walked over to the corner of the room where he kicked off his boots and slid his feet into his slippers.

'Ah,' he said. 'That's better!'

Mrs Reilly was looking up from her work. Her hand with

the needle and thread in it was poised in the air.

'It's because he believes in fairies, good fairies, that Miss Anderson does not approve of him,' she said unexpectedly. 'He *is* a good fairy.'

'Nonsense, my dear. Get on with your sewing and don't think or say foolish things. This is what Miss Anderson disapproves of.' He stood in the middle of the room pointing down to his feet.

'Carpet slippers!' he said with feigned horror. 'And in the House of God!'

'He suffers with his feet,' said Mrs Reilly protectingly.

'So do I,' I said. 'He has my sympathy.'

'Then kick off your shoes, my child. Why didn't you think of it before?'

I kicked off my shoes, not because my feet were troubling me then but because I knew it would make us all happy and easy with one another.

It was true that the Montgomeries would have prevented Sam from working. When Vicky and David arrived it seemed as if the whole world was full of Montgomeries and their voices, full of laughter, excitement and anecdote resounding through the open windows so that coming up Lessar Avenue from the last day at school I didn't know whether a circus had taken possession of the flat or whether there was an unholy row going on.

'It's neither,' said Sam consolingly when I came in and said what I thought. 'It's the invasion of England by Australia. And look at Vicky's beautiful hat. It's made a wonderful impression on the landlady. We've been elevated from colonial to dominion status forthwith.'

Vicky, as always, looked like a million dollars. She had a faultless taste in clothes and the money to spend on them. In some circles, namely at the University and St Hilda's, we were ashamed to mention her London address. It was the Park Lane Hotel.

After tea we listened exhaustively to detailed news of Mary and Denney, of Pepper Tree Bay, and the whole population of Western Australia, of whom Vicky always spoke by Christian name. There was no one Vicky didn't know intimately.

The news of Denney and Mary was fair. They were in good health except that Mary worked too hard. Of course, Denney had got herself a job. It was with a journalist on a political paper and now everyone had to suffer a rejuvenation of the

69

political arguments that once used to rend the Montgomery family in twain. Denney took her duty as political mentor seriously, and as Mary voted in the opposite camp there were occasional ructions. Denney kept the old home 'Forty-Five' in a state of rumpus and Mary spent her in-between moments tidying and polishing it up. The one subject about which they agreed to agree was anxiety for Mama.

We poo-poohed this, of course, and each privately made the mental note to write home that night and tell Denney and Mary, in our several ways, not to be silly asses. In short, to mind their own business about Mama abroad. As if anything, *anything* could happen to Mama, except at her own direction!

The schools being on vacation, so was Mama. This meant the flat was in a constant turmoil of comings and goings. The goings were all right but the comings had a disastrous effect on Sam's will to work. After a few days he developed a technique of dealing with the Montgomery invasion. As soon as breakfast was over he would clear everything from the large dining-room table that took up the centre of the one living-room, and he carefully placed piles of sacred-looking papers on the chairs, even on the sofa and sideboard. The table he would reserve for a barricade of books that extended in a semicircle the full length. When anyone came in and made for a chair he would start up with an air of impending catastrophe.

'Not there! Not there! Those papers mustn't be disturbed!'

'Well, where can anyone sit down?'

'Just a minute, please, and I'll clear a space. Just let me finish this page!' And his pen would scratch away filling up page after page. He either forgot, or pretended to forget, that he had promised to clear a chair.

After a while even the Montgomeries gave up. Most of the family conclaves took place in the little kitchen because the kettle was always on the boil and someone was always making tea. As the person making the tea had to be included in whatever was being said and as nobody could ever wait patiently for the tea, 'hot black and Irish', perforce everybody had to repair to the kitchen. Those who couldn't sit on the chair, the table or the coal-box, had to sit on the floor.

David, born and bred in Pepper Tree Bay, was quite used to this. But not so Reggie Arbuthnot. He had a horror of kitchens and swore he had never been in one in his life, except when in Australia.

My heart longed for Ireland but I knew I could not leave Sam to this menagerie. All the pleasure of seeing Vicky and David was tarnished by this inner silent longing to be elsewhere.

One night I dreamed I was on a hill overlooking Holyhead. I was waiting for a boat across the Irish Sea. I was going to jump on it from the hill, and that, in my dream, seemed quite the right thing to do. It was the way my father used to go to Ireland. Often he told the story of how he had done so little Latin he was sure he would fail and he was rushing back to Ireland to take his examination.

'I studied all the way to Holyhead,' he would say. 'My head was so full of Latin I jumped on the ship without knowing I did and I was across the Irish Sea in the worst storm that ever swept it without knowing there was a wind blowing. But I passed my examination. I could learn more in twenty-four hours of concentration than in a term of listening.'

So here I was in my dream, standing on a hill and waiting to 'jump on the ship' and there was a wind blowing off the Irish Sea. But the storm didn't frighten me. I was exultant. Soon, in a minute, I would be in Ireland.

The wind whipped the sea up into a great storm of billowing white water and suddenly, as I looked down on it, the Irish Sea had become a waterfall, and I couldn't jump.

Just to round off the night nicely I fell asleep again and dreamed I was arguing with Mama. I woke up and lay thinking with distress of these old, unhappy far-off things that still haunted me. I thought of arguing with Mama about which was the right direction to go in Piccadilly, and then of coming home, of having lunch with Sam and how peaceful and quiet it seemed.

I felt comforted. Good old Sam, I thought. I had a sudden vision of him buried from the Montgomeries behind his barricade of books. I gurgled with laughter, and turned over and slept.

'Sam is your anchor,' said the Vicar, wagging his finger at me. 'When you go to Ireland you'd better take him with you.'

'But he wouldn't like it. He wouldn't understand it.'

'That doesn't matter, so long as he's got a firm hold on you. I wouldn't let you loose among the leprechauns, my child, even if I don't believe in fairies. And I'm not saying I do, and I'm not saying I *don't*.'

'You're just saying "maybe"?'

'As a man of God I don't hold with such things.'

'But as someone who was once a little boy in Ireland?'

'Ah now, child. That was a long, long time ago.'

Gerry came into the flat a week later with the momentous news that she and Reggie were going for a hike to Cornwall.

'Who with?' demanded Mama.

'With no one,' said Gerry.

'You can't go to Cornwall and back in a day.'

'Who said we were going to take a day over it. We'll be away ten days.'

'But you can't go *alone*,' said Mama. 'What would people say?'

'Everybody goes hitch-hiking in summertime,' I said. 'They go through the Youth Hostels and Cyclists Clubs. Did you want them to take a chaperon, Mama?'

'Don't be facetious, Theodora. Do you think I'm going to let Gerry go traipsing all over England with a strange man, and sleeping . . . sleeping . . .'

'Mama, Gerry will sleep in a dormitory for females and Reggie will do likewise in a dormitory for males. If they're going to get up to mischief it won't be at night time. There are plenty of hayfields between here and Cornwall.'

Mama's face went white with crossness.

'Do you *have* to talk like that, Theodora?' Vicky intervened.

'You know as well as I do that if people are bent on doing wrong they can do it at two o'clock in the afternoon. Anyhow, they can't do it in a Youth Hostel . . . the Warden wouldn't let them.'

'As if Gerry is likely to do anything wrong,' said Mama indignantly. 'How dare you suggest such a thing?'

'Then what are you worrying about?'

Even Sam looked up from his work.

'Don't be so belligerent, Theodora,' he said mildly. He turned to Mama. 'It's really quite all right, Mrs Monty. Everybody, all the young people do it in England and Europe.'

'Well, they don't do it in Australia,' Mama said, beginning to be mollified.

'That's what's wrong with Australia,' I said.

'Anyhow, I don't think this conversation is right in front of Gerry,' said Vicky haughtily. 'Gerry's only a young girl.'

72

Gerry gave me a sardonic wink.

'If I don't put the kettle on, Theodora,' she said, 'you'd better. Looks like there's a row brewing.'

Even Reggie Arbuthnot's thunderstruck amazement at Mama's reluctance to let Gerry go off with him did not quite mollify Mama.

'I don't like it. I don't like it,' she kept saying as Gerry's preparations went forward.

I went with Gerry to the YHA headquarters and was so imbued with the excitement of seeing people buying rucksacks, sleeping bags and bicycle gear that I joined up myself.

'You're not coming with us,' said Gerry threateningly.

'Wouldn't dream of it,' I said. 'This is merely an advance movement on my part against future holidays.'

But I was green with envy.

'I'll run down to Winchester,' said Reggie, 'and see if we can hire bicycles there. It would save pedalling through London's closed areas.'

'Oh, we'll just write,' said Gerry airily.

'How can you write?' said Reggie. 'You don't know to whom to write.'

'Leave it to me,' said Gerry. 'Bet you I get a couple of bicycles in Winchester within three days.'

She'd got them within two days. Late the following afternoon she came in triumphantly with a letter from one Jas. Snooks who could and would oblige with two bicycles. One male and one female.

'How did you know about Jas. Snooks?' I asked.

'I didn't,' said Gerry. 'I just wrote to "A Leading Bicycle Firm c/o Winchester" and left it to the post office. This boomeranged.'

Vicky and David took a trip to Scotland and took Mama with them. Sam and I were left alone in the flat. Sam didn't have to be saved from the Montgomeries after all.

'Sam,' I pleaded. 'Couldn't you stop working, just for one week? Couldn't we have just a very little holiday?'

'No.' He shook his head sorrowfully. 'I took on a much bigger theme than I anticipated. I'm not through the research part yet and don't even know when I'll start on my thesis.' He looked at me thoughtfully under his long dark lashes.

'You go. You go to Ireland. You'll have Laura so you won't be alone.'

I shook my head. I couldn't leave him alone there. The very thought of his head bent over those endless books . . . and the emptiness of the flat made my heart cold for him.

'I'll finish my book,' I said brightly. 'If I work to the same routine as you do, Sam, I believe I could do it in three weeks.'

Laura herself put a period to any dreams of Magillicuddy that summer. She appeared in London herself, *en route* to Scotland, and the shooting.

Sam had never seen Laura before. He had come into our lives after she had left Australia. He was so completely taken aback by her beauty, her grand style and the queer charm that occasionally shone through like soft sunlight filtering through clouds on a rainy day that I was very nearly jealous.

For the first and only time since we had arrived in England Sam put aside his books and gave himself up to talking to Laura. She had always been beautiful, even as a child, but now soft northern climates had ripened and softened her skin. Her dark hair framed the perfect oval of her face and her teeth and eyes shone with real splendour. I had forgotten her eyes were so dark. They were the same deep violet as Denney's eyes. She had Vicky's imperious manner with something really imperial behind it. She had height and grace, and beautiful slim ankles and wrists. Her voice was soft with a faint Irish lilt to the ends of her sentences. My heart swelled with pride in Laura. She was the real aristocrat of our family.

'Oh, my,' I said. 'You've got an Irish accent.'

'In Meath they say I've got an English accent.'

'And in England,' I said, 'they say we've all got an Australian accent.'

'You don't seem to belong anywhere,' said Sam with a grin.

'Well, you haven't any accent,' said Laura to him. 'Thank God!'

She sat in the arm-chair, her hands folded under her chin and her legs crossed, showing not only a fine leg but her lovely ankles and shoes. Sam looked at her with open admiration. Laura's dark sardonic eyes turned to me to see how I was taking it.

Up to her old tricks, I thought. But I was too proud of her to let it worry me too much.

'Come to Magillicuddy for next Easter,' she said, smiling at Sam. 'I'm going to the South of France for Christmas.'

'We'll try,' said Sam. 'It all depends how far I've got on

74

with the thesis.'

It was my turn to glance triumphantly at Laura. She wasn't used to having her invitations accepted with reservations.

'Well, I must go,' she said, jumping up. 'Shopping and all that, you know.'

She moved round the room touching an ornament or two and flicking open the cover of a book.

'*Journal of the British Psychological Society,*' she read. 'Ugh!'

She looked up.

'Can you ride a horse, Sam?'

'Not yet,' said Sam.

'Then you can stay home,' she said flippantly. 'There's no place for you in Ireland. Theodora can come without you.'

Sam was so entranced with her he wasn't even offended.

'I can play golf,' he offered.

Laura paused in her progress to the door.

'In which case you can come and keep Danny company. When he's not carrying a riding whip he's waving a golf stick.'

Quite suddenly the rather wistful charm that sometimes flitted over her face smiled gently on Sam.

'Danny would like that, you know,' she added.

She waved her hand from the door and I leaned out of the window and watched her get in the taxi and drive away.

'Poor Laura!' I said.

'Poor Laura?' demanded Sam. 'What's poor about her? She seems to me to have *everything*.'

'Yes, nearly everything.'

Sometime when Sam had stopped working, and could listen to me for several hours on end, I would tell him all about Laura; and how she came to marry Danny Montgomery and return to Ireland.

Now Sam and I really were at peace and in between cups of tea and snacks of veal and ham pie, the like of which I had never tasted in Australia, I retyped my book and he ploughed through his endless references. When Mama and Vicky and David returned from Scotland I had finished the last chapter. It was Thursday and we didn't go back to school till the following Tuesday.

On Friday there came a letter-card from Gerry at Exeter. Reggie's ship was out of dock three days ahead of schedule and he had to leave to rejoin it at once. He'd rung his mother to have his things sent straight to Southampton. Would I come down and bring the other bicycle back or would she just put the two bicycles on the train for Winchester and come on herself?

I sent a wire hurtling to the Youth Hostel at Exeter.

'Don't dare do that to Jas. Snooks. Besides I want to come.'

Suddenly I lost my conscience about Sam. The book had worn me out and I had arrived at the sanguine state of mind when I could throw him to the wolves for three days. By four o'clock I was on the train, old clothes, rucksack and all. Gerry and Reggie met me at the station. I could hardly recognize Gerry. The sun had browned her skin more than the sun in Australia or the heat in the tropics.

Reggie looked like a beautiful tramp. No dusty clothes or rent sleeves could alter his handsome well-bred features. He had borrowed a tandem from someone in the hostel while Gerry had ridden the other bicycle into Exeter. He now took Gerry on behind him and surrendered the second bicycle to me. We sailed round the by-pass between a glory of trees only dreamed about.

'I never see a chestnut,' I shouted, 'without thinking of the poem—

> *"I think that I shall never see*
> *A poem lovely as a tree."* [1]

There was silence from the tandem.

'This is heaven,' I went on into the rushing air. 'You were meanies not to let me come before.'

'Nothing,' said Reggie out of the corner of his mouth, 'not even a tandem, would have divorced you from Sam.'

We piled into the bicycle shed of the hostel and while Gerry and I went to wash Reggie went into the kitchen to bag a primus and a frying pan.

'What have we got for food?' I asked.

'We've got mushrooms,' said Gerry. 'Hundreds of them. We'll have to wait and see what we can swop before we can acquaint you with the entire menu.'

'Where did you get the mushrooms?'

'Out of a field when no-one was looking.'

'Aha,' I said. 'So you've been in the fields after all. How's the hay?'

Gerry gave me such a dark look I realized my idea of humour was in poor taste.

The hostellers began to pile in with the long twilight and soon Reggie had effected exchanges with the mushrooms for three rashers of bacon, three tomatoes, six apples and a carton of Devon cream. We fed well round the great wooden table, but the food was nothing like as good as the conversation. Every nation in Europe and half the Empire seemed represented there in shorts and slacks.

'Come on France,' a blond giant with a Swedish accent called to a girl at the end of the table. 'I'll walk you down to the village to buy the breakfast.'

'Buy me two grapefruit,' said the Balliol man.

'Grapefruit? Vot eez dat?' asked a German medical student.

Gerry and Reggie had pushed their plates aside and gone outside.

'Your wash-up,' said Gerry. 'You'll have to wait your turn at the sinks.'

I sat, elbows on the table, and talked to the Canadian girl. She was a student at London University and lived and worked in a social club in Bermondsey.

'How on earth did you get there?' I asked.

She had the thickest Canadian accent I had ever heard.

'Wal, it was like this,' she said. 'I began to run out of money and I'd two terms to go. I tried to get a job but I couldn't.'

'Why couldn't you get a job? Most people do.'

'That's all right for you,' she drawled. 'Your accent's only half bad. Mine's altogether bad. No one could understand me. So . . .' she shrugged her shoulders, 'what's a girl to do?'

'What did you do?' I asked.

'I went to the police. I said to them, I said, 'I'm a good girl. And I want to stay that way. I guess you want me to stay that way too. I can't get a job because nobody can understand my lingo and I can't understand nobody else's lingo! How does a girl stay good when she's got no money, and nobody can understand her?'

'What did the police say?'

'They gave me a letter to someone or other in the London County Council who sent me to the social club in Bermondsey. They give me my bed and board and five shillings a week. I study at the University in the daytime and at night I keep order with the kids in the club rooms.'

'Can the kids understand you?'

'You don't have to talk English to kids. They know in advance what you mean.'

'How did you get here?' I asked. 'Here in Exeter.'

'I walked,' she said. She grinned at me. 'And liked it!'

I washed up. Gerry and Reggie were a long time away so I walked outside where twilight had given way to moonlight. They were standing together under a tree by the creeper-covered fence. Reggie had his arms round Gerry and they stood so still they might have been fixed in stone. Something in their silence and stillness had the tragic quality of parting. Were they engaged? Had Reggie ever seriously broached the subject of marriage to Gerry?

One couldn't ask her. Wild horses wouldn't have dragged an admission of failure from her.

As I looked at them across the moonlight I knew that as far as Gerry was concerned this was no passing 'love affair'. This was no will to defeat the Arbuthnots of Arbuthnot. She was parting from Reggie and life was bleeding out of her.

I turned away noiselessly and went inside.

In the morning we took Reggie to the train but I refused to go on to the station.

'I'll buy today's food,' I said. 'I'll meet you in half an hour, Gerry.'

I shook hands with Reggie. His eyes had nothing to communicate to me. His face was white and deadly serious. They had been utterly silent all the morning. When I went back to the station for Gerry, she was leaning against the outside wall smoking a cigarette.

'Oh, what the hell!' she said. She threw her cigarette down and stabbed at it with her heel. When she looked up, her eyes were hard and bright and her mouth set.

'Where do we go now?' she said.

'Bridgwater, wasn't it? Then the Mendips and so to Winchester.'

Reggie's name was not mentioned again.

And so to Winchester . . .

CHAPTER NINE

School in September was a hive of activity. Everyone on the staff had been away and come back bouncing on the balls of her feet. There was something intrepid in the way they went about preparing for the winter. Curtains were got ready for the windows to keep the draughts out. Never mind the light, it didn't get in, anyway. Chimney sweeps were organized to do their dirty work after school hours. Returns were lodged with the local education officer to see that sufficient coal was in. The cupboards, desks and storerooms were not so much spring-cleaned as winter-prepared. When the Vicar came in he had necessarily to hold up his cassock skirts as he stepped over piles of books, boxes of chalks and reels of cotton.

Without ado the children were put to making streamers and Chinese lanterns, paper ornaments and decorations of every kind. This, it was explained, was partly in preparation for Christmas and partly so that the school could be brightened through the long winter days ahead. One morning Miss Anderson came into my room.

'Look!' she said to the children, holding up a little brown bulb. 'Look! They have come!'

There was a 'coo' of delight from the children and some decorous handclapping. Miss Anderson turned to me.

'The tulips,' she said. 'The tulips have come. And look ... daffodils, too!'

There was another 'coo' of delight from the children.

I dutifully said, 'How very interesting!' I remembered the boxes and pots of tulips that had grown along the window edge in spring, but I hadn't really thought very much about them except to remember to water them if I didn't want a scolding. I had not then learned to look with desperate eagerness for the first tiny shoot, the first streak of colour and know that, soon, spring would come.

Miss Anderson left my share of bulbs on the table and disappeared through the door into the school. A few minutes later she came back buttoning on her coat. Her funny, plum-coloured fur felt hat was pulled down over her brows. I never saw Miss Anderson in any other hat. I often wondered in the years after I left St Hilda's how long that hat lasted. For ever and ever, I imagine, by its texture and quality. Its fashion was of no importance whatsoever to its wearer.

'I'm going, children,' she said. 'I'm going at once to County Hall. We haven't received "earth" and I feel we should not wait another minute. Tomorrow we will plant our bulbs!'

This she said with a flourish in a manner in which I might have declared: 'Tomorrow, *tomorrow*, I am going to Buckingham Palace!'

Alas, when I did say those momentous words I was not believed. That was a long way off yet. Spring and Buckingham Palace came together and, in the meantime, we had to begin the groundwork with the tulips.

I did not go so often into the Park for lunch now. I stayed around the lunch table on the side nearest the fire for somehow I felt the cold of my second winter in the north country even more than the first. I was afflicted with rheumatism. Not very badly but somewhat embarrassingly.

Somewhere in the small hours of the morning I would wake up with the pain in my left leg. By breakfast time I was stiff and I had to hobble my way down the long slippery road towards the bus. By the time I reached school I was only limping slightly. One day Miss Anderson was following me across the Park and the playground and saw me.

'I've noticed you limping quite a lot lately,' she said.

'It's rheumatism,' I said ruefully. 'It wears off as the day goes on.'

'I've noticed you start off the day with a stiff leg and seem to have forgotten all about it by morning tea time.'

This, I fancied, she said rather tartly.

'I don't *forget it*, it forgets me,' I said. 'It comes back again in the night.'

'Very peculiar rheumatism,' she said. 'Are you sure you're not worrying about something?'

I looked at her in astonishment.

'What would I have to worry about?' I asked.

'One never knows, one never knows.'

At morning tea-time and at lunch-time for several days we discussed the vagaries of my rheumatism. Even Miss Bernard shook her head doubtfully.

'Very strange,' she said. 'Very strange.'

'Nothing like as strange as that each season one finds last year's clothes don't seem to fit one,' I said, by way of changing the subject. 'I've let everything out, and I'm still *tight*.' I tugged at my skirt for it was uncomfortable.

They looked at me in a concerted silence. I looked back in equal surprise. My skirt wasn't as tight as all that! Why did they take everything I said so seriously? What was wrong with putting on a little weight, anyway? Last winter I had been afraid to get on the scales because of loss of weight, and here I was blooming with health and they were all shaking their heads. Was one supposed to get *thin* with rheumatism? And the rheumatism wasn't as bad as all that, anyway!

Next day I went out into the Park for my lunch. Somehow that communal lunch hour sometimes got me down. I just couldn't understand them, or they me. There was, for instance, the silence with which they greeted my statement that when I had seen Pavlova in Pepper Tree Bay she had made one leap that extended from one side of the stage to the other. Didn't they think Pavlova could fly through the air? They must have seen her themselves . . .

And the time we had sat on the stage behind Galli Curci because the theatre was full and I could see the muscles moving up and down her fabulous throat? And Melba buying ice-cream in Boans Ltd in Perth and nobody, except me, of course, knowing who she was?

Why were they silent when I told these little anecdotes? Or was it just that I talked too much anyway and they didn't really want to know what Pavlova and Galli Curci and Melba did beyond the confines of Covent Garden?

Maybe I just talked too much!

The lunch in the Park wasn't a success because the cold damp stiffened my leg again and I had to limp back to school. I was ashamed of my rheumatism by this time and I crept in the side door from the playground. I was so silent I couldn't believe they heard me, and yet I had barely taken off my gloves and coat when Miss Bernard was at the door. She had a steaming cup of tea in her hand which she set on the table for me.

'So late?' I asked.

'We decided to wait for you, dear. In future we'll have the tea *after* lunch. Then you can have yours whether you go out or stay in.'

I was deeply touched. I wanted to thank her, them, but I didn't know how to get beyond their reserves, and sound genuine.

'I won't go out any more,' I said. 'It wasn't much fun.'

Nevertheless the tea was from then on made after lunch and just a few minutes before the bell went.

'In case you go out, dear.'

There was the most astonishing change of front on the part of the Misses Anderson, Illington-Etc. and Bernard. They did little things for me. When I jumped up to poke the fire somebody was there first. Somebody got a chair for me. Somebody hung up my coat when it fell off the peg, somebody would answer the door if I went to answer a knock. I looked from one face to another. They were chatty. They seemed to like me.

Miss Anderson didn't worry me any more about registers, and the tulips and daffodils were always watered so it didn't matter if I forgot.

They inquired solicitously after Sam, Gerry, and everybody in Pepper Tree Bay. I couldn't think what had come over them. I told Sam.

'Perhaps they've realized that under your brash exterior your sterling qualities are worthwhile,' he said with a smile.

In my room I had an ancient gramophone and with the gramophone went one record: 'In Your Easter Bonnet.'

As the winter thickened and darkened even I began to take an interest in the gaily-coloured pots with the bulbs just showing their brown, scaly tops above the earth. When would they shoot? Once or twice, when the children weren't looking, I scraped the earth away to peer down at the roots. Like a child making sure that something was going on!

Sometimes in the afternoon, just at the end when the children were hatted and coated and gloved I would put the gramophone on, and we would hear 'In Your Easter Bonnet'. Instead of getting tired of the one record I began to get very fond of it. Somehow it brought Easter flowers, sunshine and the Hyde Park Parade into the little cloistered schoolroom.

The children began to recognize this weakness for the record as a vagary in me. When I would take it out they would all smile.

'Now we'll have a little spring all our own,' I would say. The tables and chairs were put away and the children stood waiting for the door into the playground to be flung open. I would sit at the table and put my hands under my chin and smile benignly on them.

'In your Easter bonnet,' I would sing with the record.

'With the thingummies upon it' . . . and my hands would twirl above my head stroking the invisible flowers and feathers and cherries. The children would stand still and watch me.

'I guess they think I'm a bit of a circus,' I said to Sam.

'Teach them the words,' he said. 'The real fun of a circus is when all can join in.'

So we all used to sing it, and sometimes dance around. Until one day Miss Anderson flung open the inside door, just as I was twirling a little girl nearly off her feet.

'Mrs Richardson, if you can't buy another record I'll buy one for you. We are *tired* of Easter bonnets.'

Sure enough, she did buy me three new records. They were pretty and gay and pleasantly suitable to children. We dutifully played them, and even liked them. But just occasionally I would give the children a conspiratorial smile, we would tune the soundbox very low and put on 'In Your Easter Bonnet'. Their faces would light up and we would dance our Easter Parade on tip-toe.

Meantime, Mama had had an invitation to visit the Arbuthnots at High Wycombe from Saturday afternoon till Sunday evening. Gerry had gone back to live with the Girls' Friendly Society so she was not there when the letter arrived. It threw me into a flutter of consternation.

'Mama,' I said. 'I think it's all over—Reggie and Gerry, I mean.'

'That's nothing to do with my visiting Mr and Mrs Arbuthnot,' Mama said. 'They probably never thought there was anything in it, anyway. Who would know better than they that a sailor has a girl in every port? And how do you know it's all over?'

'I don't. I just suspect it.'

'If you knew as much about young people's love affairs as *I* do,' said Mama, 'you would never make conclusions. I've had five daughters, don't forget. And I'd hate to tell you the number of times I've been wrong about *you*, Theodora.'

'Anyhow, what are you going to wear?' I said anxiously. 'And they do everything differently from the way we do it in Australia. Their customs are different.'

I looked up to see Mama sitting with a very straight and dignified back. Suddenly she wasn't the County Council School Nurse any more. She was what she had been long ago, a rather great lady, the wife of a distinguished Churchman who entertained Bishops and even an Archbishop occasionally. Why

83

should I have feared that the English customs would worry Mama?

Mr Arbuthnot might be a very rich man, but he wasn't an Archbishop. Nothing short of Canterbury would have intimidated Mama on the social side. So she shed her navy blue gaberdine uniform and emerged as she really was—a woman of great and simple dignity who had been buffeted by Fate in an engagement in which Fate had come off worse.

Gerry evinced little interest in Mama's visit to High Wycombe.

'They do that out of good manners,' she said. 'Because Reggie's been so often here and had our hospitality.'

Nobody dared to ask her what of Reggie now.

On the Saturday Mama took the train to High Wycombe and left us to our speculations. On Monday I had a letter from the publishers to whom in anxiety and a terrible sense of pretentiousness I had sent the manuscript of my book. They were interested in my book but before they could make any comment would I call and see their editor on such and such a day at such and such an hour.

I could hardly do any work at school and 'In Your Easter Bonnet' was played dangerously often to keep me thinking of spring and not of publishers. The fateful day came and Sam rose one minute earlier to polish my shoes for me. Sam always noticed people's shoes and was convinced that a shining shoe was an *entrée* into anybody's goodwill.

The publisher's editor was charming. Yes, they were interested in my book but there were just one or two little things —quite minor, you understand—not more than a few hours' work. Was I prepared to make those alterations?

Was I prepared to do handsprings down the Strand? Swim the Channel? Deflect the course of the Thames? I would do anything they asked!

For once Sam had put down his work. Through the window he had watched for me and the kettle was on the boil. He knew before I could open my mouth. 'Because,' he said, 'you were dancing down the street.'

We hadn't enough money to go to the West End and the theatre but we had enough to go to Streatham and the cinema, and thither we went. Mama wouldn't come.

'I've got a headache,' she said. 'Besides, I don't like going out in that black fog. I'm frightened of it.'

'But it's a celebration, Mama,' I said indignantly. 'Two aspirins will fix the head and Sam and I will fix the fog.'

Mama shook her head resolutely. 'I'm not coming.'

Half-way to Streatham I turned to Sam. 'I think that was downright funny of Mama. She didn't look to me as if she had much of a head.'

'I don't think it was funny,' said Sam. 'I think it was very nice of her. When did we last go out together?'

He looked downright smug, as if he'd written the book himself, and as if going to Streatham *alone* with me was a very clever thing to do.

I was too afraid to mention the book at school yet. To begin with I had to do the extra work on it and the final edition had yet to be formally accepted. I hadn't yet a contract signed on the dotted line. However, everybody went on making me cups of tea and opening doors for me, and even enduring 'In Your Easter Bonnet' more often than was necessary. After a few weeks of this treatment I had not only grown accustomed to it; I began rather to bask in it than to doubt it. It was very pleasant to be liked and fussed over and so obviously thought something of. I spoke of it to the Vicar.

'I don't know what's come over the school,' I said. 'But it's very nice.'

'There always comes a time, my child, in every woman's life when she has a right to a little fussing.'

I stared at the Vicar in astonishment. Suddenly he blushed to the roots of his thin, untidy hair.

Could he possibly mean . . .?

'You're not . . . not . . .?' he asked. His eyebrows danced all over his forehead.

'You mean I'm not? I'm not . . .?'

'Yes. That's what I mean. At least, it's what Miss Anderson and the staff think.'

'I'm *not*,' I burst out. 'I'm just *fat*. Just fatter than I was. I was too thin. I've been eating bread and sweets to put on weight.'

The Vicar threw up his hands and roared with laughter.

'I knew I'd get some fun out of that school before the year was out,' he said, and he wiped the tears from his eyes with the edge of his cassock.

When I got home I threw open the door ceremoniously. Mama was sitting on the sofa showing Vicky a crochet pattern. David was reading in the arm-chair and Sam was at the table. They all looked up startled by my dramatic entry.

85

'Whatever's the matter?' Mama spoke first.

'Sam,' I said. 'I don't care how poor we are. You've got to buy me a new skirt.'

'If you say so—but what's wrong with what you've got?'

'It's tight,' I said. I sat down at the table and rested my elbows on it.

'Do you know why they've all been so nice to me? They think I'm going to have a *baby*.'

The family guffawed with laughter.

That night when Sam and I were alone he tried to tease me out of my seriousness.

'Why are you so silent, dear?'

'Do you know,' I said, 'I never even thought of it before. I just thought we had to have the Ph.D. first, so I haven't even thought of it. But I'm sorry I'm not going to have that baby. They're always doing something to upset me in that school. Now they've gone and put *ideas* in my head!'

CHAPTER TEN

Christmas came and went. Mama went on a Cooks Tour to Italy and Vicky and David went to the South of France. Gerry went on being at the Girls' Friendly Society, went on working, and went on saying nothing about Reggie Arbuthnot. Mama had come home from her visit to High Wycombe and declared it to have been a success.

'Charming, charming,' she said. 'The kind of people that make one believe the English are the salt of the earth.'

'Did they say anything about Reggie and Gerry?'

'Of course not; why should they? Perhaps they don't know any more than we do.'

'But they must have mentioned their son's name?'

'Well, once or twice,' Mama conceded. 'His name did come up. There were school trophies about, and books, and a lot of naval gadgets. They would mention they were Reggie's.'

'Did they say where he was right now?'

'Yes. They did mention that he was in Colombo.'

'And did you mention Gerry?'

'I did not.'

'If Gerry had had a father, or even a brother,' I said crossly, 'they'd have gone down there with a stock-whip and demanded somebody's intentions.'

'Don't be silly,' said Mama. 'Those days died out with chaperons. If Reggie and Gerry can go off wandering round the countryside for ten days, then they are responsible for their own conduct and what comes out of it.'

I looked at Mama in astonishment.

'Look who's talking!' I said. 'I thought you were the one who objected to hiking and hayfields.'

'You are all very wilful girls,' said Mama. 'I've learned to accept defeat when I couldn't do anything else about it. Somehow you seem to be coming out of it all right. I suppose Providence is looking after you. *I* gave up years ago.'

We heard no more of Arbuthnots though on one occasion shortly after Mama's return from High Wycombe Gerry had come down to Clapham Common for high tea on Sunday. She left her handbag in Mama's room and as I was going there for some other purpose she called out:

'Bring me my cigarettes, will you? They're in my handbag.'

Gerry's handbags were quite different from mine. Inside mine I always carried at least three months' souvenirs of bus rides, receipts, broken stubs of pencil and an indescribable litter of old and forgotten correspondence. Gerry never carried anything but the bare essentials for the day so that if there were some foreign body in her handbag other than a money purse, a powder compact, a handkerchief and cigarettes, one couldn't help noticing it. In this day there was a solitary letter and it bore a Colombo postage stamp.

'So they write to one another,' I thought. I wondered why Gerry never mentioned the letter, or Reggie.

When the family scattered, Sam was left alone to his thesis. It was a happy period in spite of being cut off from a social life. The bitter cold outside made the fire-warmed room in the flat a kind of comfortable haven. Sometimes, just towards the end of the day, Sam would have the urgent need of fresh air and we would walk across the Common. We always looked longingly towards the great blocks of modern flats rearing themselves on the west side and think longingly of central heating, and fruit salad and cream for tea every night.

When school resumed the little extra attentions the Staff had been bestowing on me waned and fell away. Either the Vicar, or the fact that I was now dieting *off* the extra weight instead of dieting it *on* as formerly, had roused the dreadful suspicion in their minds that I was not, after all, *enceinte*. Somehow they felt a little cheated and probably visited their misunderstanding on me. I hadn't done the right thing by them at all. Somewhere along the line I had deceived them.

When I told them reports of Pavlova and Melba way back there in Pepper Tree Bay they got that cold, disbelieving look in their eyes and I stopped my accounts in mid-flight. Nobody asked me to go on and finish what I was saying and I knew, finally and irrevocably, they didn't want to know about Pepper Tree Bay.

'I suppose it's rather naïve of me to think the rest of the world ought to know about Pepper Tree Bay,' I said to Sam.

'Well, do you want to know about the night life of Saskatchewan?'

'Not particularly.'

'Then why do you suppose anybody from Saskatchewan to London wants to know about Pepper Tree Bay?'

'Before I came here I wanted to know about London.'

'London is the centre of the world, my dear. Pepper Tree Bay is just something that bobbed up down under, and is probably inhabited by people too odd to be British.'

I thought ruefully on this for a few minutes.

'I got a kind of a feeling,' I persisted, 'that they didn't *believe* me. About Galli Curci, I mean.'

'Well, you did let them down about the baby, you know.'

So I gave up talking about the wonders of Pepper Tree Bay and never again mentioned any celebrity who visited there. It was a pity. It was such a beautiful place. Nobody noticed the omission so I had to concede that Sam was right.

At last the bulbs were shooting in the window boxes and I knew that the end of winter was in sight. Every day I examined the chestnuts as I came through the park and every day I wondered more, as I had never wondered in Australia, at the inscrutable workings of Nature. The sleeping world was awaking. Nothing looked old, as it always looked in Australia. Everything was new and beautiful and fresh with the promise of life. The trees didn't look as if they were made of wood any more.

Reggie Arbuthnot's ship should have been home surely.

There was no sign of this event from Gerry. And no appearance from Reggie. Perhaps their letters had been the trailing ends of something they wished, or had to end! Then one day the Agent General to whom we had gone about some technical details of Sam's scholarship, told us that the Lord Chamberlain would be sending twenty-five invitations to a garden party at Buckingham Palace to West Australians and what did we think of including the names of a couple of struggling students amongst the wool-growers and goldminers and cattle-dealers, who mostly could afford to visit the Mother Country in the *de luxe* fashion? We thought it was such a sound idea and we were speechless for fear of over-estimating our worth in the Agent General's eyes; and that he meant some other two more worthy and humble students.

In due course the great gilt-edged invitation came . . .

By Command of His Majesty the King, the Lord Chamberlain invites, etc. . . .

Oh, fabulous dream! The King of England had commanded Sam and Theodora to attend his party in Buckingham Palace!

I broached Miss Anderson for leave on that fateful day. To my consternation she received the intelligence of this remarkable invitation coldly. She stood looking at me for a minute.

'I don't know that the London County Council Education Authority gives leave to attend *garden parties*,' she said. 'To visit another school, in the event of illness, they send us a relieving teacher, you know. An absence on the part of a member of the staff would not then dislocate the routine. It would not impose hardship on the other teachers. But a garden party? No, I'm sorry. I don't think the Education Officer would concede that!'

'The Board of Managers? The Vicar?' I asked hopefully. But that was the wrong tack altogether. At the mention of the Vicar's name Miss Anderson's mouth set firmly.

'We'll leave the Vicar out of this,' she said. 'He has no authority over the absence or presence of teachers.'

That day I did go out into the park for my lunch. It was spring but still cold. I sat on a bench and let my leg get stiff. I didn't read the *Telegraph* and I didn't eat my sandwiches. I couldn't really believe she wasn't going to let me go and yet at the bottom of my heart was the cold knowledge that Miss Anderson never retracted a decision. When she made a decision it was final.

When I went back to my classroom, driven a little early by my stiffening leg, the other teachers were busy putting away the lunch things. They barely acknowledged my greeting. Clearly I had been sent to Coventry again.

'They're jealous,' I said to myself. 'The old meanies!' Yet somehow I knew that was wrong. They were not jealous, they rejoiced in other people's success. They were full of praise when I even pulled off some minor achievement in the schoolroom. Even the Vicar they praised when he delivered a fine sermon.

'What am I going to do?' I asked Sam.

'You're going to the garden party,' he said firmly. 'The King does not invite you to see him. He commands you. And not the whole of the London County Council can disregard the command of the King. You go back tomorrow and just say that. Just say "The King Commands . . ." If you don't I'll go and see the Education Officer myself.'

But I couldn't do that. And I couldn't let Sam go to the Education Officer. There is something about the discipline of English institutions that puts a person outside the pale if they go beyond their immediate superior.

I let a week drift by. Sometimes I made up my mind to rebel and just go. At heart I was a coward, however, and knew I wouldn't be able to face the staff after the event. At last, taking my courage in my hands, I broached it to Miss Anderson again.

'The day of the garden party is a Wednesday,' I said tentatively. 'That is the afternoon the children have painting. Couldn't I set them an assignment? Then Miss Bernard or Mrs Illington-Wharton would only have to bob their heads in now and again. I needn't go till recess time. Say half-past two.'

'And would you propose to come to school in a garden party dress? This was said as if Miss Anderson was asking the fantastic.

'I wouldn't wear one of those *very* garden partyish dresses in any event. I've got a pretty navy-blue dress that's not very elaborate. I could change into it at recess time.'

'Oh, very well,' she said at last. 'You may go.' She turned away before I could thank her and almost flung herself through the door. I was too happy about going to the garden party to be long depressed about Miss Anderson's disapproval. I stopped worrying about it before the day was out.

Our greatest problem now proved to be Sam's dress. A morning suit and hat were required and Sam didn't have one, and we certainly couldn't afford to buy one for one occasion probably in a lifetime. Morning suits and hats were never worn nowadays in Western Australia.

We confided our troubles to the Agent General who confided them to the Secretary. The Secretary, with a twinkle in his eye, whispered that the other twenty-three invitees were hiring them from Moss Brothers. At first we were horrified at the suggestion, but we still wanted to go to the garden party. At last an embarrassed Sam took himself off to the city where he interviewed Messrs Moss and Moss. He came back full of spirit.

'Do you know,' he said. 'Would you believe it? They've hired out one thousand morning suits for that garden party. Even the English have to do a spot of borrowing from Moss Brothers.'

On the great day I told the children where I was going and appointed two to keep guard at the door while I changed my dress at recess time. I put on powder and rouge and lipstick . . . things I never dared admit existed on ordinary days. I pulled on my nice white gloves and put on my hat. I let the children into the schoolroom again and I turned around and around and begged them to admire me. They did. Their eyes bulged. Here was Theodora transformed. I hadn't got any more beautiful, I'd just got different. The make-up on my face translated me from the world of schoolteachers as they knew them at Denmark Hill.

I didn't dare present myself thus arrayed to Miss Anderson. I took off my hat and just poked my head around Miss Bernard's door.

'I'm off,' I said. 'Will you keep an eye on the children? They've all started work.'

I withdrew my head quickly before she could take off her spectacles to examine me. I gave a last twirl for the children, kissed my hand to them and let myself out of the door on to the playground.

What would Sam look like? I was sorry for the discomfort, even the embarrassment he would suffer, in that morning suit. And a top hat! Poor Sam, I hoped it would fit him.

I had to meet him on the platform of the incoming train at Trafalgar Square. What an ass he would feel in the train in that garb! But lo and behold, a most extraordinary being emerged from the sliding doors of the train. He had been perfectly fitted. His suit was as immaculate as if new. His top hat shone, and fitted, and sat on his head at a gay angle. He actually advanced towards me twirling his beautifully furled umbrella.

'Sam!' I said, incredulous. 'You don't *mind* being in that thing?'

'Mind? Why should I?' he asked loftily. 'I think I look very good. What's more I feel good. The damn thing fits me perfectly.'

With a whoop of laughter we ascended the stairs and passed under the Arch into the Mall. A taxi cruised near us. Sam held up one finger. It stopped and we got in. Sam leaned back, both hands resting on his umbrella.

'To Buckingham Palace,' he commanded. One would have thought he had been doing it all his life.

The next day I entertained the children at great length on the wonders of a palace. I told them about the taxi and the top hat. About sailing into the forecourt of Buckingham Palace as if we really belonged there. About the red carpet everywhere—just a little shabby but I left that part out. About the long corridors of paintings of past royalties, about the wide, bare, polished drawing-room that led on to the gardens, and then about the fabulous people walking there in the glorious clothes. The ladies with their floating organdies and their wide-brimmed hats; the men immaculate in their tails and grey-buttoned waistcoats. Of the splendour of the Royal Family and how the Princess Royal had the kind of peaches and cream beauty I had not expected. How the little Princesses when rejoining the King had curtseyed. How the Duchess of Kent was the cynosure of all eyes. So gay, so charming, so *svelte*, with nothing of her future personal tragedy overshadowing her sunny face.

Then, of course, I had to tell about the strawberries and cream eaten under marquees and of how even the English people stand on chairs to see the Royal Family go past. In retrospect I took the children to the party with me. First, there was the gold-edged invitation—I showed them that—and, lastly, there was Sam and me going home to Clapham Common in a daze. For just one day of our lives we had walked with Kings.

'In Your Easter Bonnet' was put on and we gave vent to

our gay spirits with the old favourite. Suddenly the classroom door burst open. Miss Anderson stood in the doorway.

'Mrs Richardson, there's such a hullaballoo going on in this room. And that wretched record on again!'

'We were just having a party,' I said apologetically. 'We've just got to the strawberries and cream stage, and the Queen has just gone by.'

Miss Anderson looked at me as if I had taken leave of my senses.

'You see, we started at the beginning,' I said, handing her the Lord Chamberlain's command, and not knowing what I was saying, or what to say, to bridge the awful silence that had fallen on us all.

Miss Anderson took the great pasteboard card and looked at it. For the only time in our two years' acquaintance with one another I saw Miss Anderson lose countenance. Her mouth puckered in at the corners. Her fingers twitched at the card. She looked at me puzzled and then confused. She looked back at the card. She put it uneasily on the table.

'I see,' she said. 'I'm sorry I've disturbed you. Well, go on, children, you may go on with your game.'

Miss Anderson very nearly fled through the door. I gazed after her. I picked up the invitation and looked at it again. What was there about the invitation that had had this extraordinary effect on the Headmistress? Then it dawned on me. The thing that was odd about it was that it was addressed to people so humble as Sam and Theodora Richardson. She hadn't believed me when I had said we had been invited to Buckingham Palace! I had needed evidence. The evidence of an invitation card!

'Why?' I asked the Vicar. 'Why should she have thought it was not so?'

'My child, schoolteachers in England do not get invited to Buckingham Palace.'

'It was because we are from Australia. A number of people are asked from the Dominions and Colonies.'

'I know. But Miss Anderson doesn't know that. Probably she has never been in contact with anyone from the Dominions or Colonies before.'

'But why should she think I would make up such a thing? It's such an impossible thing to make up.'

'Not any more impossible than a tarantula as big as your

hand or the snake that reared hissing behind you while the Curate went to get a gun and then shot it over your shoulder.'

'But it *did happen*,' I said.

'I know. But they don't think it possible, and then, my child, there was the baby that wasn't . . .'

'I didn't make that up. They did.'

'But you didn't disabuse them.'

'How could I? I wasn't supposed to know what they were thinking. Besides . . .'

'Besides what?'

'I suppose I hadn't the moral courage straight away. They would have looked so silly; and they were being so nice.'

'It was easier when they were being nice, eh? When they were making allowances and forgiving your shortcomings? It smoothed the path? It was hard to change back to the old relationships? Isn't that it?'

'Well, perhaps,' I said weakly. 'I just kept putting off saying the fateful words. Then, of course, they realized.'

'So now, my child, they don't take anything at face value. I'm afraid you've got yourself to blame. Now sit down and I'll make some tea. Don't sail under false colours or your friends will mistake you for an enemy. A cut from a friend is the unkindest cut of all.'

I was not to be mollified by the Vicar's words. I was angry in a kind of way I had never been before. Usually my temper, if aroused—which wasn't very often—flared badly. This time it was just deep and cold and was there to stay. The worm had turned. I sent them all to Coventry. They were sorry and they resorted to the tactics of my supposed *enceinte* stage. They plied me with cups of tea and now and again a lightly-boiled egg.

Boiling eggs lightly was Mrs Illington-Etc.s special prerogative. She did it with an air of ceremonial. The eggs were always exactly right and everybody always said so. They were savoured and commented on and praised—as if the boiling of an egg lightly could only be achieved by genius. Eggs or no eggs, I was not to be won over. They made the tea wishy-washy, anyway!

One lunch-time Miss Bernard commented on the fitful vagaries of the spring weather. Tentatively she inquired after the manners of 'weather' in Pepper Tree Bay. They all put down their spoons and leaned an attentive and interested ear.

But I was not to be drawn about talk of Pepper Tree Bay. I merely replied that they had weather in Pepper Tree Bay, too.

I didn't like them any more and I didn't care how soon Sam got his Ph.D. and we all returned to Pepper Tree Bay.

I suppose I had to be cross until I had some tangible way of expressing it. With spring, along with the tulips and daffodils and leaves on the chestnuts, had come my contract with the publishers. The book was actually going into production.

Vicky and David had found a 'Colonel' somewhere, or rather the 'Colonel' had found them and he was introducing them to a racecourse here and there. Also West-End restaurants. They were still at the stage when they couldn't understand why they didn't win at the races. Somehow the 'Colonel's' bookmaker kept letting him down.

Reggie's ship must have been back in home waters but there was no evidence of Reggie about. Every time Gerry had scraped enough money to pay her fare to Ireland thither she went.

'I don't need any money in Ireland,' she said. 'I just live on Laura and Danny.'

Mama's independent soul was outraged.

'You can't do that!'

'But I can and do,' said Gerry. 'Remember how Aunt Shelagh and Laura used to live on us at the Rectory, for weeks and weeks on end. And they had so much money they could have bought and sold us!'

'That was your father's doing,' said Mama. 'He had pride if you girls have none.'

Every time Mama scraped a few pounds together, and had a long week-end or an Easter break, she got together with Thos. Cook and motor-coached to the Lakes or the Fens, or even the coal-mines of Wales. There was nothing Mama was going to miss.

'I don't smoke, and I don't eat sweets,' she said. 'All I want is an occasional cup of tea, hot, strong and Irish, and as I can never get it that way unless I make it myself I take my little primus and kettle with me. All I want is my tour ticket and a couple of pounds in case of need.'

Dressed in her blue gaberdine raincoat, she was an indefatigable traveller.

Meantime the 'Parish Night' at St Hilda's drew nigh. The school was properly dislocated this time. Desks and tables were cleared and two of the schoolrooms were opened up by means of folding doors to make a hall. The children made more paper-chains and Chinese lanterns. Trestle tables were set up in horseshoe fashion and sheets were starched and laundered to look like table-cloths. To the parish dinner came the parishioners of St Hilda's and 'Friends' of St Hilda's. These latter were people who perhaps long ago had had some connection with the church and had continued their interest by sending an annual donation to the parish funds. Quite the most impressive of these friends was a General out of the West End; and a theatre *entrepreneur*, a man who consorted in his daily life with people like Noel Coward and Laurence Olivier and Sybil Thorndyke. In the candelight of the parish dinner they looked just the same as anybody else.

Sam being a visitor from overseas, and (who knows?) a student of whom they might one day be proud, was seated at the end of the top table. Just being one of the teachers I sat at the bottom of the horse-shoe.

During the dinner somebody got up and sang 'Trade Winds'. The local bootmaker played the 'cello and two of the church-wardens, with their wives, sang a quartet from *Lucia di Lammermoor*. The Vicar made a speech, each paragraph of which ended with a Latin tag, and the man next to Sam got up to reply to the toast to the Visitors and made his speech in rhymed couplets. This particularly pleased the Vicar and annoyed Miss Anderson.

'As if the parishioners of St Hilda's understand Latin tags and rhymed couplets,' she said indignantly. The Vicar's wife worked anxiously at conversation with the General and the editor of the parish magazine, little Miss Carpenter, listened spellbound and visibly shocked to the theatre *entrepreneur*. Across the distance I noticed that Sam, and the man who made rhymed couplets, were deep in the kind of conversation they both enjoyed.

As soon as the dinner was over the choirboys began to clear and move the tables for more concert items; Sam came eagerly across the room to me. He had his dinner neighbour in tow.

'Theodora,' he said. 'May I introduce Mr Rushton? He knows all about you.'

'Who's been talking to you?' I said. 'The Vicar or Miss Anderson?'

'According to the teller, so is the legend . . . is that it?' Mr Rushton asked with a smile.

'I've been talking to him,' said Sam. 'Do you know what Mr Rushton is? He's a publisher's reader and he does work for your publishers.'

I was suitably awed.

'I didn't read your manuscript, I'm sorry to say,' he said. 'But I recollect it being discussed. Congratulations on being in with the firm.'

I glowed. I really felt like a writer. We sat down together and talked at length about writing and publishing. When the Vicar came towards us Mr Rushton explained our mutual interest. The Vicar poked his long forefinger through his thin, scrappy hair.

'So,' he said. 'We've got to writing about tarantulas and snakes, have we?'

'You'd be surprised,' I said. 'I've written a harmless little love story and there isn't a single snake in it.'

'Not even a villain?' asked Mr Rushton.

'Not even a villain,' I said.

The next morning when I entered Miss Anderson's room to sign the time book she was standing in one of those solemn conclaves with Mrs Illington-Etc. and Miss Bernard that always made me think they were planning a funeral. As I came in the door they turned and surveyed me. Mrs Illington-Etc. coughed. Miss Bernard smiled and fussed about finding the pen for me to sign. Miss Anderson stood looking at me with a half-smile that made her face unexpectedly human.

'Mrs Richardson,' she said half playfully. 'Why didn't you tell us you were a writer? Why didn't you tell us you had written a book?'

Now came my great moment for revenge, and I took it.

'Because you wouldn't have believed it,' I said. 'Any more than you believed about tarantulas and Pavlova and Buckingham Palace.'

I drew off my gloves and with a flourish I signed the time book. I looked at them coldly.

'Yes, I've written a book. And it's going to be published soon. Shall I tell someone to ring the bell, Miss Anderson?'

Miss Bernard said 'Oh!' in the manner of a balloon slowly deflating. Mrs Illington-Etc. said:

'Oh dear! Oh dear, what a *situation*!'

Miss Anderson looked at me for quite a long time.

'Never mind about the bell, Mrs Richardson. I don't think

we need to ring it quite so early today.'

This time she really smiled. I retreated, not quite as victoriously as I had expected. They were obviously so very sorry my feelings had been hurt.

After that the school returned to normal. They didn't fuss so much and I didn't talk so much. There was a kind of truce and, anyhow, soon it would be summer, and there would be roses in the park.

CHAPTER ELEVEN

Through the post there came another imposing gilt-edged card. There was one for Mama and Gerry, too. Lloyds of London were having an evening reception. They had the honour of inviting, etc.

We had the honour of accepting, too. Even Sam emerged from his thesis to put on his tails and white tie. Gerry, it was agreed, would come to Clapham Common early in the afternoon and we would all dress there and proceed together. Gerry didn't bring a dress; instead she brought about six yards of satin and tulle.

'You can't make that up in time,' I complained.

'With you and Mama assisting I can make anything up in time.'

'I'll give my assistance in the kitchen,' Mama said firmly. 'I'll get the meals and do the shopping. Theodora can help you.'

I either had to help Gerry or lend her my blue dress again. I chose the lesser sorrow and we got out pins and patterns. The landlady from downstairs lent us her hand-sewing machine.

Gerry was the perfect figure for making a dress *on to* a person. We made a straight slip in an hour, then Gerry put it on, stood on a stool while we, the landlady and I, pinned satin and tulle in strange places until she looked like a dressmaker's model. Every time Gerry wilted or complained of the standing I stuck a pin in her.

'That will teach you to leave it to the last minute to make a dress!'

At last the arranging and pinning were done. It took less than an hour to sew the main seams, the shoulders and the waist on the machine but the yards of hem and drape that needed hand-sewing looked as if it would take us for ever to complete. We sat on the floor, Mama and the landlady included, and held bits of hem in our hands while we sewed furiously.

Strange though it may seem, the completed article made Gerry look better than I had ever seen. It was an off-white with a hint of pink in the sheen of the satin. She wore Mama's silver shoes while Mama wore my black satin ones. For once I was able to claim my own silver shoes to myself.

We stood, bathed, powdered and dressed, demanding admiration from Sam.

'There'd be some who'd be intimidated by taking out three Montgomeries,' he said. 'But I must confess I'm proud of you. You all look beautiful, and, Mrs Monty, you look like their sister.'

Sam always said the right thing to Mama, and indeed she looked twenty years younger.

Gerry was beautiful. Her love affair, with whatever aches it had brought in its train, had given her a touch of seriousness and even dignity.

'We ought to have a taxi,' said Sam.

'No,' we all said firmly.

'What's wrong with the Underground?' asked Gerry. 'It's still running, isn't it?'

'Besides, we might need a taxi home,' I put in.

'I've been in England a year, and I haven't been in a taxi yet,' said Mama.

So to the Underground we went. The only hitch in our arrival at Lloyds was Sam's temporary loss of the cards. We stood in anguish while he searched all his pockets.

'What made me give him *my* card?' said Gerry querulously.

Sam had been through every pocket twice and there were no cards.

'Think back to what you did after we handed them to you in the hall, Sam,' I pleaded. 'Where did you go from there? To the bathroom? The living-room? It might help you to remember what you did with your hands, and where you put the things that were in your hands.'

A seraphic smile spread over Sam's face.

'In your handbag, Theodora. That's where they are. I was afraid I might forget them. Besides they make my pocket bulge.'

I opened my handbag and there were the cards.

'Idiot!' I said under my breath.

'You should have paid the fares at the Underground, then you'd have known,' said Sam imperturbably.

We presented our cards, were announced, and walked in out of the drab street into a heavenly world.

I had seen flowers, but never flowers like Lloyds of London had arranged. The Chelsea flower show was dimmed. The vast reception hall was walled with flowers from the floor to the ceiling. The air was pungent and cool and sweet with them. Across the polished floor a young man detached himself from a group and came forward to meet us. He introduced himself as one of the underwriters and he was to be our host for the evening. Each party or couple who arrived were thus received and our hosts took us at once to a buffet against the wall.

'You must have a drink,' he said. The cork in a bottle popped and between the folds of the white napkin a fine stream of pale bubbly poured into the shallow glasses. We sipped delicately. I thought it was a nice innocuous drink and quite good for my thirst.

Uniforms gleamed, jewellery sparkled and glorious ladies willowed across the polished floor like flowers on long satin stalks.

Our host, tall, handsome and reminiscent of a Guard's officer, watched them through hooded eyes. It occurred to me that he was getting some enjoyment as his friends amongst the young officials advanced to meet a newly-announced couple.

'Ha!' one imagined him saying to himself. 'Young Forsyte has bagged a knight. There goes Thorndyke getting in first with the bishop. He always was for the Church. Here come another couple of Colonials—that ought to be Smithson's meat and drink, preferably drink.'

We moved around the great hall and were introduced to others. The underwriters never forgot their perfect manners but every now and again two would converge together, their guests be introduced and while polite small talk was interchanged the two hosts would cause another cork to pop at yet another buffet. They would drink and so would we; they would speak to one another out of the corners of their mouths but their faces would never, even for a moment, lose their expressions of bland interest in their protegés.

After this kind of minor sortie we would move on. Our host explained to us the wonders of Lloyds and stories of the Lutine Bell. And so to another buffet.

Gentlemen bowed, ladies inclined their beautifully coiffured heads, friends would meet and part and all the time the pretty, pale, bubbly drink flowed from thousands of bottles at hundreds of buffets. Caviare, chicken, turkey, ham, salads, fruits, bonbons and nuts were toyed with. In the distance a glorious string orchestra touched the air with sound as gently as a zephyr.

Our host lost his Guards air. He held firmly to Gerry's arm and engaged Sam in his own subject. Mama was always bowed first through a door and I was always handed first the little shallow glass. He was the Englishman at his best.

Perhaps it was halfway through the evening that I saw Reggie Arbuthnot. We had reached one of the upper reception rooms and the crowd was particularly dense. Over the rim of my glass I noticed the back of a young man on the other side of the room and I idly thought how much it looked like Reggie's back. Then he turned round and I saw it was Reggie.

He saw Gerry and stood looking at her a minute. His face had a strange, stern quality and his lips closed in a straight line over his beautiful white polished teeth. I glanced quickly at Gerry. She had not seen him. She was laughing at some joke just told her by our host. Sam was looking down at his hands as he twiddled the stem of his glass. Mama was behind me. I was on the point of saying something but stopped. I looked back. Reggie was gone. I stood on tip-toe to look over the heads of the crowd to see where he had gone, but I could see him nowhere. I glanced towards the doorways. There was no evidence of his departure. I could have dreamed it.

I shook my head and put my glass back on the table. Sam had seen my puzzled gesture.

'What's the matter?'

I shook my head again.

'I could have been dreaming, but I'm sure I wasn't.'

'How much of that stuff have you been drinking?'

'Oh, don't be silly, Sam,' I said. 'That's only a sort of dry lemonade—as if that would affect me.'

Our host coughed behind his hand. Sam's eyebrows shot up.

'Lemonade?' he said. 'Blasphemy!'

'Well, what is it—a sort of light wine?'

'A sort of light wine?' Our host coughed again and took

out his handkerchief and delicately blew his nose.

'Theodora, do you really mean to say you don't know what you've been drinking?'

I looked at the bottles but I wasn't wearing my reading glasses and I couldn't decipher the labels. Anyhow, they were in French.

'Well, what is it?'

'*Champagne*. Darling, don't tell me you've been seeing champagne flowing like rivers and didn't know. Haven't you ever tasted champagne before?'

'No,' I said. 'I haven't. And if that's all it is . . .' Then I remembered our host. I also remembered a night in Pepper Tree Bay—long, long ago. There had been champagne, and gipsy music. And a damaged heart.

'I'm sorry,' I said apologetically. 'I suppose that's rather naïve of me.'

'Have some more,' he commanded. 'Now you know what you're drinking you'll enjoy it.'

I reared back.

'No. I've had about twelve glasses already.'

'Twelve glasses!' said Mama, alarmed.

'Do you feel all right?' Sam asked.

'I feel perfectly all right. If it's champagne, why don't I feel queer?'

'You will,' said our host with an air of amusement. 'It has a delayed action.'

'Don't you drink any more,' Mama and Gerry said in a chorus.

'When I come to think of it, I would like to drink some—just to know what champagne really tastes like. I wasn't thinking about it before.'

There was a guffaw of laughter but Sam looked concerned.

'What were you shaking your head for? Are you sure you're all right, Theodora?'

'I'm perfectly all right,' I insisted. 'I was shaking my head because I thought I saw someone. Then when I looked again he wasn't there. He'd just vanished, and I'm certain he didn't go through the doors.'

There was a burst of laughter again and Sam decided to take me under his arm.

'I'm all right,' I kept saying. And I was, but no one was going to believe me. It was useless to say I had seen Reggie

Arbuthnot. It would have ruined Gerry's evening, and they would all insist it was the champagne. I was so clear-headed I resolved to have one more glass when we took our final supper. I couldn't bear to think that I had drunk the stuff all night and couldn't tell what it tasted like.

This time I savoured my glass, and thought it was very fine indeed.

'Why had I forgotten what champagne was like,' I wondered sorrowfully. Sam kept me pinned to his arm, however, and was reluctant to let go even when we went to the cloak-room for our coats.

We were ushered down the long flower-lined hall and the commissionaire saluted us.

'Taxi, Sir?'

Because we were always afraid of disappointing the servants, Sam said.

'Yes, please. A taxi.'

The commissionaire's finger went up and a taxi moved up two yards. The door was opened and Mama and Gerry got in. I had a sudden urgent knowledge that I couldn't get into that confined space.

'Sam,' I implored. 'Let's walk. I couldn't get in . . .'

'Nonsense,' he said. 'You're perfectly all right. A shocking waste of champagne.'

'I can't get in the taxi,' I said stubbornly. Mama and Gerry were expostulating with me. Sam was propelling me from the rear.

'Nothing on earth will induce me to get in it,' I said.

Behind us the commissionaire was getting restive with the door. Departing guests were piling up on the carpet under the canopy. Taxis along the rank were crawling up, their drivers' heads out to see what was the cause of the delay. I turned away and took a few steps along the footpath. Sam gave up the struggle. He gave the driver the Lessar Avenue address for Mama and Gerry and walked towards me. I took hold of his arm.

'Word of honour, I'm all right, Sam,' I said. 'But I couldn't have got in the taxi if you'd crowned me.'

I never felt more clear-headed in my life. We walked to the embankment. 'It's too late for the Underground,' Sam said. 'Would you call the top of a tram a confined space?'

'I don't mind the top of a tram. It was just the taxi, and

Gerry's scent, and Mama's powder.'

We got on the tram and ricocheted our way south of the river and homeward bound. I didn't tell Sam about Reggie. I was perfectly certain he would have thought it was the champagne.

Next morning, however, after Gerry had returned to her tabernacle in the West End, I broached the subject with Mama. To my surprise she told me she, too, had seen him.

'I said nothing to Gerry,' she said. 'If he had wanted to see us he would have come over.'

'He did see us. He was looking right at us.'

'I know. I saw him.' With that her lips clamped together and it was quite clear Mama had nothing more to say about Reggie Arbuthnot to me, or to anyone else.

'Just as a matter of courtesy,' I persisted. Mama went on saying nothing. I fell silent, too.

Poor Gerry. Then the break had come from Reggie and not herself!

I washed up the breakfast things and didn't know I did it— I was so engrossed in a conversation I was having with Reggie Arbuthnot in which I told him in detail what I thought of him.

'Mama,' I said, stamping up the three steps to her room. 'We ought to send Sam along to demand an explanation.'

'You ask Sam,' she said with a small smile. Well, at least she hadn't said the age of chivalry died with chaperons!

'What do you suppose he was doing there?'

'I suppose he was invited. Lloyds have more to do with ships and men that sail them than with anything else.'

'A third officer is not such a very high rank . . .'

'Neither is a travelling student.'

Was that the cause of the disruption of Gerry's love affair? Weren't we good enough?

My heart squeezed when I thought of Gerry and her lessons in voice production, and her flights to Ireland. She didn't get on very well with Laura but Magillicuddy established her position in life.

'Mama, we've got an archdeacon and a canon in our family. Not to mention the Montgomery seat . . .'

'If I know the Montgomeries, Magillicuddy is not much more than a barn of a place. What it was once is not what it is now, except what Laura is making of it.'

'I hope you mentioned the archdeacon and the canon when

you were at High Wycombe,' I said.

'I did nothing of the kind,' said Mama. She said it in the kind of voice that accused me of being a snob. I was ready to bite the dust for poor Gerry's sake. Mama had often said when all went well with the Montgomeries we were at sixes and sevens with one another. Let one be in need or trouble, however, and the clan spirit brought us out battling.

Later in the day Vicky and David arrived. There was something pert about Vicky, and David looked like the cat that had licked the milk and discovered it to be cream. They talked about frivolous things but every now and again a happy glance would pass between them.

'What's on your mind?' I asked at length. 'You two found a fortune?'

'No. Just saved it, that's all,' said Vicky, shaking her shoulders.

'How can you save a fortune unless you've had something to begin with?'

'We caught a fish,' said Vicky. 'A nice big, slippery one and we put salt on his tail and caught him.'

'It's a bird you catch with salt on its tail,' said David.

'You must admit he was some bird,' said Vicky, and then added in a voice heavy with satisfaction. 'A gaolbird he'll be now.'

'The Colonel?' I asked, one eyebrow cocked.

'The Colonel,' said David. 'One of Vicky's finds.'

'I like that. It was I who guessed he was a fraud first.'

'You found him. Then you found him out. Granted.'

'For goodness sake, tell us and stop talking in riddles,' said Mama.

'There's going to be a court case,' said David. 'And we've been warned by the police to tell the details to *no one*. It might prejudice the case.'

'We're no one,' I said hastily. 'Nobody in England ever heard of us.'

'We'll tell you just a little bit,' said Vicky. 'When we first met the Colonel he seemed to know, or know of, everything in Western Australia. He'd been there and was quite an intimate friend of all the first families. Or so you'd think. I did for quite a long time.' She turned to David. 'You must admit he was pretty good. After all, I've *lived* on Innanup station and been an intimate of the Bastons all my life. He knew all about

Innanup and he didn't make a mistake there. No, it wasn't the Bastons.'

'Who was it then? Who did he make a mistake about?' I asked.

'It wasn't a person. It was a word.'

'Ah, ah!' said David reprovingly to Vicky. 'That's the evidence. You're not to divulge it now.'

'All right,' said Vicky. 'You'll have to come to court to hear all about it.'

'There's no harm in you knowing that once we guessed,' said David. 'We also guessed that sooner or later we were going to be caught for money. So we went on fooling him, just waiting.'

'He couldn't be so blatant that he'd ask you straight out for large sums of money?' I asked.

'Oh no. He worked up to it. He was on all sorts of committees, so he said. We guessed that we'd be roped in for one, sooner or later.'

'What was it? Starving Abyssinians?'

'No. Starving students. I guess Sam gave him the idea,' David said with a grin.

'Sam?' I said indignantly. 'He hasn't even seen him.'

'No, but Vicky's told him all about Sam. And Thora, the Canadian girl. You've no idea how Vicky's heart had been wrung for all you unfortunate students. The Colonel's heart was wrung, too. He promptly got up a committee in aid of them.'

'But that's so obvious . . .' I said.

'Not the way they do it. Confidence tricksters like the Colonel are artists at it. That's why Vicky's so smug. The police have been trying to catch this fish for a long time. When Vicky landed him they looked like giving her a medal.'

'I was taken in about the Bastons. You wouldn't believe that possible, would you?' said Vicky.

'To cut a long story short,' David said, 'his committee were buying a hostel for indigent students. He wanted us to act along with a lot of other high-sounding names, as guarantors. In good faith we were asked to show the money, just as a matter of routine. We weren't going to be asked to hand it over. So, as a matter of routine, I mentioned it to the police. There were two detectives sitting at the next table when we had lunch at the Trafalgar Palace. I had a really big time preventing Vicky from looking at them and tossing her feather—you know the way she does.'

'I didn't even know which were the detectives, or where they were,' Vicky said haughtily. 'To be perfectly honest, I had cold feet. I began to wonder if I was wrong after all.'

'Go on,' Mama said impatiently. 'What happened next?'

'I had the money with me. Two hundred pounds in my wallet. I handed it over to the Colonel and his friend, the "Chairman of the Committee" to examine. They expressed satisfaction and handed me back my wallet. Two minutes afterwards the Colonel left to ring up his solicitors and two minutes after that the "Chairman" remembered something he had failed to remind the Colonel of and which he wanted reported to the solicitors. They're certainly a fine pair of actors. I don't know how the West End stage gets on without them.'

'Seems like you two were no mean actors yourselves,' I said with undisguised admiration. 'Do you mean to say you looked unconcerned throughout all this?'

'I didn't feel quite so good,' David admitted, 'when I examined my wallet. Of course it was empty. In fact, it wasn't my wallet at all. It was its exact replica. They'd probably been studying it for a long time.' He took out his wallet and showed it to us. 'Not hard to ring the changes,' he said. 'It's a standard plain black morocco case.'

'Is this yours or the one they gave you?'

'This is mine. The police got it back inside ten minutes, and the Colonel and the "Chairman" along with it.'

'The detectives went after him?'

'As soon as the wallet came out one of them ducked for the door. The other followed when the Colonel left the table. They nabbed them doing a quick change with a duplicate set of overcoats left in the waiting-room.'

'You must have had a few unhappy moments all the same.'

'I did,' said David.

'I spilled the wine right down my new suit,' said Vicky. 'But it was worth it.'

True to the Montgomery pattern we all began to be sorry for the under-dog.

'Couldn't you have told him you'd found him out and let him go?' said Mama. 'It would have been a lesson.'

'He was going to take our money,' said Vicky indignantly. 'And nobody knows how many others he's taken in. Besides, when we went to the races it was always David who paid for the outing and though we seemed to win in the beginning, we always came out losing. Not much, certainly. Enough, however, to have given the Colonel a good day.'

'Don't waste your sympathy on him, Mrs Monty. When you see him you'll understand why,' David said. 'Like the chameleon he changes his character and his appearance according to his surroundings.'

'You're not going to tell us how you found him out then?'

'Not yet,' said David. 'We'll give you a tip though. It was the way he spoke. You see, we understood he was an Englishman. It was Vicky who tumbled to something in his speech that proved that a lie.'

CHAPTER TWELVE

It was a lovely June. The whole world, even the world of Clapham Common, smelt good. The seagulls had gone away and there were yachts on the pond and kites on the green. People promenaded the South Side and as fast as they threw papers and ice-cream cartons on the ground, keepers speared them up and incarcerated them in cavernous bins. The pigeons and the sweethearts were settled in what they were going to do for the next summer and there was sweet-smelling peace everywhere.

On a Saturday afternoon, after the shopping and the flat-cleaning and the laundry bag had been attended to, I wanted to drowse the afternoon away. Mama, up in her room, would literally sleep it away.

On one such day we decided sleep was a crime against England and Mama and I went on the Putney bus to Richmond. Never in our lives, down under, had we seen trees and foliage as in summer-dreaming England. We ate maids of honour in the right place in the High Street and walked along the embankment of the river watching the boating.

Richmond had a fascination for Mama and after that we nearly always went on a Saturday or Sunday. When funds were low we forewent the maids of honour and took our own Thermos and biscuits. Always we had to leave Sam behind. I felt sad leaving him and sadder still that he did not have the opportunity of eating maids of honour and looking at chestnut trees with their white candles.

The law case against the Colonel had not yet come off, and Reggie Arbuthnot had not reappeared though Gerry had another letter from him postmarked Colombo. She happened to mention it.

To me it wasn't possible that Reggie was in Colombo again, and why did he send his letters from there? I decided there was something mysterious about Reggie, yet this was hard to reconcile with his open face and clear, firm eyes.

In spite of summer and the roses, trouble for the Montgomeries had to come in threes. The third was a deluge of trouble, and I brought it all on my own head.

In accordance with some ancient precaution and tradition the school gates as well as the school doors were kept locked at lunch-time. The wall around the pocket handkerchief playgrounds, one in the front and one off my own room, was eight feet high. It would require some venturesomeness to get in. To get access into the school itself from the playgrounds would have been like assaulting an impregnable castle, unless the great heavy doors were unlocked.

There had been a truce between Misses Anderson, Bernard, Mrs Illington-Etc. and myself, and the air between us was zephyr-like. Life at St Hilda's was in perfect accord with the roses and bus rides through Putney to Richmond. Then one afternoon, shortly after school had been assembled, Miss Anderson came into my room with an air of perturbation.

'Mrs Richardson, did you unlock the front door by any chance at lunch-time? We can't find the key to lock-up. Meekes, who is monitor this week, says the door was unlocked when he went to open the school gate.'

Lunch-time had been an unusual one. Miss Anderson and Mrs Illington-Etc. had taken a flying visit to the West End and had been absent. Miss Bernard had lunched alone in her own room and I got on with some picture-making in my room. There had been nothing but a brooding silence over the school for nearly two hours.

'No,' I said. 'The only door I used was the one into my own playground. I have the key here.'

'Let me see it,' she said. 'There may have been some mistake.'

I took the key from my drawer. It was the right key and belonged to my room. Miss Anderson stood puzzled. It was useless to ask the children for guidance because they all went home, and the outer gates had remained locked.

'You are quite sure?' She looked at me uneasily. I was surprised.

'I'm quite sure,' I said. 'I don't ever use the front door if I go out. I use my own door.'

'Yes. That is so. Then what can have happened to the key?'

'Meekes has looked in the usual place? The key hasn't fallen down?' It was kept on a nail on the inside wall.

'We'll all just have to look again,' said Miss Anderson. She was visibly annoyed and for once did not close the schoolroom door quietly as she went out. There was nothing I could do about the school key so I went on teaching. Twenty minutes later Mrs Illington-Etc. mountaineered her way into the room.

'The whole school's upset,' she said. 'Now cast your mind back. Are you quite sure you didn't have occasion to unlock the front door?'

'No, I didn't unlock it,' I said a little edgily. 'I've already told Miss Anderson that.'

'A key can't disappear into thin air.'

'Of course not. It's been mislaid. Perhaps Meekes might have taken the key down and then forgotten he had done so.'

'Meekes has been searched and so has his desk. He insists the door was open. Miss Anderson and I locked it when we went out. We gave the key to the caretaker who returned it to its proper place. The caretaker says the door was locked and the key hanging on the nail when he went to lunch. He *never* makes a mistake.'

'Between everybody someone has mislaid it,' I said sympathetically.

'You're the only *forgetful* person, you know,' she pursued.

'I haven't forgotten on this occasion,' I said firmly and politely. 'I didn't use the front door at lunch-time.'

Mrs Illington-Etc. retreated. Half an hour later Miss Anderson appeared again.

'I must be frank with you,' she said. 'Miss Bernard says she is quite certain someone went out of the front door at lunchtime. She heard them. You and she were the only people in the school.' This time I was really indignant.

'If I had done so, I would say so, Miss Anderson. What object would I have in losing the school key without admitting it?'

'When a school key is lost the Board of Managers and the Education Officer have to be notified. A locksmith has to be sent at once and the locks changed. This is not only a confession of carelessness to the authorities but it occasions inconvenience and expense.'

'I didn't know that,' I said. I couldn't explain that in Australia nothing was locked up, not even the front door of our home, 'Forty-Five'.

'Well, you know now,' she said, making a visible effort not to sound annoyed. 'If the key is not found by half-past four I will have to remain here till the locksmith arrives.'

'Surely not,' I expostulated. 'The caretaker might find the key while cleaning the school.'

'It's against the regulations to leave the school unlocked.'

'Well, I'm very sorry. I wish I could help you.'

'You can help me by casting your mind back. What did you do at lunch-time?'

I cast my mind back for her.

'I made some tea and ate my lunch. Then I took out two of those big three-ply cardboard sheets and posted the illustrations on them. I varnished them, glued the tape bindings round the edges. They were just finished when the bell went. I went out into the playground, outside my door, to the washbasins.'

She stood looking at the cardboard-backed pictures as if they could substantiate my story. Clearly they were still sticky with the varnish I had painted over them. The bindings were still wet.

'It's very strange Miss Bernard should have heard someone going through the front door. Miss Bernard *never* makes rash statements.'

When I went to her room to sign the time-book after school she was sitting at her table angry and forbidding. She did not acknowledge my 'Good afternoon' and I felt certain she thought I was the guilty party. As I went across the park I was torn between anger and miserableness. My short coat which I had worn in the morning, indeed, right up to midday because of a small chill in the air, now weighed on my arm. I felt damp with perspiration. It was not a warm day but my crossness oozed out of my skin as well as put an edge to my tongue.

Sure enough, next day there was a new lock and a new key.

111

By some subtle conveying of an unexpressed wrath, the atmosphere of the whole school was heavy with guilt. Every child was aware that some dastardly crime had been committed in the losing of the school key and everyone obliquely felt he had some share in the guilt we all must suffer from such incompetence.

During the afternoon Miss Anderson and I went into the church to prepare the hymn books for the next day's weekly service. As we entered the church door there was the faintest sound, almost as of mice scattering through the church.

'What was that?' I said.

'Merely the Vicar escaping in his carpet slippers,' Miss Anderson said. 'He's probably in the Lady Chapel and thinks I don't know it.'

My heart went out to the Vicar. Somehow in this mood Miss Anderson made me want to run for cover, too. Several times during the day when I had heard her step outside my door and her hand on the knob I wanted to dive into a cupboard and pretend I wasn't there. I began to think myself that in appointing me to the school the Vicar had been playing something of a practical joke on the staff, a form of retribution for the hundreds of times he had had to scuttle before the foreboding tread of Miss Anderson and her friend, Mrs Illington-Etc. I wondered if it was only the carpet slippers that made him an offender in her eyes.

By Friday the school seemed to have become accustomed to the ignominy of having had to send to the Board of Managers and the Education Officer on account of its carelessness. One felt, however, there was a blot on the escutcheon. Never had a confession of mismanagement gone forth from the school to higher authorities before.

On Saturday morning Sam went to Russell Square to see his Professor about a preliminary examination of his thesis. He came home looking tired but with a light in his eye.

'I don't think I'm going to have to worry,' he said.

'Did he tell you your thesis was good?'

'No. He didn't discuss the thesis, only the formula I had used in analysis. Just as I was leaving, however, he asked me if I would be prepared to have the work published by the University.'

'What does that mean?' I asked. 'It must mean it's all right.'

'Of course, he means it's all right. The mediocre stuff doesn't get published.'

'Oh, Sam!'

He was so undemonstrative I could hardly sing a song or dance or corroboree. I could only look at him and take a mental flight into realms of hope and ambition. I could only show him how I felt by giving him York ham and fruit salad for lunch, his favourite fare.

I did all Sam's day-dreaming for him.

The next morning I went to St Hilda's as usual for the children's service. I had one of those awkward twists of conscience because I did not go to the eleven o'clock Mass. I loved Father Reilly so much that I couldn't tell him that I didn't know how one made Confession. I wasn't ready for such a change in thinking. I loved and was deeply moved by the solemn beauty of the service in the High Church, but I didn't know how, and I couldn't bring myself to partake in those aspects, such as Confession, which had never been part of my training before.

I went home across the park towards the bus route just as the deep bell tolled its call to those who went to Mass. I didn't feel quite so happy and carefree as I had the afternoon before. It was all very well to dream Sam's dreams for him, but what about myself? I always seemed to carry around something about myself that was left undone or, having been done, was wrong.

In the afternoon Mama and I decided to take a bus to Putney and Richmond. 'We might vary it by going to Kew Gardens,' Mama said.

'We'll take a Thermos,' I added. 'Pay day's a week away.'

There was a faint chill in the breeze so I put on my short woolly coat, the one I had worn to school the day the key was lost.

We were standing by the bus stop, our Putney bus lurching round the corner, when I put my hand in my pocket. I felt something hard and flat. I knew instantly it was a key. I think I knew instantly it was the lost *school key*.

For a dreadful minute of hope I kept it pressed down into the seam of my pocket. Then, as Mama stepped on the bus, I looked at it. It was the school key. I pushed it back and mounted the bus in Mama's wake. It was nearly full and we had to sit apart. I was thankful for that. I took the key out again and looked at it but I felt so sick I could not see it. I felt as if I had gone white all over, as if I would like to lean out of the window and be very sick indeed.

How . . . how?

I tried to tell myself that someone had put the key there. Some frightened child, unable to confess, someone picking it up from the floor and slipping it in the pocket of my coat as it hung on the nail in my room. But I knew that was not the answer. It couldn't be, because it could never be proved. It had to be something that could be proved.

I had taken my coat off at midday. I remembered that I felt hot as I knelt on the floor dipping the brush in the hot glue and painting it across the back of the illustration I was about to spread over the big cardboard frame. I had felt hot rolling the little smoothing roller backwards and forwards, backwards and forward, over the shining poster so that not a wrinkle or air-bubble would spoil the completed picture. I had got up and taken off my jacket and hung it on the children's pegs near the door.

If I put the key in the pocket myself, then I must have done it before then! After Miss Anderson and Mrs Illington-Etc. had gone out and handed the key to the caretaker. That left about half an hour during which I had eaten my sandwiches and prepared the materials for making the pictures.

The materials? The picture, the cardboard, the glue, the tape binding? Nothing rang a bell.

All right, I would take each article as I had prepared it. I had got up from the table, put my lunch wrapping in the paper basket. I had gone out to the wash-basins in my own playground and come back. I hadn't locked that door, indeed, I had left it ajar because already it was warming up and I had let the air in. I had lifted up the big map hook and opened the windows high up over-looking the street on the opposite side of the room to the door. I got out the two cardboards on to which the poster had to be pasted. I estimated I could finish two pictures by two o'clock. They were heavy, cumbersome things and I kept them standing against the wall behind the stock cupboard. There had been eighteen in all, and I had that day finished the twelfth. I opened the stock cupboard and selected the illustrations from the supplement to the *Child Education* that were in a neat pile at the bottom of the cupboard. I got out the bag of little glue pellets to make the glue. I had been irritated that I had not made the glue at eleven o'clock. Now the water would not be hot, I would have to go . . .

That was it! I would have to go to the caretaker's shed, the place where he kept the coal and a coal-burning stove, leading off the front playground. Miss Bernard had heard someone go out of the front door. That was me. I had gone out to get the glue-can, always kept along with other messy things in the caretaker's shed. I had put it on his stove and let the hot water dissolve the glue pellets. I had come back and because I had the bag of glue in one hand and the hot billycan of melted glue in the other I had not locked the door. I must have put the key in my pocket when I went out and there it had stayed. I had been hot because I had stood over the caretaker's stove, so I had taken off my coat.

'Why do You let me *forget* things?' I cried in angry despair to God.

Why had I *forgotten*!

I could see myself standing in my room looking at Miss Anderson in polite surprise and saying firmly—

'I did not go out of the front door!' And looking at Mrs Illington-Etc. in barely suppressed indignation and saying,

'I did not go out of the front door.'

My denial had been emphatic and final, not to be retracted. I would have sworn my honour away that I did not go out of that door. Alas I had sworn it away!

I do not know how I got through that afternoon at Kew Gardens. Mama would keep prodding me and saying:

'Look at this' and 'Look at that'. Until in the end I snapped at her.

'For goodness sake, stop poking me, Mama. I'm *looking*.'

'You don't seem to be, you're not taking any notice.'

'I am. I just don't talk about it, I *think* about it. If I burst into a flow of words I can't concentrate on what I'm *thinking*.'

'You've got a very peculiar way of showing appreciation,' said Mama. But she was hurt by my shortness of temper and stopped prodding and even commenting.

'I've got a headache,' I said lamely. 'I didn't say so before.'

'We'll go home early. We can always come another day. Thank heavens it's not far and not expensive from Clapham Common.'

I couldn't have borne to stay another minute. Back in the

flat I went straight to the kitchen and began to prepare supper. Thank God there was no Gerry and Vicky and David this week-end.

'You certainly look as if you're got the hump,' Mama complained while we had our meal. 'What's wrong with her, Sam? Yesterday she was walking on air, today she can't even be civil.'

'What's that?' said Sam looking up vaguely. 'I don't see anything different. Anything wrong, Theodora?'

'You wouldn't know if there was,' I said angrily. 'The roof could fall in and you wouldn't know unless it fell on your beastly books and you couldn't see what you were writing.' I burst into tears and fled to the kitchen.

I lay in bed and stared through the window at the tracery of the tree from which the nightingale sang last summer. The nightingale had sung for Mama. Not even an owl would hoot for Theodora. I couldn't tell Sam.

If I told Mama she would have out-hooted any owls. She would have come down flatly on the side of Misses Anderson, Bernard and Mrs Illington-Etc., not to mention their silent and sympathetic opposites in the School Upstairs.

I couldn't tell Sam because I was ashamed. It was the sort of thing about myself I couldn't tell Sam. He wouldn't have minded the 'forgetting' but he wouldn't have understood my flat denial, my absolute certitude, unless my certainty had been as inviolable as a scientific law. Then, because there were no nightingales for me, and partly because of an overwhelming self-pity, I began to be angry with Sam. I lay there and listened to his quiet breathing and seethed with anger and frustration that Sam was the sort of person to whom I couldn't tell this awful thing that I had done.

Somewhere in the corner of my mind a second self stood and admonished me for my suffering. A lost key was not the end of the world. I had not committed theft, murder or rape. I had not broken one of the ten commandments. I had not even broken the eleventh, 'Thou shalt not be found out.' I had broken the twelfth, 'Thou shalt not forget,' and even Moses had not seen fit to record that one on the tablets.

Periodically, through the night, I would wake up and think;

'Oh well, I don't have to say anything about it—it's over

116

and done with now.'

I would fall asleep again, lulled by false security.

I went to school early, but not as early as Miss Anderson. She was sitting at her table making up her stock book. When I came in she slammed it shut and pushed it into her long drawer.

'Must be nearly time for school,' she said.

'No. I'm early, Miss Anderson.'

'Oh well, you can get on with the pictures,' she said. 'I'd like them finished and hung by the summer holidays.'

Her manner was polite but curt. She turned the time-book towards me and went downstairs. I bent to sign it. Miss Bernard came fluttering in.

'Dear me, dear me. Miss Anderson's beaten me again. She *does* get up early these days. I do hope she doesn't overdo it. Once I was *always* the first . . .'

I handed her the pen and she glanced at me to thank me.

'You look very peaky,' she said solicitously. 'Are you all right?'

'It's the heat,' I said weakly. I had wanted to tell Miss Anderson, but she had gone away. I couldn't tell her after all. I couldn't face that absence of a 'Good morning' and the dreadful living with them after the confession.

'The heat?' said Miss Bernard in astonishment. 'I thought you came from a *hot* place.'

'That's where I'm going,' I said grimly. I picked up my bag and gloves and went to my classroom. I couldn't face them at lunch-time and I went into the park. I couldn't eat my sandwiches and I couldn't read the *Telegraph*. I didn't mind the Board of Managers, or the Education Officer. I'd never seen *him*. He was a shadowy figure who loomed over Miss Anderson but not having seen him he had no terrors for me. I didn't mind the whole of the Board of Education or the London County Council. I only minded Miss Anderson and Mrs Illington-Etc. I didn't even mind Miss Bernard. Underneath her appropriate air of being shocked she would really be grieved for me.

At last the day ended. I signed the time-book and left the school. My legs, without any request from my head, took me straight to the Vicarage. Mrs Reilly opened the door to me.

'He's in there,' she pointed to the study, 'doing pamphlets. If you go in he'll make you work.'

I smiled wanly. Sure enough there stood on the desk a pile of circulars and a pile of envelopes. The Vicar looked mischievous.

'Take off your gloves,' he said. 'You can work while you talk.'

'You always know that I come to talk. Maybe I would have done better in life if I'd listened, and *remembered*, instead of talked so much.'

'What's the trouble now, my child?'

As I sat down at the little chair beside the desk I put the key in front of him on the table. He looked at it, and then at me. He picked it up and held it in the palm of his hand.

'The school key?'

I nodded.

The Vicar began rapidly folding circulars and I began putting them in their envelopes. I could hardly keep the tears from my eyes so he waited a little while.

'Well, go on, my child,' he said at length. 'Tell me about the key.'

'It was in the pocket of my coat.'

I told him the whole sorry story. He folded circulars and I put them in envelopes.

'If it weren't for the various incidents of the carpet slippers,' he said with a grin, 'I would think it was funny. But I know just how you feel.'

'But, Father, if you feel like that why—why do you wear the slippers when you go into the church?'

'Bravado, my dear. And always the hope that today I won't be caught.' He looked under the table.

'How are your own feet?'

'Sore. They always are in summer time.'

'How're Sam's feet when he's working at that table in winter time? Don't the draughts get him?'

I nodded.

'You buy him a pair of carpet slippers, m'dear. They're heaven's greatest comfort.'

He jumped up and thumped round the study, his hands clasped behind his back and the skirts of his cassock, faded and frayed at the hem, swished a little as he walked. He pulled up in front of the table and looked at me sternly.

'Well,' he said. 'You've reported to the Chairman of the Board.' He wagged his finger at me. 'No more such carelessness, young lady. You have grievously embarrassed your superiors.'

I nodded.

'The incident is closed,' he added. He picked up the key and dropped it in the Toby jug on the mantelpiece.

'Now go home and get Sam's supper for him, and don't forget the carpet slippers.'

He let me out of the front door of the Vicarage and I went off with the feeling that a terrible load had dropped from my shoulders.

Two days went by, and I felt all right. School seemed bright and easy and the staff were so preoccupied with fixing the school so they could leave it in absolute order when the holidays came that the incident of the key seemed forgotten. But at night I couldn't go to sleep. It wasn't so much the key that worried me as that I couldn't tell Sam about it. It made me angry with Sam. I wished I either had no conscience at all or could conduct my life without mistakes so that I would have the peace of mind that was always Sam's lot.

On the third morning I knew that I could never have acquitted myself in Sam's eyes by hiding behind the Vicar's skirts. After school I went once more to the Vicarage.

'What's the matter now?' the Vicar asked. He turned abruptly away from me and went to the mantelpiece. He lifted up the Toby jug and shook its contents out on his hand. There were screws and safety-pins and old stamps, a broken stump of pencil, and the key.

'I suppose this is what you want?'

'I'll have to tell Miss Anderson,' I said.

He poked his forefinger through his hair. It was nearly always standing up around his head like the halo. He waved one hand vaguely in the air.

'There's something in the old saw, "he who fights and runs away, may live to fight another day". If it were me, now, I'd run for the Lady Chapel. The Lord loves most those he can pity, and the pitiful are the cowards.' He sighed deeply.

'I sometimes almost *bask* in cowardice,' he added. He folded my hand round the key.

'Run along, child,' he said. 'An old coward like me has no business to pose as spiritual adviser to the Theodoras of this world.'

119

All the same I knew that Father Reilly was not a coward. If he had been a coward he wouldn't have put on his carpet slippers at all. I was yet to discover the quality of his courage and that underneath the frusty cassock there was a knight as chivalrous as any in Christendom.

I went back to the school. I knew Miss Anderson was stock-taking and would be alone in the school. I let myself in my own playground and room and went into the classroom where Miss Anderson was on her knees in front of a vast stack of paraphernalia just removed from a stock cupboard. She looked up.

'Have you forgotten something?' she asked.

'Not today, Miss Anderson. But I did the other day.' I put the key on the table.

'The school key,' I said. 'I had it in the pocket of my jacket all the time.'

She got up, dusted her knees and sat down at the table. She picked up the key and sat looking at it. Her mouth had a grim 'I told you so' look about it. If she uttered the words out aloud I would have nothing to say.

'Well,' she said at last, as if taking a breath and a new decision with her intake of air. 'There's nothing more to be said about it, is there?'

'Would you like me to explain?'

'No. You *forgot*. That's the answer to it, isn't it? You quite often *forget*, you know. Perhaps this will be the last time.'

I stood in silence. I wished I could promise that but I'd lost my confidence in myself for all time. My flat denials of having gone out of the front door mattered more to me than the key. They would ring in my ears for ever. It was no use to talk about them.

'Very well,' she said at length. 'You may go.'

She sat looking at me, tall, cold, stern. When I reached the door she halted me.

'When did you discover you had this key?'

'On Sunday.'

'And this is Thursday?'

'Yes,' I said. I hoped she wouldn't ask me what I had done about it in the meantime. I wanted no more subterfuges but I didn't want to give away the Vicar and his advice to 'cowards'.

'It's been weighing on your conscience for four days then.'

'Four nights and five days,' I said.

She did not soften.

'Then my last word on the matter is to thank you for bringing the key to me now. I suppose you realize you needn't have done so?'

'When one works at school, and housekeeps at home, and keeps a weather eye on one's husband's thesis, one has to get some sleep sometime,' I said wearily.

'Very well,' she said again. 'You may go.'

I went slowly home. I didn't have any feeling of a load having dropped from my shoulders this time. I felt worn out. And I still couldn't tell Sam.

'Some day,' I thought. 'Some day, when we've been married for years and years . . .'

I judged my arrival at school the next morning so that I would arrive exactly on the required time. I didn't want to be signing the time-book when the others came in. Or worse, come in upon them when they stood in solemn conclave, planning a funeral, as I used to think with an edge of laughter at their expense. I didn't want to laugh at them any more. Or at anything, for a while.

They didn't exactly send me to Coventry and they didn't exactly make me cups of tea or open doors for me. They did just enough of both to make me feel their pride in their school was taking the offence hardly, but they didn't want to carry on the punishment, so just occasionally someone opened a door for me and every now and again Miss Bernard would slip me in a cup of tea.

'Just in case you need it, dear . . .'

But not a word was said to me about the key. The nearest reference was at morning prayers. It was one of those days when neither the Vicar nor the Curate came in and Miss Anderson said prayers. Just when we had finished all our usual ones she added one in of her own.

'Let us pray for those amongst us who sometimes err. Guide their footsteps, their actions and their words, dear Lord, so that we all might see and understand; and with Thy forgiveness learn also to forgive.'

I knew by their tight-folded hands and their tightly closed eyes they were all praying for me. I wasn't praying to God, however.

'Why did You make me this way?' I reproached Him. 'That I have to be prayed for in public?'

121

I would like to have added, 'It is all Your fault.' But I didn't quite have the courage.

However, this time I was going to Ireland. The whole incident had been enough to drive that tiny wedge between Sam and my care for him.

There was only just enough money to pay for our flat and our housekeeping, and an occasional trip to Richmond or window-shopping in the West End, so any holiday money would have to be taken from our tiny little bank hoard of twenty pounds. If one took it then the other went without, so to date neither of us took it.

'Sam,' I said, 'when you've finished your thesis you're to take a week off and go to Whitby, the home of your fore-fathers. If I go to Ireland, will you promise me?'

'Yes,' he said. 'I'll promise you anything, even a big emerald studded with diamonds.'

'Don't forget the diamonds,' I said. 'And just in case you can't rise to it, I'm going to Ireland.'

CHAPTER THIRTEEN

The case of Rex versus Archibald Rennie Winsop in which David and Victoria Browning were to appear as witnesses for the Crown took place on a Friday. As luck would have it we had a holiday from St Hilda's that day.

It was one of those parish holidays granted by the Education Authority when the school premises were needed for parish affairs.

The Montgomeries—that is, Mama and Gerry, Sam and myself, David and Vicky—repaired to the court in mass formation. By the crime standards of a great metropolis it was a trivial case and attracted little attention. There were very few people in court. The counsel for the defence was tall, bulgey-eyed, supercilious and clever. When Vicky entered the box he looked faintly amused. One imagined the thoughts that flitted through his head were to the effect he would soon tie *her* up in knots. He bargained without the fact that Vicky was a Montgomery. Scratch her pretty soft skin and the Irishman would come out battling.

122

In the meantime the accused had appeared in the dock. I have never seen such a disgraceful looking scallywag. Mama began to make noises indicative of her disbelief that this was 'the Colonel'.

'They've got the wrong man,' she whispered to Gerry.

'No, they haven't,' said Gerry. 'He's just got himself up that way to try and make a fool of Vicky and David. To make their evidence unreliable is the only way to get him off.'

The Colonel was unshaven and unclean. His dirty-coloured shirt was tieless and open at the neck. His hair had not been cut and if he had been instructed to use a comb he ran his fingers through his hair sufficiently often to make it rumpled and dishevelled. He slouched as he walked across the court. He sat dejected and when he spoke he sounded illiterate.

The police case was handled quickly and expertly.

'Is this the man you knew as "Colonel Winsop"?'

Vicky nodded. 'Yes,' she replied clearly.

'How do you recognize him?'

'He is the man I recognized in the line-up the day after the arrest.'

'The man in the line-up, this man, is the man you knew as "Colonel Winsop"?'

'Yes.'

David was called and he gave evidence that the man was Colonel Winsop.

The detectives were then called and gave evidence of how they had sat at a table adjacent to David and Vicky in Trafalgar Palace; had seen the wallet passed over and passed back; had detained the man in the lobby and retrieved the wallet from him. He was unable satisfactorily to explain its presence. Moreover, he was unable to explain two overcoats left with the attendant, and two tickets for them.

Every time Mama looked at the prisoner she shuffled her feet and looked as if she would get up and make a speech.

'Vicky hasn't explained he didn't look like *that* when they went out with him,' she complained.

'The case isn't finished, Mama,' I answered tersely. 'Wait till his defence goes into action.'

'Order in the Court!'

Gerry and I each dug an elbow into Mama.

The prisoner was put into the dock. He looked so lost and bewildered that if David hadn't warned us he was a first-class actor our hearts would have bled for him.

123

He had a garbled and hardly intelligible story that he'd got the wrong coat ticket and, being poor, was tempted by the coat. The wallet was in the coat.

Mama looked as if she would break into speech again, and again Gerry and I applied our elbows. Then Vicky was called by the defence.

The lawyer asked her where she shopped. Where she spent her leisure hours. How much it cost her to make the journey to England. Then, with a gesture of astonishment, he turned to the prisoner.

'With all that background, am I to believe you allowed yourself to be accompanied to the racecourse, into various restaurants in the West End, by *that*.' He pointed with contempt at the 'Colonel'.

I could see it all. That was the defence. No one as well-dressed as Vicky would be seen anywhere on earth with anyone as disreputable-looking as the prisoner at the bar.

'Yes,' said Vicky coolly. She was the perfect witness. No matter how wide the gap counsel for the defence drew between Vicky and the bogus Colonel, she remained monosyllabic and unconcerned.

'Why doesn't she tell him the brute wasn't dressed like that?' Mama demanded. I wondered why myself.

David was called. The same performance was enacted, with the same results. Then the police asked leave to introduce further evidence and recall Mrs Browning.

'Had she recognized the "Colonel's" companion?'

No. She hadn't met him before and in his unshaven disguise had not been able to pick him in the line-up.

How had she been so certain of the 'Colonel'?

Vicky's answer came simply.

'He has brown eyes with a fine purple line round the pupils. I looked for that first.'

There was a little murmur of approval in the court.

'Are you in the habit of noticing such small details of personal appearance?'

'Yes. I've lived on a sheep station in Australia and when there's thousands of sheep you can pick one from another by the eyes.'

A laugh broke out in the court-room but was instantly silenced by the magistrate.

Mama said, 'Bravo!'

'Order in the court!'

'Was it by a similar small detail that you were suspicious of the prisoner in the first place?'

The magistrate intervened.

'Is this question consistent with fresh evidence?' he asked the prosecuting counsel.

'It is evidence of identity, Your Worship.'

'Very well. Proceed.'

The counsel for the defence demurred but he was waved aside.

'It was a word he used. I mean, the way he said a word.'

'Would you like to tell the court in your own words, Madam?'

'Colonel Winsop told us he was English, and we believed him. It seemed to us that he spoke like an Englishman, an Army Englishman.'

The magistrate allowed himself the hint of a smile. 'Proceed.'

'He said he'd been in Australia but only for two years. Then, on one occasion, I noticed he said "ver-ee" for "very", the way Australians do. There were some others with us so I didn't comment on it. I was thinking about it, however, when I noticed he said "Sun-day" instead of "Sundee".'

There was another smile in the court at Vicky's attempt to say the Sabbath in the manner of an Englishman.

'So I listened, and quite a number of times I noticed he accented the second syllable the way we do. And no English person does that unless he's been a lifetime in Australia. Sometimes he gets the Australian intonation, but never the pronunciation of words. I began to suspect that the Colonel had either been many years in Australia or was originally an Australian and had by living in England acquired the English intonation but not always the pronunciation. When I pointed this out to my husband we began to set tiny traps to catch him. When he fell into them we guessed he was "bogus". The wallet incident proved it.'

The police inspector in charge of records was called and it then appeared that Archibald Rennie Winsop was indeed born in Australia. At a very young age he had gone to Britain with his parents but returned to Australia about ten years later. There he had worked as a jackeroo on sheep stations around Australia and later in New Zealand. He returned once more to England where he rapidly acquired an English intonation and a bogus army rank and proceeded to lie in wait for his former countrymen. His knowledge of the pastoralists and first families of Australasia had been from the paddock end of the binoculars.

The case ended with the collapse of the defence. The Montgomeries proudly escorted Vicky and David into the outer world of London.

'Fancy an Australian doing a thing like that,' said Mama sadly. 'And to his own people, too.'

'He wouldn't have got away with it with an English couple,' David said. 'They would have picked the difference in accent at once. Most Australians don't know they say "ver-ee" and "Sun-day" so they would hardly notice it in him.'

'How did you notice it, Vicky?' I asked.

'The Saturday night before someone in the hotel told me she recognized me as an Australian. When I asked her why, she said it was because of the way I said "ver-ee", amongst other things. The next day I noticed someone saying "very"— you know, the way the English do—and I was just trying to imitate it to myself when blow me down, the Colonel said to me, "You are looking ver-ee thoughtful today, Mrs Browning." So I said, "It must be the day of the week—what day is it?" And he said, "Sun-day". Just like that!'

'All the same I'm sorry he was an Australian,' said Mama. 'And I'm sorry it had to be fellow-Australians to expose him here in England.'

'Set a sprat to catch a mackerel,' I whispered to Gerry. I wouldn't have spoiled Vicky's day by saying it aloud.

David looked positively proud of her as he bore us all off to lunch.

'Not to the Trafalgar Palace?' I asked in astonishment.

'No place other,' said David 'This time *not* accompanied by the police.'

The day had yet a final surprise for us. At five o'clock the front-door bell pealed through the house and presently the landlady came upstairs.

'A gentleman for Miss Gerry,' she said. A head appeared over her shoulder.

'I've brought myself up,' he said. 'Do I throw my hat in first, and see what happens?'

'Reggie!' I cried. Then remembering the night of Lloyds' reception I abated my enthusiasm. I held out my hand. 'How do you do, Reggie?'

I said it loudly enough for Gerry to hear from behind the living-room door and be prepared for her visitor.

It was Mama who came forward.

'Well, well, well!' she said. 'We are glad to see you.'

Mama was master of the situation. Her manner was pleasant but not exuberant. I remembered that in all the years of our growing up Mama must have had a lot of experience in receiving chastened lovers or repenting wooers for her five daughters. There was no evidence, however, that Reggie was either chastened or repentant. As he came into the tiny hall he gave me an informative wink. It said, 'You and I know about Lloyds . . . I hope you've been discreet!'

I pursed up my mouth and refused to return the wink. I gave him a dark look. It said, 'Watch your step, young man. Any monkeying with my sister and you're for it.'

He smiled rather gently, and there was something so direct in the way his eyes met mine, and a touch of seriousness about his smile that I thought I had perhaps done well to keep my own counsel about the reception. There was a reason lying behind Reggie's recent conduct.

Perhaps; after all, it had been Gerry who had put a period to their love affair!

That was only wishful thinking, and I knew it.

By this time Reggie was inside and Gerry, tall, cool, and slim, was shaking hands with him. They might have met last week. Reggie shook hands with Sam and said:

'What's wrong with you?'

'What should be wrong?' asked Sam in surprise.

'You don't look as if you're working.'

'That's an unkind cut,' said Sam. 'You wait till I've really finished. I'll show you how well I can sit about and loaf.'

We told Reggie in unison about the court case. He looked at us sympathetically.

'There's one on every voyage,' he said. 'Those fellers are waiting for you fellers.' He looked at Vicky with a twinkle in his eye. 'You certainly do a tired sailor's eyes good to look at, Vicky. I'm glad you've as many brains as you have nice dimples.'

Vicky looked at him gratefully. Her pretty china-blue eyes smiled back at him.

'Where have you been, Reggie?' asked Mama,

'Round the world twice,' he said casually. 'That's my job, you know.'

'And how's the weather *round the world*?' I asked innocently.

'Just variable,' he said, still smiling at me.

'You look very well, Reggie,' Gerry said easily. 'The weather of the world must suit you surely.'

Reggie stood with his head a little on one side.

'Sounds to me as if you've been in Ireland,' he said. 'It could almost be Laura speaking.'

So Gerry's lessons in voice production had borne some fruit! And how well did Reggie know Laura, anyway? When Laura was around I had misgivings.

Gerry and Reggie, after tea and some discussion, decided they would go out for dinner. Vicky and David decided they would take Mama back to their own hotel for dinner, and Sam and I decided we would have veal and ham pie 'all by ourselves'. When this was over Sam said he was not going to work tonight. I looked at him in surprise.

'Reggie thinks I can't do anything but read books,' he said almost indignantly. I burst out laughing.

'Are you really surprised?' I asked.

'I'm not going to work tonight,' said Sam stubbornly, as if such rebellion would reinstate him in Reggie Arbuthnot's eyes. 'Shall we go to the Old Vic or Sadler's Wells?'

'Have we got enough money? You can't get in for less than ninepence at Sadler's Wells.'

'Let's look and see.'

He turned out his pockets and I turned out my purse.

'It looks like Sadler's Wells,' Sam pronounced over his pile of coins triumphantly. 'What's on?'

'Don't know, and don't care. I only care we're going!'

At Sadler's Wells it was *Carmen*, and the star performance came from the orchestra. I thought I had never heard anything played with such felicity. Sometimes it is inevitable there should be a crumb of gilt jolted from the gingerbread. This night it happened as we hurried in the evacuating throng to the Angel Underground. It didn't seem right that jostling elbow to elbow with the lately enthralled audience in the lifts and on the platform were little men in dinner suits with cornet and flute and violin cases tucked under their arms. These who had so lately transported us to other realms now

128

became no more than other men, people who are tired, hungry for their supper, a little shabby, eager to escape the theatre and return to the fastnesses of their castles in Tooting, Brixton and Camberwell Green.

A week later Mama had the bright idea that we couldn't face Denney and Mary and all the other inhabitants of Pepper Tree Bay without being able to report we had been to a café in Soho. David had taken a flying business trip to Paris and Reggie Arbuthnot was in the bosom of his family at High Wycombe.

'We can go without the men,' said Vicky. 'In Soho we can do *anything*. Nothing's conventional in Soho.'

'Where exactly is Soho?' I asked. They got out a map of London and showed me.

'Anywhere round here,' said Gerry, weaving a pencil in and out between East End of Oxford Street and Regent Street. Reggie and I've had lunch, or something, round about there dozens of times. I don't see there's anything different from anywhere else.'

'You don't know where to look,' said Vicky. 'If I know you and Reggie you just go into the first place you stumble your toe against when you're hungry.'

'We have mightier things than food to talk about,' said Gerry.

'Exactly,' said Vicky. 'You should have more regard for your figure.'

As Gerry had youth's superb slenderness Vicky's remarks were ruled out of order.

'It's what she *will* become,' Vicky said. 'The foundations of a good figure are laid down *now*.'

'Wrapped round is more to the point,' said Gerry. 'I haven't had to get into anything tighter than a four-inch belt yet.'

'All this has got nothing to do with a café in Soho,' said Mama. 'We'll all go to Regent Street together and I'll pick the place we'll go to, then there won't be any arguing.'

'As if you'd know, Mama,' I said. 'Your beat is always between Woolworths and Marks and Spencer's.'

'And a very good bargain I've had,' said Mama staunchly.

Sam looked up as much as to say, 'When you've stopped arguing I'll get on with my work.'

'Come on,' I said. 'Let's go.'

As it was an evening out we went by bus so that we could

approve or disapprove of London according to how the weather permitted us to see it. It was early twilight and the towers and reaches of Westminster lay before us in their sombre glorious beauty as the bus turned over Vauxhall Bridge. I felt a sudden deep love surging from me across the river with its boats and barges to the far embankment. How much more deeply had London woven itself into the warp and woof of my own being because I had been here living and working as part of it than it would have been if I had been skating across it like a gilded tourist. It hadn't been easy but I'd always be glad I had worked in London and not played.

'Next time I come,' I thought, 'I'll play. Now that it's nearly over I'm glad I've lived the way I have lived here. This way London is my own.'

We left the bus at Piccadilly and did our usual window-gazing round Swan and Edgar's and the neighbouring shops.

'Down here is a place that looks very interesting,' said Mama. 'I've noticed it before.' She led us off Piccadilly to where a restaurant presented to the world a façade of black marble and glass. There were circulating glass doors in the modest entrance and no commissionaire. In green neon light over the doorway was the modest legend, 'Café Marseilles'.

I had an unhappy feeling that Mama was being misled by the modest dignity of the frontage. Anything as simple and unostentatious as this can be very misleading in the West End. I put a hand on her arm.

'This is the west side of Piccadilly,' I said. 'I don't think this is what you'd call Soho really.'

'Of course it is,' said Mama with the kind of certitude that brooked no interference. 'It's near enough, anyway.'

'I've got a feeling it's not the kind of place we really want.'

'Let's go in and see. That's simple enough.' This was from Vicky who had been around the West End enough to have known better.

Mama led her contingent through the door. Immediately we were inside we knew we were in the wrong place. Then was the moment to retreat but we were too unsophisticated to manage it. We were invited to wait in the drawing-room annexe to the polished dining-room. We were a little early.

The apostle of dignity who thus guided us was not to be denied and we found ourselves sitting upright and uncomfortable on chairs of such solid worth and irreproachable dignity that they alone bespoke the class of restaurant into which we had intruded. Beyond and opening out of this annexe was a vast polished floor on either side of which were arranged little tables snowy with white cloth and shining with solid silver. On the other side the members of a string orchestra were hastily composing themselves before their instruments. Waiters stood as stiff and impeccable as statues near the exits to the culinary departments. The apostle of dignity who had led us to our chairs glided from one to another with an air of authority. There was not another soul present but ourselves and the staff. We looked at one another uncomfortable.

'Let's run for it,' I said.

The other three were uncertain. I had spoken what was in their minds but nobody could move quickly enough. They sat fastened to their chairs. The head waiter as if sensing our intentions, moved across the floor. He bowed to Mama.

'If Madam is ready?' his eyebrows hovered near his hairline.

'Thank you,' said Mama with matching dignity.

'Would Madam prefer a table next to the orchestra?'

'That would be very nice,' said Mama. She thought the head waiter was being kind to her. Gerry clutched her arm as we turned to follow our escort.

'Mama,' she begged. 'We have to tip heavily for a ringside seat.'

Mama, who had refused to understand or comply with the tipping system of England, ignored this.

We were led to a beautiful table where we all had a near vision introduction to the orchestra. The conductor rose and bowed.

'Would Madam care to suggest a number?'

'What will we have, girls?' Mama beamed on us. Even if we were the only people present she was going to enjoy herself. Vicky said 'The Bells of St Mary's,' because it was the first thing that came into her head. The orchestra struck up and the first violin played straight to Gerry's blue eyes.

'Why do you suppose nobody's here yet?' Mama leaned across the table and asked Vicky.

'It's too early, people don't come to this kind of place until theatre and after theatre time.'

'You'd better not ask the orchestra for too many numbers,' Gerry said. 'They'll expect to be paid for it.'

'Nonsense,' said Mama. 'I don't believe in tipping. We get on in Western Australia without it.'

'The basic wages makes it unnecessary,' Gerry began wearily. We were tired of explaining this to Mama.

A waiter had come and straightened our already straight spoons. Another brought a water jug. A third undid our napkins for us and moved the little cubes of white bread nearer the plates. Mama went on admiring the dance floor, the curtains, the flowers and the beautiful silver. Vicky tossed her beautifully groomed head so that her tall feather in her little green toque waved about like the conductor's baton. Mama smiled encouragingly to the conductor and nudged Gerry to notice the fiddler was playing to her specially. The first waiter picked up the menu and collected some others from neighbouring tables and firmly placed them in our hands.

'Yes, of course. We must eat.'

I looked at Vicky.

'How much money have you got in your purse?'

'None,' said Vicky airily. 'I didn't ask David for any. I suppose you can lend me some between you.'

'Just take one look at the top of the menu,' I said. 'You won't have to go any further.'

Under the word 'Menu' was printed in modest and shrinking type:

Minimum charge thirty shillings each.

The second waiter returned and lifted the water jug and asked us each in turn would we have some water. We all nodded dumbly. We waited in silence until he went away.

'How much have you and Gerry got, Mama?'

After some consultation with their memories—no one had the courage to open a purse and look—they confessed to roughly a pound between them.

'I've got ten shillings and Vicky none. That makes enough money for one to eat and the rest to look on. Then there's the tips.'

The word 'tips' provoked Mama into saying 'Nonsense.' again.

'Have some sense, Mama,' said Gerry. 'We're in a spot. How do we get out of it?'

For once Mama saw the situation as it really was. She stopped having the world the way she thought it ought to be and acknowledged the world was not to her ordering.

'We'll have to think,' she said quietly.

The menu waiter returned and stood almost menacingly beside Mama.

'Your order, Madam?'

Mama looked up at him.

'Why do so many waiters come to this table?' she asked. 'Isn't it usual for *one* to look after a table?'

The waiter shrugged. There was obvious contempt in his face. Clearly they'd all been trying us out to see what we were really made of and they had come to the final and right conclusion. We were a bunch of Colonial wops who had got into the restaurant by mistake.

The orchestra had ceased playing and the conductor lounged back in an easy chair at the side of his stand and lit a cigarette. The members of the orchestra turned their backs on us and began talking to one another. The waiters around the room relaxed from their statuesque stillness and slouched against the walls, tilting their silver trays in careless disdain. Every piece of furniture seemed to stare at us in unfeigned contempt.

Mama let her eyes rove round the faces, round the room. Imperceptibly her back straightened. She spoke very quietly to the waiter.

'Send the head waiter to me.' She did not say 'please' yet the command was a request. It was as faultless a way to handle an insolent servant as only the highest integrity and best manners would dictate.

The waiter shot an uneasy glance around his colleagues. They leaned against the walls in open derision.

'The head waiter,' Mama said quietly.

The man turned and went towards the entrance. A minute later he came back with the apostle of dignity.

'Madam?'

Mama pointed to the heading on the menu.

'I regret that we have come by mistake into your restaurant,' she said with great dignity. 'We cannot afford to dine as is indicated here. Would you like us to leave?'

The head waiter suddenly became human.

'No, Madam,' he said. 'That is a caution to those who come here to use the dance floor. Without that warning customers would come and order coffee and use the floor and the orchestra for the whole evening.'

'Could you suggest something modest that would be suitable.'

'Certainly, Madam. I would like to suggest a grill. We have a special. You see here,' he pointed to the menu. 'Steak, mushrooms, crisps, tomato purée.'

'I see,' said Mama. We all did a rapid calculation. The grill was priced at eight shillings.

'If Madam will permit,' the head waiter said with a dignity that matched Mama's, 'I suggest you have the grill without the mushrooms, then coffee to follow. That, together with any incidental expenses, would come to twenty-five shillings for the party.'

Mama's back was very erect.

'Thank you,' she said. 'We would like that.' She looked at the waiter man to man. 'And we would like *one* man to attend us.'

'Certainly, Madam.'

He flicked his hand and one of the waiters detached himself from the wall and took the order from the head waiter. The others had suddenly frozen themselves back to their original positions at attention.

The head waiter gave the tiniest clap with his hands. The conductor put out his cigarette and resumed his baton. The orchestra took up the instruments. Mama suddenly was a very great lady again and we ate our grill in an atmosphere that accorded full recognition of the fact that the honours of the occasion went to her. Our own backs were straighter. We consciously held our heads a little higher. We spoke politely to one another and expressed admiration for the cooking, the service and the delightful tones of the orchestra. We might have been only formally acquainted with one another. We were all conscious of the fact Mama had set us a great example. However humble were our origins we were not so humble that servants could deal with us shabbily.

For once Mama made no difficulties about leaving a modest tip for the waiter. When we left the restaurant we crossed the great floor with a last mustering of pride. From the distance the head waiter returned Mama's bow. He did not come forward to receive a tip, even if there had been enough left to give him one. That was the highest compliment he paid us.

Outside in Piccadilly we let our shoulders droop in unison.

'Phew!' said Gerry.

'*Awful creatures!*' said Vicky. Mama was exuding complacence.

'Hold your heads high, girls,' she said. 'You never can tell .. they might have thought we were impoverished duchesses.'

'With our *accents*,' Gerry and I shrieked in unison. 'Mama, when will you learn that even when we don't open our mouths they know we're not English.'

'I don't see how they can possibly tell. We're all white, aren't we?'

'So are the Swedes and the Germans and the Canadians,' I said. 'You can always tell the difference. They *look* different. They carry themselves differently. They wear different clothes.'

'Stop arguing,' commanded Vicky. 'I call that an *unpleasant* experience and I don't intend it ever to happen again. I shall see that I always have money.'

'I think it was a very good experience,' I said thoughtfully. No one asked me why, so I reserved my comments for Sam.

'It's funny,' I said. 'Of all the lessons I've ever had from kindergarten to college, and even at St Hilda's, that's one of the best.'

'What was good about it, Theodora?'

'I won't ever be afraid of English servants again, to begin with. I'll remember that though I mightn't have done much in life I've done a little better than they have. I don't mean I'll be snobbish about it. I just mean that I won't let *them* make me feel they're snobbish about it. I won't ever be afraid to go anywhere again. I'll just remember to hold my head up and be dignified—that's what Mama was.'

CHAPTER FOURTEEN

Reggie's visit must have been a flying one for once again he disappeared.

'His ship left almost at once,' Gerry said.

'Did you go to High Wycombe?' I asked her tentatively.

'No. I wasn't asked,' she said laconically.

'Aren't you and Reggie . . .?'

'No love affair lasts for ever,' Gerry said haughtily. 'Of course, there are always tail ends about these things . . '

There was a little hard note in her voice and just at the end of her sentence it faltered. Gerry had lost her manner usually so full of joyous wit and had become quieter and more reserved. She came less often to the flat and seemed to have taken up with some artists and pseudo-intellectuals who had a flat in Bloomsbury. She smoked too many cigarettes and her slimness had a hint of thin-ness about it. Her eyes were bright and when she was being amusing it had a brittle quality about it.

I thought a lot about Reggie Arbuthnot. He was a very attractive man and I had no doubt that every voyage produced its admirers. There was something warm and sterling about him, however, and it was hard to reconcile the philanderer with him. His eyes were very direct, even when he had winked at me and given me the unspoken direction to say nothing of Lloyds of London.

I wondered about Laura, too. Somehow Gerry's brittle manner reminded me of Laura at her worst and I wondered if Gerry's recurring visits to Ireland and Reggie's reference to Laura on the day he 'came back' had anything to do with whatever was wrong with their hearts.

Then the thought of Laura and Ireland squeezed at my heart again. This August I was going to Ireland. Really and truly going there. I felt I had mis-managed myself over the last eighteen months. When we had left Pepper Tree Bay going abroad had meant going to Ireland and here I'd been nearly two years within forty-eight hours of *home*, and I hadn't been there. In this mood I saw Sam's work as a tyranny.

I did not speak to the family of this thing in me that was almost a need . . . this wish for Ireland . . . because I knew their attitude would be disdainful and condemnatory.

'Where there's a will, there's a way,' had been Mama's battlecry all her life. If I wouldn't divorce myself from Sam and his domestic requirements, then—too bad!

'It would do Sam good,' would have been their united cry. I thought so too. I fretted against the tyranny of that thesis, but I could not walk out on it before. Now I could do so because the last periods were being put to that tome, and my spiritual bastions had been reduced to rubble by the mere matter of a school key. I needed a holiday. I had to go. No one was more pleased than Sam. He was absolutely unconscious of the struggle in me. He would have been delighted if I had gone at any time, if I could do so without going broke. He would have been astonished and puzzled if it had even occurred to him that I thought he needed me.

Such is the silly state of any woman's heart.

I wrote to Laura and said I didn't care whether she would be there or not, come August I was coming to Magillicuddy. It looked as if Mama would take a flying visit thitherwards, too.

Laura wrote back and said she wouldn't have us unless Sam came, too. Sam said that though his thesis would be in the hands of the University he had to go to an Approved School near Dorking to do some intelligence testing for the Home Office. It had a bearing on the work he had been doing. He would be there two to three weeks, but he had also been invited to give an address to a staff group at Queen's University in Belfast at the end of August. He might get as far as Belfast and take a flying trip to County Meath.

Belfast! Laura wrote at length of her opinion of Belfast. You can't come to Meath from Belfast, she said. In the first place you can't fly. Trains in Ireland crawl. In the second place, the correct and invariable procedure is to visit Dublin *first*. You can finish up in Belfast.

Sam smiled and said something inaudible about the 'troubles of Ireland being visited even unto the Montgomeries' but persisted in his intention of visiting Belfast. The correspondence between me and Laura ceased on that note. I did not worry. Whether Laura was there or not to Magillicuddy I was going.

In the last week before the holidays we moved from Clapham Common to Streatham. All on account of the cat.

Our landlady had a beautiful tabby cat. It used to come upstairs and rub its legs against Sam while Sam sat at the table. Sam liked this. I think he liked the pussy's company. He would sit with his pen in one hand and his left hand dangling below the table where he could stroke the cat's head when it came a-visiting him.

The cat's name was Mrs Brown, and we all liked her. Mama was given to putting down saucers of milk, and I was given to letting the creature curl up beside me on the sofa when I was reading.

Mrs Brown, like all females, had one terrible fault. She liked sharpening her claws. Not on persons but on things. Now the furniture belonged to the landlady and if we had been indifferent to her belongings we would have passed over Mrs Brown's failing without correction. As it was we had considerable respect for the fine old leather arm-chairs and the big leather sofa. The only cross words the cat ever heard us utter was when she reared herself on her hind legs and sharpened her claws by scratching them up and down on the legs of the upright chairs, or, worse, on the leather-covered furniture. Someone would say:

'Get down! Naughty!' in a sharp tone. Sam would then remonstrate.

'Don't talk to the poor thing like that,' he would say. 'It's such a nice friendly cat. Just lift her down.'

Sam would suit the action to the word. He wouldn't notice when I came in, or Gerry. He wouldn't hear us when we spoke to him. He always knew, however, when the cat appeared in the doorway and he would call to it and proceed to do his work while stroking with one hand. When once or twice Mrs Brown decided to sharpen her claws on Sam's legs he almost wept with sorrow in having to remove her from his trousers.

The only frictions that occurred were when the landlady suspected Mama was putting down saucers of milk for her.

'She won't come downstairs for food if you do that,' remonstrated the landlady.

'She's got two homes,' said Mama gaily. 'One here and one there.'

This did not please the landlady at all.

'She's my cat,' she said. 'If you want a cat you should get one yourselves.'

'There's no entrance to a backyard from the flat,' I said. 'The cat couldn't get out when you lock up.'

'Use a sand-tray in the bathroom like everyone else.'

We couldn't bring ourselves to go to that extreme, however. It was much easier to have the landlady's cat on friendly terms, and leave the trouble of trays to her. Maybe the landlady suspected this.

One day when we were all out Mrs Brown visited the upstairs flat and since I had left our bedroom door open she had called in there. Seeing a beautiful rose-coloured eiderdown within reachable distance of the floor she must have thought it something new and exotic upon which to try her claws. Evidently she enjoyed the sensation of claws tangled up with satin for she didn't limit her tears and frays to a few inches. She nearly ripped out the side of the eiderdown. When I came in I let out a cry like a wounded animal. Mama and Sam rushed to the scene.

'Whatever's the matter?'

'Look what Mrs Brown has done! Look at my beautiful eiderdown!'

There was a shocked silence while all viewed the mess of feathers and torn satin.

'Wait till I get that cat,' I wailed. 'That's the only possession I really cherish.'

'Don't blame the cat,' said Sam immediately taking Mrs Brown's side. 'After all she didn't know what she was doing. You should have closed the door.'

'It's your eiderdown, too,' I said. 'Don't you *care* that it's ripped to pieces?'

'Yes I do care, but you can hardly blame the cat. After all, you've encouraged her up here, you know.'

'Me? I don't sit talking to her all day, and stroking her, and taking her part, and giving her more attention than I do to my own people.'

Sam had never seen me doing what the family called 'taking off'. He might have understood my distress at the torn eiderdown but he didn't understand my making a scene. It shocked him and he looked it. That only made me worse.

'It can be mended,' he said.

'It can't! It can't!' I wailed. 'It's ruined!'

Mama had been pushing down back into the covers and drawing the torn pieces together.

'I think something can be done about it,' she said. 'But for goodness sake stop taking off, Theodora. You can be heard all over the house.'

'You, too!' I cried. 'You're taking Sam's part and he's taking Mrs Brown's part!'

'What's the matter with Mrs Brown?' It was the landlady in the doorway.

'Nothing that can't be remedied,' said Sam in a soft, soothing voice. 'Unfortunately we left the door open.'

I knew I ought to be quiet and let the scene die out but somehow it now seemed that Sam had joined forces with the landlady, too. They were all, including Mrs Brown, ranged up against me. At that moment Mrs Brown reappeared, and, walking calmly up to Sam, proceeded to rub her back against his legs. This infuriated the landlady for clearly Mrs Brown had omitted to notice her mistress's presence and had shown a preference for Sam.

'You will encourage her up here,' the landlady said tartly.

'What do you expect?'

I had referred my anger to Sam now.

'He goes to the greatest trouble to remove her claws from your leather furniture, but *my* eiderdown . . .' I began.

'Don't make a fuss, Theodora,' Sam said uneasily.

'Fuss?' I cried. The very fact that I was shocking Sam made me worse. I knew I was appearing in a bad light and the only way to save myself from making it worse was to flee. I ran down the stairs and out of the door. I walked round and round the Common. The words I uttered in the soft evening air were words of vilification against Mrs Brown and the landlady. Yet deep down it was Sam I was fighting. He didn't mind about the coal buckets and the dustbin or the poky kitchen. He didn't mind about Miss Anderson and Mrs Illington-Etc., and all the hardships of shopping in the Abbeville Road. He didn't mind about Ireland, because you can never tell another person, even one as close as a husband, what you feel unless you can compose a symphony.

My rage, for some extraordinary reason, fed itself on buckets of coal. This was mid-summer but I thought only of winter, and buckets of coal. In my anger I omitted to think of the eiderdown.

When walking to school the following Monday I confided my hatred of buckets of coal to Miss Anderson's niece. She had a solution ready for me. A colleague of hers was leaving her rooms in a house in Streatham within three weeks. Miss Anderson, Jr., knew the rooms quite well. They were in a newly-renovated house and had new modern furniture. The big room, divans one end, dining-table and chairs in the middle, and a sink, and gas-ring curtained off at the end, was over the main kitchen of the big house. So it was kept warm in the winter. Furthermore, the hot-water pipe running into the bathroom ran along the inside wall of the room. This also kept it warm. Finally, there was a hot-water tap over the sink and though there was a shilling-in-the-slot gas-fire it was not expensive on account of the general warmth of the room's position. There was attached a modern kitchen to be shared with the occupant of the opposite suite of rooms. That present occupant was a Danish woman, very clean, who went to work six days a week. The kitchen would be virtually mine.

I conjured up pictures of heaven. No coal dust? No dirty fires? No dustbins? There was a chute to the lower regions. A hot-water system for the wash-basin!

I confided my information to Sam that evening. I couldn't say anything in front of Mama because so far I didn't know about accommodation for her.

Sam was silent.

'Sam,' I begged. 'We'll be in England for half the winter, the worst half. I couldn't stand any more buckets of coal.'

'I thought I carried up the buckets of coal.'

'Darling, you do. You carry up about half of them. You just don't notice how often I go down for coal.'

'Why do you? Why don't you ask me?'

'Because the only time you've got your head out of a book you're in your best suit and going to the University.'

Sam was silent again.

'Hot water in the sink,' I said hopefully. How that would facilitate the shaving process!

Sam certainly cocked a listening eyebrow on that one.

'And my rheumatism. Oh Sam, you don't know how much I would like to live in a *warm* room and *not* have rheumatism.'

It was the rheumatism that did it. Sam agreed that we should go to Streatham and investigate these apartments. Everything, of course, depended on our getting a room for Mama. I wanted to go so badly I wasn't going to believe there was no room available for her. There just *had* to be one.

One glance at the interior of the big Georgian House was enough for Sam. It was clean and newly-decorated. The big room that would shortly be vacant was all that Miss Anderson, Jr., had said and the cost was no greater than the flat at Clampham Common. The kitchen that was to be shared had two gas stoves, one for each occupant, and separate cupboards, sinks and saucepan rack. The landlady had a sympathetic approach to us. She was a widow and her husband had been a Proctor at Oxford. The problem was the room for Mama but after much consultation with calendars and diaries we found that Mama could be arranged for.

There was a room falling vacant half-way through September. If we took possession on the first of August, Sam would leave on the same day for Dorking and that left Mama and me sharing the room till we both left for Ireland on the Tuesday.

Sam now disclosed the fact that he had been invited by the Home Office to proceed from Dorking to Ardale and carry out further tests at a school there. This would take him a

141

further six weeks. In the meantime the other room would fall vacant. There would be one week-end when Sam would be back in London between his Belfast visit and Ardale. Mama would stay an extra few days with Laura.

Nagging at the backs of our minds was a secret anxiety about Mama. How was she going to get back to Australia?

Mama herself was sanguine. She'd work her way back. This filled us with horror, for though she was on the look-out for a patient to take, nothing had come forward from the various travel agencies with whom she had placed her name. Sam had a travelling scholarship that provided his return passage and mine had been paid before we left Australia. We did not have to worry about ourselves.

The only cloud in all the sky was the little shadow that settled on Sam whenever the cat was mentioned. Unconsciously he had recorded a black mark against me, and I knew it. I thought there was a chill between us.

At night time, or when I walked on the Common awaiting the day of our removal, or when I met the landlady in the passage, or when I sat eating my sandwiches and glancing through the *Telegraph* at lunch-time I would think about it and fret. Not about the cat and the landlady, but about Sam. He was a long way away from me.

The thesis was finished and sent to the binders who would send it to the University.

Sam was very tired and very white. Now that the long strain was over he was inert and had no interest in his food. Instead of sleeping at night he went out for long walks on the Common, and did not ask me to go with him. This I fretted about, too. It would have been absurd for him to ask me because I had to get up in the morning and go to school, and it was in the early hours of the morning that Sam walked. He never told me what he was thinking about in those lonely vigils and now that I'm older and wiser I realize it was just reaction; but at the time I worried and was as lonely as if he had gone away. Indeed, he had gone away, a long, long way away.

Sam did all the packing up for Mama and me when we left the flat and indeed on the day of removal—it was the last day at school before the holidays—Mama and I left for work in the morning and returned in the evening by a different bus route, to Streatham.

After dinner Sam took his portmanteau and departed for

142

Dorking. We had been married one year and eleven months, and when Sam went away I felt as if the world had come to an end. He had not forgiven me about the cat and I had not forgiven him for my not telling him about the school key.

Mama slept in the other divan bed, and I excused my nose blowing by saying I had a cold. It was a cold in my heart and not my head.

On Saturday Vicky and Gerry arrived to view the new accommodation and pronounced it fine. Vicky and Gerry and I wanted to go down to the Crown and Sceptre just to say we had been inside an English pub but we hadn't either the courage to tell Mama or the heartlessness to go without her. It was Laura, arriving from Ireland, who resolved the issue for us.

'We can't eat dinner in this place,' she pronounced. 'There's not enough room. I know where we can get a good meal down the street.'

Remembering our Soho experience we exchanged uneasy glances.

'I'll shout you,' said Laura. 'You needn't run for your purses.'

Amidst gales of laughter we told her about the Café Marseilles.

When we later walked down Christchurch Road towards the Crown and Sceptre the other three walked in front and I walked with Laura.

'How did you meet Reggie Arbuthnot?' I asked her.

'Gerry brought him over in the winter. Later Danny asked him for the hunting.'

'Did he go?'

'Of course he did. Everyone comes to Ireland for the hunting.'

'Except Gerry.'

Laura flicked one beautifully plucked eyebrow.

'My dear, if Gerry wants Reggie Arbuthnot all she's got to do is hang on tight enough.'

'That's your philosophy.'

'I got what I wanted,' Laura said flatly. 'I meant to marry Danny. And I did.'

I thought back on Gerry's defiant challenge to the Arbuthnots: 'I'll fight for him,' she had said. Had she thrown in the sponge? I wasn't going to ask Laura anything more for it was like throwing Gerry's pride to the lions. Laura would be merciless. As it was she had to get one home on me before

143

we turned into the pub.

'I see you took good care to pack Sam off a day before I came over.'

'We didn't know you were coming, to begin with,' I said amiably. 'And I don't know anyone, *anyone*, who would stop Sam working if he had his mind set on it.'

In the twilight Laura's face had a delicate pallor and her blue eyes looked dark as pansies.

'I came over expressly to take Sam home. Now I'll go back empty-handed.'

'You'll have Mama and me.'

'You and Aunt Helen can come on Tuesday. I'm going back tomorrow and if you ask me why it's because I can't stand the sight of Irish emigrés returning to their home country. They all do the same thing.'

'What?'

'You'll see. And you'll do it, but I'm not going to stand around and watch.'

The dinner was all that Laura promised. The best beef of England, a light ale, and the Montgomeries inevitable order for dessert, fruit salad and cream.

'Why didn't we think of this sort of thing before?' I asked.

'Why go to Soho?' demanded Gerry.

'Trouble with you all is you haven't bothered to *find out*,' said Laura.

Mama was looking from one to another of us. I began to feel restive. In a minute she would burst out with her pride in her children and say something embarrassing and doting.

'When I look at you girls . . .' she began.

'You can see the map of Ireland all over our faces,' put in Laura. 'For goodness sake, don't say that in Ireland, Aunt. Nobody can stand the Irish at Magillicuddy.'

'I wasn't going to say anything of the kind,' said Mama tartly. 'I was going to say you all need powder on your noses. Including you, Laura.'

There was a guffaw of laughter.

'The last word's yours, Mama,' I said.

CHAPTER FIFTEEN

On Tuesday Mama and I took the four o'clock train to Liverpool. It was the 'Irish' train and everybody aboard was bound for the green isle. When we went on the platform at Euston there was the long, black monster puffing and steaming as if rearing to go. On the front carriages were huge signboards, 'Belfast, Northern Ireland,' and on the end carriage the simple statement, 'Dublin'.

We found our seats, and left our cases on them. We then repaired to the buffet for the last bad cup of tea for three weeks. I was swallowing my tea too hot.

'There's another ten minutes,' Mama said. 'The train won't go without you.'

'I'm worrying about my case,' I said. 'The galley proofs of my book are in it.'

That morning the proofs had arrived with the admonition not to delay too long with the corrections. For a moment even the journey to Ireland had been paled beside this glory.

Galley proofs! I've often wondered what galley proofs looked like.

Mama obligingly swallowed her tea hot and we hurried back to the train. There were three others in our carriage, all hikers. It transpired they had been in the Tyrolean Alps. I don't know where the legend arose that English people in trains are uncommunicative for it was never my experience to remain silent or not to be on the receiving end of information. The three ladies, all with greying hair and weather-beaten faces, instructed us on the art of hiking in Europe.

'We are going to Dublin,' was all I could say. For once I had to remain quiet while Mama maintained the reciprocal courtesies. My heart was too full for speech. I was thankful Mama's attention was elsewhere.

Sometimes in life there come unexpected moments of grand experience. Sometimes it is on the backs of the commonplace that the spirit is suddenly released and reaches, for one glorious moment, the purple heights.

Such a moment came to me when we stepped out of the train at Liverpool. The station was dingy and ill-lit. Drawn up against an asphalt kerb, right on the station itself and within a few feet of the train, were several shabby buses. A uniformed bus driver stood at the side of his door.

'Dublin this way! Dublin this way!'

His voice rose over the hurry and scurry of dithering passengers. I stood outside the railway carriage, my case in my hand, and looked at the buses.

'Dublin this way! Dublin this way!'

The words struck me with terrific impact. Something in me rose and went out into the night air. It soared beyond the earth or even my own comprehension of what was happening to me. It went straight to heaven. Here had my father, and his father before him, stood. I was going back to the beaten way of my origins.

'Dublin this way!'

No other words have ever had the same effect on me. It was the grandest moment of all.

The bus was crowded, shabby and rackety. The way to the docks was dark, ill-lit and sinister. The Irish ferry was just a ship and that was all. But I was following the way to the stars.

On the wharf was a collection of Irish shawlies singing and crying a sentimental farewell to their boys. Under the swinging yellow light that hung beside the custom house a young man and a young woman, she in shawl and clogs, stood in passionate embrace. When the young man pushed his dark soiled cap back on his head and folded the black woollen scarf around his neck, she clung to him tearfully.

'One over the eight, the lad's had,' said a man standing beside me on the deck.

Perhaps he had. He weaved his way up the gangway to the pit at aft end of the ship.

'Och Paddy! Give my love to Dublin, dearr, dirrty Dublin!' wailed the Irish voice of the bedraggled colleen on the dock.

The ship moved out and the group of shawlies on the shore sang the 'Londonderry Air' with tears in every word. The man at my side had gone away and there were two American girls, perhaps twenty years of age, who wept unashamedly. Their father, dressed like an American but speaking like an Irishman, came up behind them. He placed a hand on each shoulder.

'It's only an act they're putting on,' he said. 'They know

every ferry is half full of tourists.'

One of the girls sobbed bitterly at his words and they turned and walked away along the deck.

Mama was making sure that all was well with our cabin so I walked around the deck, too. I came to the place where the first-class passengers could look down into the pit where the poor Irish sat huddled on the floor, their shawls and coats over their heads to protect them from such rain as might fall. They were singing, all the Irish songs one knew and many that one didn't. The American girl was standing there sobbing against her father's shoulder.

'I can't bear it. I can't bear it,' she said. 'They can have my cabin.'

'I've seen worse sights than that in Brooklyn,' he comforted her. 'They don't mind it. They like it. It makes 'em feel martyrs. It improves their singing no end. Without a grievance there'd be no songs in Ireland.'

In a pale grey dawn we came to the Liffey and to Dublin. When I opened my case in the Custom's shed the officer picked up the galley proofs of my book.

'Phwat might this be?'

'My book.'

'Your book? You've been after writing it yourself?'

I nodded.

'Glory be to God,' he said in undisguised admiration. 'You've written a book? Faith and I don't know how you do it!'

He passed us on with a wave of his hand.

Somewhere I read in a book that when you set foot in Ireland the spirit of the Irish rises up out of the ground and you feel a beating of wings in the air. Even Mama was silent as we mounted a jaunting car and were driven around the dock road, across O'Connell Bridge to our hotel. The driver flicked his long ivory-handled whip in the air and pointed out the scenes of interest. His thick Irish voice curled lovingly round the words and every now and again he would turn his head and smile knowingly at me.

'Would your honours be from Boston now?'

'We're not American. We're Australian.'

'God bless us now, that's a long way to be coming. Over there's where the Barracks were after being when the British were here.'

When the British were here!

147

Mama and I had arranged to stay in Dublin over night because we wanted to see the ancient gracious Georgian city. We wanted to walk up Grafton Street; we wanted to sit on College Green. We wanted to go to Trinity College where Burke's name was carved on the panelling of the rooms my father occupied.

It was in the morning that we first saw the policeman on the corner that led to O'Connell Bridge.

'Oh Mama,' I cried. 'Look at him!'

There he stood, a big man, his beautiful uniform immaculate and his white gloves spotless; his hat at so slight an angle it was hardly an angle at all. Yet there was a jauntiness about it. He held his head high and when he raised his hand it was as if he stopped the traffic of all the world. His flashing white teeth matched the white of his gloves. His blue eyes challenged the world and the wave of his hand directed the destinies of a city.

'You stay here,' I said to Mama. 'I'm going to speak to him.'

Four lines of traffic seemed to converge on the policeman's island. I skipped about between cars and bicycles and a pony trap or two. The policeman saw me coming and the high hand instructed Dublin stand still in patience while Theodora Richardson asked her way.

'Where does the Meath bus leave for Kells, please?' I asked.

'Have you come all the way from Australia to be asking me the way to Kells?' he said. His voice was like the little breeze that used to come in across the sand dunes on a summer afternoon in Pepper Tree Bay. I flushed with pleasure.

'How do you know I come from Australia?' I asked.

'It's the sound of you, and the way you have of walking. And the cock of your head.' He moved his cap to a greater angle and bent his head sideways and smiled down on me. 'It's not the look of your face now,' he said. 'For it's an Irish face. And is it from Kells you went out across the water to Australia?'

'My father did,' I said.

'Och,' he said with a sigh. 'It's always the best that goes from here. 'Tis the flower of the country that lives across the water.'

Dublin traffic stood mute and silent. It looked on with approval while the policeman at the corner near O'Connell

148

Bridge made me welcome home. He pointed along the shore of the Liffey.

'On straight,' he said. 'God bless you!'

There were champagne sparkles under my feet as I went back to Mama.

'What on earth were you talking about?'

'I asked the way to Kells.'

'But we're not going till tomorrow.'

'I had to ask him something, and he told . . .' I faltered. No, I could not tell Mama what the policeman had told me in words and told me with his blue eyes. 'He told me on "straight",' I said, pointing along the quays.

We made our obeisance to Trinity College and walked up Grafton Street till we found a restaurant. There we had the best tea we had drunk since we left Australia. When we returned to the hotel the lounges were full of young men in riding clothes and young women in jodhpurs. The air was blue with smoke, and ribald with wit and scintillating conversation. There was music in the sound of every word and a scratch under the wit of every sentence. They laughed mercilessly at one another. One imagined the greatest social asset was a stream of anecdote and a bright vocabulary, for clearly no one minded if there was mud on his leggings or turf in his hair.

After lunch we were loaded on to a bus outside the bus office on the quays by a posse of young men who, dawdling about, were quick to perceive that we were 'foreigners' who needed every available friendly hand to keep us 'on straight' and in a manner of style appropriate to our importance. One interviewed the bus driver and another ushered us right into the bus, felt the seats for us and found us one that he promised was 'away and the best for your honours'.

When I went to tip him he threw up his hands in horror.

'It's an honour to be knowing you,' he said and would not take it. Someone else piled our cases on and the entire passenger load turned around and nodded and smiled. I wished the bus could have been as comfortable as their smiles. Sad to say, it was one of the worst sprung and one of the worst driven vehicles it has ever been my luck to ride in. It rattled at a terrific pace down country roads and around country lanes in a manner that was terrifying. Every now and again the bus would stop and the driver would lean out and give the day's news of Dublin to some peaty passer-by. In return he would hear what O'Flaherty's mare brought at the sale and this intelligence he would pass on at the next stop. By the time we were well into the meadows of Meath he had a news service at the tip of his glib tongue that would dwarf Reuters.

Mama was at her poking business again.

'Look at those green fields,' she would cry, accompanying her words with a knuckle tapping at my hip-bone. 'If you squeezed the grass it would drip green lush.'

'Did you ever see cows like those?' This was a forefinger prodding into my arm. 'Lying down and full up.'

'Oh now, isn't that pretty?' This was a nudge from her elbow.

'Mama, will you leave me alone? I can *see*. I'm looking all the time and I don't want to be knocked about in the process. And I don't want to *talk* about it, I want to *think* about it.'

'As a travelling companion,' said Mama crossly. 'You have no good points whatever. If you want silence why didn't you go and travel on a deserted island in the Pacific?'

'Why didn't I?' I moaned. 'Or why wasn't I born into a world of dumb people, preferably without arms, too.'

I wanted to sit and let Ireland lave over me, but I didn't have a dog's chance with Mama beside me.

At Kells we were set down on the grey stone path by the great Cross. On the steps of the Cross were half a dozen of the usual street gallants, all with black caps and dark peaty clothes. There was no sign of anyone else in the street.

'This is where we were to be picked up by Laura,' said Mama, looking round. 'By the Cross,' she said.

'Perhaps she's late,' I ventured. 'Let's look around.'

A grey street wound past grey buildings up a hill and we walked up it. At the top of the hill we could see the incredible green of the fields stretching away into a misty blue. How many times had my father and his brothers tramped thuswise up this very hill? I could almost hear the sound of their boots in the hollow echo of our own footsteps.

'Not much to see there,' said Mama, who having seen one aspect of the countryside had seen all.

'Let's go back to the Cross,' I said.

There were only dawdlers on the steps looking curiously at us from under the peaks of their caps.

We went into a shop strangely reminiscent of the little tuckshops that settle down beside schools all over the world. There was a middle-aged woman weighing out bags of boiled sweets and she looked up at us with a fine smile. I bought a packet of cigarettes and one of the bags of sweets.

'Could you tell me how far it is to Crossakeel?' I asked.

'On straight, past the Cross,' she said. 'Seven miles it is by the road; and would the two of you, sisters that you are I can see that, be coming from Boston?'

'One day,' I said to Mama, 'I'll have to go to Boston.'

'We're not sisters,' said Mama happily. 'We're mother and daughter.'

'I don't believe a word of it. Which would you be after telling me is the mother of the other now?'

'Go on, Mama,' I said. 'Tell the truth.'

The flattering attention the two middle-aged ladies paid each other for the next ten minutes left me free to go out on to the footpath. Two of the dawdlers had left the Cross and drifted near the shop where they had been listening to the conversation.

'You would be going to Magillicuddy through Crossakeel, lady?' one asked.

'Yes. Someone was to pick us up at the Cross. Have you seen anyone about?'

'That would be Johnny Lenehan who comes in the pony cart. If he's not late then he's early. Everything depends on God and the drouth that's on him whether he comes early or late. Whichever way it's after being he goes to the Sergeant's. If you ask there you'll get yourself one way or another, lady, to Magillicuddy.'

'Where is the Sergeant's? Do you mean the police-station?'

'God save us, no, lady. Don't be after mentioning the station to the Sergeant.' The man bent forward on his hips and lowered his voice.

'He was in the Constabulary before the troubles, lady.'

'Where can I find him then?'

'Up the other hill. 'Tis the cottage set back from the road before you come to the Round Tower. You can't miss it, and there's all the world know the Sergeant if you do miss it. Just be asking after him.'

I stepped back into the little dark shop to ask if we could leave our cases there while we went in search of the 'Sergeant'.

In front of the Sergeant's cottage stood a jaunting car,

151

which Johnny Lenehan was to swear was nothing of the sort but an 'outside' car. Whatever one called the little pony cart with seats at the side so that passengers could look out on the world, was according to whether one was of English or Irish descent.

In the Sergeant's parlour Johnny Lenehan sat slaking his drouth.

'God save us,' he cried, nearly weeping with apology. 'Jimmy Boyle and his bus from Dublin must have been an hour early.'

The Sergeant was elderly, conversational, and not to be rebuked or refused.

'It's a foine cup of tay I'll give you if you'll but stay a while. Johnny Lenehan here is not fit to travel with until there's a cup of tay on top of the whiskey that's in him.'

We accepted the idea of a cup of tea and sat down in the dark parlour. It was like Father Reilly's study and my own father's study: warm, lived in, smelling of tobacco, and dreadfully untidy.

'Did you ever know my uncle, Rory Montgomery?' I asked the Sergeant when he brought us the tea. He was a bachelor and there were no women about.

Mama's back stiffened with my question and Johnny Lenehan looked shocked.

'Did I know the rascal? Sure and I spent years of my loife cleaning up the mess after him. A divil he was for keeping books and record.'

'What was he like?'

'He was like the rest of the Montgomeries, save your honours, and it's God's truth you want. A wild lot they were, ridin' down to the river instead of away to school. They all came to a grievous end so they tell me. Rory himself went away to the Canadian Mounties and the snow was the death of him. Then there was William, him that was the father of the young missis out there at Magillicuddy now. A pile of money he made in the mines in Australia, so they're after telling me, then lost it all in the wild gambling of the stock exchange. He died of a broken heart, so they're telling me. And what I'm telling you ladies is God's truth as it came to me.'

Mama was holding her head very high.

'I was with William Montgomery when he died,' she said haughtily. 'He died of a coronary thrombosis.'

'And the same thing and all it is, lady. When you get to

152

being my age you learn there's different names for the same thing.'

The Sergeant was not going to admit we knew more about the Montgomeries than he knew himself.

'Then there was Timothy and Joseph. And a terrible wild one was that Joseph. To the Church they both went, Church of England, you understand me. 'Twas as well for Joseph his brother Timothy rescued him from being after poaching his own pheasants for he'd gone to gaol instead of to Church if Tim hadn't come home from the Colonies and put him to school and university.'

Mama drank her tea. All this story we knew, and told in the Irish brogue with a lot of hand waving and 'God save us' was amusing. For Timothy it had been a lifetime of self-sacrifice, we knew. He had foregone his right to Magillicuddy to finance my father, Joseph the wild one, because he foresaw that Joseph had the qualities of leadership and the Church needed leaders. For ten years he lived as a poor clergyman in Ireland after he returned from South Africa to keep a home and a stern, overseeing eye on Joseph, the brother who was twenty years younger than himself.

In telling us the story of Timothy and Joseph the Sergeant forgot to tell us the end that had come to the brothers. Uncle Tim had died in the finest way that a great Churchman and Christian gentleman could die, pronouncing the blessing at the end of a sermon.

'Then there was Dennis, the one in between. Him that's the father of Master Montgomery out there at Magillicuddy now. Would have broken Tim's heart to have seen the way he let the old place go to rack and ruin. Drink and horses, it was. And wild riding. There was not a steeplechase that Dennis Montgomery would not win, or the back of his hand to the world and the hay-ricks in all County Meath come down in a blaze to the ground. In the troubles he was, right up to his neck. There at the very cross-roads, Crossakeel, and you'll see the place this very day, they rode him down. Got him from behind a hedge with a pitchfork they did. Och!'

The Sergeant sighed.

' 'Twas no way for an Irish gentleman to die. 'Twas the blessing of God that Tim never knew the end of him.'

The whole of this story had been accompanied by sighings and exclamations of woe from Johnny Lenehan. So lowered in spirit was he by the sad end of the Montgomeries that he jumped up and helped himself to a liberal allowance of rye whisky.

Mama, seeing this, set down her cup and announced that we must be going. I would have liked to sit listening to the Sergeant for a long time but even though the twilight was long there was a long way to go to Magillicuddy and a pony cart is not the fastest means of locomotion.

'Come again, and come again. Welcome you are, the both of you.'

The old Sergeant led us to the door and putting his long forefinger against his nose, whispered to me.

'Don't be after letting Mrs Montgomery out there at Magillicuddy know you've been talking to the Sergeant now, will you? God bless you! We're no friends but that's a sorrow on me and not on herself. A foine young woman she is, and making something of the ould place, too.'

'I don't believe a word he said,' said Mama, not seeing the romance for the sorrow in the story of the Montgomeries.

'They don't like the Sergeant all on account of Rory that was in the Constabulary,' said Johnny Lenehan, eager to explain. ' 'Tis best not to mention the visit, and all.'

I knew very well that Johnny Lenehan didn't want Laura to know where he had been in between times. And what doing. Laura, I imagined, might be something of a martinet out there at Magillicuddy.

The dark was falling when we turned in a gate and drove at a spanking pace up the long curving drive between wide green lawns and old gnarled trees to the house. It was a big grey house. Old and shabby. Away to the right we could see the stables and lanterns moving about them. On the steps was a man in a shaped coat and leggings.

'A welcome to your honours and who's coming down first?' he asked. He gave Mama his hand and helped her to the ground.

'It's a foine time you've been, Johnny Lenehan,' he said.

'And a foine time it was, the bus coming late like that. Me sitting on the Cross there without a soul in sight to have a drop of conversation and not even three ha'pence in me pocket for a cup of tay with Mrs Shannahan. The divil and Jimmy Boyle, him that drove the bus out of Dublin this day, must have been takin' with all the news of the sale that he stayed talking instead of getting the ladies here to Kells in foine time.'

'Then you must be full of the news yourself?' said the man, swinging down our cases. 'What did the young colt from Farmer Holland bring now? Will you be after telling me that for I'm sure you wouldn't let the bus go by without inquiring?'

Johnny Lenehan was not lost for an answer.

'Jimmy Boyle wouldn't say a word of it, him having an interest in the colt from Mullingar. Adding things together, man, I would say by the look in Jimmy Boyle's eye the lad from Mullingar took second place to the colt from Holland.'

Laura had come out of the hall on to the steps.

'Well, here you are!' She kissed us both and commanded the two men to bring in the cases.

'Just who are those two?' asked Mama.

'Grooms, I'm sorry to say. We haven't any real servants but little Bridget in the kitchen. Johnny Lenehan looks after Danny as well as work in the stables and old Mulligan is butler, cook, housemaid and groom all in one. Mulligan *is* Magillicuddy, so don't cross him, Aunt Helen; he always wins in the end.'

We had entered a lovely big drawing-room. It was a square room with a wide window embrasure at the end. Mulligan came in and drew the heavy tapestry curtains across them. There was only darkness outside but I guessed the windows gave a wide view of all that was in front of Magillicuddy.

The furniture was old and much of it shabby yet it was solid and beautiful. The ornaments, beautiful Chelsea china pieces, added charm and taste to the big room. An apple-green carpet stretched from wall to wall and was in a sufficient state of good repair for me to guess it had been one of Laura's acquisitions. Everywhere throughout the house was this combination of the old and worn with the new and taste-ful. Slowly, over the years, Laura was bringing the old place back to life.

'You've two rooms at the back,' Laura said. 'You can't have the front rooms for the damp in the walls wouldn't do the family rheumatism any good. Not even in summer. It rains here all the year round. It's the guttering in the front, and Danny won't pay for the repairs so long as he can use the money to foal a mare.'

The two rooms were comfortable and well-furnished. When we came downstairs there was a small fire in the drawing-room because a mist and light rain had settled over the county and it was quite cold.

Danny came in, still in short coat and breeches, his face, almost unearthly handsome, was lit up with a welcoming smile. His eyes were a paler blue than any of the Mont-gomeries and he was the only one that I knew who had fair hair. When in repose his face was beautiful and sulky but when he smiled a sudden warmth came over it.

'The cousins from the Colonies,' he said. 'Well, what are you going to drink? There's sherry, and I drink whiskey. Laura, God save us, drinks claret.'

Mama looked as if she wanted to say, 'What! Whiskey? At this hour? Hasn't the whole history of the Montgomeries cured you of whiskey for ever?'

She bit her lip, however, and said:

'Sherry, please, Danny. It's good to see you again after all these years.'

'And how's that goddamned country of yours out there? The heat and flies still with you?'

'At least it's a country and not a "colony", Danny,' I said, trying to remember that the charm of the Irish way of speak-ing was as much in the softness of the voice as in anything else. I could understand Gerry's preoccupation with Ireland. So I spoke softly—well, as softly as I can!

'God save us!' said Danny, in gentle surprise. 'What's the difference?'

'Don't start Theodora off on that one,' said Mama.

'The difference is . . .' I began.

'Don't bother to explain to him,' said Laura. 'He knows very well. It pleases him to believe the opposite to what are the facts. There's not an Irish farmer who hasn't the same attitude to change.'

When we went in to dinner Danny went dressed as he was, riding breeches and all. He sat at the head of the great old table and as the meal wore on he drank more whiskey and presently his legs were sprawling out under the table and his voice, though charming and full of anecdote, was thickening a little. His pale blue eyes became tired and even paler. A lock of his thick fair hair fell over his brow. He was a very beautiful young man but getting just a little drunk. Mama looked at him in sorrow. He was the whole history of the

Montgomeries all over again.

Laura took little notice of him and her greatest and longest contributions to the conversation were made to Mulligan as he served the dinner. Mulligan was putting up a fine case for Johnny Lenehan and Laura wasn't believing a word of it.

Back in the drawing-room by the fire Danny drank more whiskey and Mama was silent and heavy with sadness.

Danny, a little drunk, was gentle and winsome and kind. He was argumentative but always deferred to other points of view with a gallant wave of his hand. When, quite early, he stood up to go into bed he weaved his way to the door, came back for his riding-whip which he had left on a small table before dinner, and asked Laura where in damnations she had put Ruff's *Guide to the Turf*. Laura, without looking up, said he would find it on the dining-room sideboard if Mulligan had finished with it.

Danny went through the house shouting 'Mulligan!' and when silence had fallen on him one imagined that Mulligan had found him rather than that Danny had found Mulligan.

This was the pattern for every night that we were at Magillicuddy except on the occasion when Danny brought his friends in after they'd been to a grouse shoot, and they all stayed drinking and talking till a late hour, and the night when we all went from Magillicuddy to the dance at the 'Big House' at the cross-roads.

In the morning Danny and Laura had finished their breakfast when we came downstairs. Danny, in riding breeches, was reading his letters and Laura was reading the paper.

'Help yourself from the sideboard,' she said. 'Mulligan will make some more tea.'

On the sideboard there was porridge, grilled kidneys and lamb chops. On the table there was thick, fresh home-made bread, strawberry jam and a bowl of clotted cream.

Mama thought there should be a judicious sprinkling of early morning conversation mixed in with the kidneys and strawberry jam so she inquired first after the weather and then if Danny was 'going out riding'. By the time she had reached comments on the excellence of the new tea Mulligan brought in, the monosyllabic replies that she received indicated to her that no matter how brilliant Irish conversation was after eleven o'clock in the morning it was non-existent before that hour.

'Eat your breakfast, Mama,' I whispered. 'And *ignore* them.'

Laura folded up her paper and said she was sorry—no one, no one at all in Ireland had any manners at breakfast-time.

'Your father, Laura, and Tim too, were always perfect in their manners,' Mama said severely. 'I can't say as much for Joe, but I thought it was peculiar to him.'

'Danny takes after the tail-end of the Montgomeries,' said Laura. 'He drinks too much whiskey before going to bed.'

Danny ignored this and presently stood up, picked up his whip and turned towards the door.

'I'll be down at the stables, Aunt Helen,' he said. 'When you've finished your letters you might like to come down.'

'My letters?' said Mama. 'Where would I get letters from?'

Danny looked surprised and then as he could think of nothing to say went out of the door shouting for Mulligan.

'Mama,' I said. 'Don't you realize that in Ireland ladies don't go to work after breakfast in the mornings. They retire to their boudoirs to *write letters*. In other words, they get out from under the feet of their hostesses.'

Laura laughed.

'It's a damn good idea, anyway. If you have any correspondence you do get it done that way and it fills in the blank before midday. Theodora, do you want to borrow some riding togs?'

'What am I going to ride on?' I asked warily. 'And how many hedges are there on the route to wherever I'm going to ride?'

'You needn't ride at all, but you'll look funny down at the stables in those clothes.'

'Then lend me something, if it will fit. I might just oblige and get up on a horse.'

'Mighty nice of you,' said Laura. 'We've got the best bloodstock in Ireland.'

'Every Irish farmer says that.'

Down at the stables the sole conversation was of horses. All the grooms and stable boys looked as if they were related to one another. It was certain they had all descended from the Goidels and Brythons. They had wide, low-hanging foreheads and high cheek bones. Their cheeks and lips were red with sun and windburn. Their eyes were blue and their hair straight and a light brown. Their brogue was as thick and un-understandable as the cockneys in the North End Road.

Danny on the subject of the mare, or the filly, or the gelding, spoke with them man to man. Wherever he moved a small posse of them moved with him. They chided him and praised him. They reproved him and smoothed his path for him with one another. They called him 'Master'. But every now and again their eyes would slew cunningly round to Laura to see how she was taking things. Danny, they thought, was the 'master' but clearly Laura was Magillicuddy's 'master'.

When Danny had ridden off to see the Colonel 'up at the Big House,' Laura then took over.

With conversation at an end the stables became a hive of activity. When the grooms had taken out half a dozen horses to exercise, Laura stood over the stable boys while they cleaned out the boxes. Mama and I walked around the house and explored its shabby barns and outhouses. Everywhere there was dilapidation standing side by side with some new or repaired piece of building.

'You know, Mama,' I said, 'I think Laura's got a life's job in front of her. I'll bet Danny never did any of that repair work.'

Mama shook her head.

'It's an awful pity,' she said. 'They ought to have been born with silver spoons in their mouths to live the way they want to live.' She meant, of course, the male end of the Montgomeries.

In the afternoon Laura took us driving round the countryside in the trap and we called in at the Rectory for tea. There the Rector's wife received us in a rose-embowered drawing-room, and she wore an enormous hat on her head. The hat, like the mantelpiece and the tables, was also surmounted with roses like cabbages.

Mama remembered the customs of the days before we were poor and went out to earn our livings. She reminded me to eat my afternoon tea with my gloves on, the silliest custom I ever heard of. I always got cream on my fingers.

Twenty minutes to the dot and Laura rose.

'Another silly custom,' I said. 'What sort of conversation can you squeeze in in twenty minutes?'

'Who wants to *talk*?' said Laura. Living in Ireland she had a surfeit of it.

With darkness Danny came riding home again, and we had the same drinks, the same dinner, and the same after-dinner hour of watching Danny growing sweeter and more mellow, just a little pathetic, as he drank his whiskey.

Finally, 'Damnation, Laura, where's the *Guide to the Turf*?'

Laura's reply: 'On the sideboard, if Mulligan's finished with it.'

Then Danny's beautiful Irish voice: 'Mulligan, where the devil are you?'

When I got into bed I lay thinking about it all. This was Ireland, my Ireland.

It was better than I had dreamed. And worse. The green of the fields was greener than all the songs of Ireland had ever said. Magillicuddy was not as tumbledown as I had feared. Danny was the Irishman of books, and the servants were as picturesque and their speech as witty and musical as an Irish play. Yet in two days I had sensed the inner frustration of the life. It was a routine of farming, horse-rearing and racing, conversation that would not always be wild and witty; and drinking. As my father had said, drinking was a social grace in Ireland and it was an insult to a man's cellar not to drink yourself under the table at night. If you couldn't talk politics, horses or religion you might as well fold up and pass out. It was the life.

My thoughts were like Tomlinson's soul, flitting perpetually between two worlds. What was Sam doing? Why hadn't he written me a letter? Now if I'd had a letter from Sam there would be some point to that after-breakfast hour when guests retired to 'do their correspondence'. Didn't Sam know that when I came home to Ireland he ought to have put pulling strings around me? If he didn't know, why didn't he know?

Then from being profoundly unhappy at Sam's defection I turned to thinking again of the stables and the cobbled paths, the cracks of which were filled with dandelions, of Johnny Lenehan saying, 'The top of the morning to your honours, and phwat would you like to be riding today?' Of Mulligan putting his hand under Danny's arm and saying, 'Sure and you'll do as you're told, sirr, if you're after knowing what's good for you. If you don't take your boots off I'll take them off meself, and it won't be the first time I've laid out the maister of Magillicuddy to have me own way in the end.'

I thought of the Rector's wife with her hat like a field of roses; of the peasants who crossed themselves with the ringing of the Angelus three times a day; of Mike Finnegan who had come across from Mullingar to sell Danny a 'little red horse' and found only Laura with whom to do business.

Mike Finnegan didn't want to do business with Laura and spent his time, in between flattering her, her cousins and all her relatives, trying to wheedle out of her where Danny might be. The stable boys hovered around at a distance trying to convey to Mike Finnegan that 'let the Missis be out of the way, and we'll be after telling you where the master is gone.' Laura, however, knew her men and she on her part was trying to get rid of Mike Finnegan and keep the stable boys at bay.

'The only way not to buy that red horse, Mike Finnegan,' she said, 'is to ride with you to the cross-roads and even as far as the river.'

'Never let it be said that Magillicuddy turned a man away without a cup of tea.'

'I'll not turn you away. I'll take you away.'

The stable boys scowled and only Mulligan brought them to order. Yes, Laura was a taskmaster, but if anyone ever made anything of Magillicuddy again it would be Laura.

On Friday we went to the 'Big House'. It was a spacious and ancient country house with big, high-ceilinged rooms furnished with heavy mahogany pieces that looked as if they had been in their places hundreds of years. The great hall was arranged as a waiting gallery and on either side the dining-room and the library had been cleared and the floors waxed for dancing. A group of Irish fiddlers provided the music.

In spite of his easy and friendly manner there was something of grandeur in the Colonel's way with his guests. Mrs O'Connell was transformed. The riding habit and high stock were gone to reveal the loveliest neck and shoulders. She was a glowingly beautiful woman and made one banish fears of the fifties for ever. In her satin gown showing just a little bosom and all her back, with her shining, soft brown hair, her flashing teeth and glorious skin, she was the most beautiful woman I had ever seen.

All the men danced with me. They looked at me and talked to me in a way that made one feel their eyes and their voices made love.

It was a brilliant and happy evening. Mama was alternately charmed or alarmed by the terrific stories that were told of Rory Montgomery.

'It's something I've never been able to put my finger on,' she said. 'What was the cause of the trouble between Rory and his father?'

There was a shout of laughter.

'They were born in trouble, so I've heard,' one man said. 'No doubt it would have been no different than the troubles of all Ireland if it hadn't been for a matter of a horse.'

Then everyone told a different story about Rory Montgomery and how he had gone to County Down to buy a horse for his father and come back with a different one. They also told hair-raising stories of his activities in the 'troubles'.

When we drove back to Magillicuddy in the small hours I never wanted to leave Ireland again. When I got into bed I did not feel anxious about Sam, or wonder why he had not written to me, or wish that he, too, were here, or that I would want to tell him all that had happened to me.

I felt happy, and beautiful, and brilliant and exactly like all the others who had been up there at the 'Big House'. I even thought I had glorious, shining teeth and a beautiful skin; not to mention the 'best seat on a horse in all Ireland'.

I didn't think about Sam at all.

CHAPTER SIXTEEN

I lived in this state of bedewed wonderment all the following week. I resented Mama's insistence on our going to Belfast and Sam only came back into my life when Mama reminded me that Sam would be coming to Belfast.

While I was half-way in my descent from the clouds, Laura announced she was going over to England and while we spent a further two days in Dublin and three or four days in Ulster she would hunt out Sam in Dorking and see that he packed himself off to Belfast.

Both my feet seemed to hit the earth with a bump.

'You leave Sam alone,' I said to Laura. 'He won't forget to go to Belfast. He's been invited to give a lecture there. That's *work*. And he never forgets *work*.'

'I know,' said Laura. 'I think I can make him forget it for a day or two beforehand. Did you say he was returning to London on the twentieth?'

Never let it be said that I was a jealous woman, yet somehow my heart dropped when I visualized Laura 'hunting out' Sam. Laura had the real beauty and some of the charm of these Irish of whom I had been pretending I was one. Laura had something that I didn't have and I knew she would wreak it on Sam . . . as doubtlessly she had wreaked it on Reggie Arbuthnot. She had no fundamental interest in book-learning or the men who went in for it, but a man on the loose end of a string had an irresistible attraction for her. She meant no harm but she did it.

'You leave him be,' I said. 'Sam's got no money for your kind of "forgetting", Laura. You'd embarrass him.'

'Fiddlesticks!' said Laura, and I knew she was going to do just what she threatened.

Thereafter my heart was divided against itself.

I left Magillicuddy with the determination to return before we went back to Australia so I suffered no last farewell pangs. In Dublin I stood on the footpath and watched the policeman on the corner near the O'Connell Bridge. Suddenly he wasn't just a policeman whom I was teasing myself about, just for fun. He seemed as if he stood for something more, even than Danny and his kind in County Meath had stood for.

Danny and the O'Connell's led their kind of life only while the land they lived on gave it to them. Their wit and charm were social graces just as good manners are in an Englishman.

The policeman had something else. He worked. He was of the people, yet he, too, had kindness and a flick of fantasy in his eye. If there were fairies in Ireland, as Father Reilly would have me half believe there were, it would be the policeman who would know all about them. Not Danny or Colonel O'Connell. The only fairies they believed in were at the bottom of a quart flask at the end of a hunt. No doubt they often saw fairies then.

Mama and I spent our second day in Dublin at the house of Mr Hanrahan. He was a very old man now, with silvery hair. Once when I was a child he had come to Pepper Tree Bay and I remember him asking my father to bring in his entire family of girls. There were five of us, and Gerry, only a baby, had had to line up with us along the wall while my father repeated our names. Victoria Yvonne Montgomery; Denille Shannon Montgomery; Geraldine Rory Montgomery.' Theodora Eileen Montgomery; Mary Cathleen Montgomery;

Mr Hanrahan had laughed and teased my father about the

sound of Irish waters in a distant land. Vicky he had not thought to have an Irish name.

'Is she a swan amongst the geese or a goose over the Magillicuddy mountains?'

My mother said she was a swan and my father said that, though she had the colour of Limerick skies in her eyes, her heart was made of North Country. This was his way of disparaging Mama, for Vicky was as beautiful as a doll and the idol of her heart. Mama came from North Country stock.

I remembered Mr Hanrahan often coming in the Rectory but he was very different from this old and gentle man. In those days he had been big and red-cheeked and had had a habit of righting my father in argument that had made my father's fingers on the arm of the old leather chair dance with rage.

Now, in Ireland, he greeted Mama and me with courtly simplicity. He lived in one of the lovely Georgian houses near College Green. We sat in the library with him, for he was a bachelor and he complained of the lack of service to keep his drawing-room fit for the 'grand and gracious ladies' that used to visit him in his palmier days. Clearly he lived in great comfort, however, and by palmier days he must have meant days of his youth.

Until lunch was served from the sideboard in the dining-room we had to tell him all that had befallen the Montgomeries who had left their native land and what we had recently seen of the last remaining ones at Magillicuddy. Laura, he said, came to see him whenever she was passing through Dublin. He professed a great affection for Laura. Then he turned to me.

'And you remind me of your father. It was Tim and your father that always had my heart. Come here whenever you're in Ireland. This house could tell you stories of your father that no history will ever relate. Its door will always be open for you.'

This he said so warmly in spite of the frail quality of his voice, almost as if he wished that I would come often. His voice wavered a little as he looked away through the windows.

'I could show you wonderful things,' he said. 'There's the Dublin Horse Show, now. 'Tis the grandest sight in the world!'

But he was too old, even for the Dublin Horse Show.

'I would love to come,' I said. 'Whenever I'm in Ireland, that's a promise.'

He did not call it 'Eire' or the 'Free State' so I didn't either.

In the afternoon we were shown up to bedrooms so that we might 'rest'. We understood perfectly that Mr Hanrahan had to rest and though Dublin outside the windows called we obediently went to bed.

Dinner was like the dinners at Magillicuddy. Pheasants, roast mutton and fruit pies weighed down with clotted cream.

Mr Hanrahan, too, drank whiskey and continued to do so afterwards until we departed.

'It's part of the life, Mama,' I said.

'Then I'm sorry Laura's come back to it,' was all she said. 'No wonder the Irish leave Ireland.'

'It's not on account of the whiskey, Mama. They take it with them. It's on account of it being too small an island for the population.'

Mama borrowed Laura's favourite word and said:

'Fiddlesticks!'

The next morning we went to Belfast. We put up humbly in the Presbyterian Girls' Club and Mama was able to demonstrate joyfully to me that it was worth coming to Belfast.

'Look how *clean* it is,' she cried. In the hotel in Dublin we hadn't been sure whether we had company or not when we went to bed. Certainly we both had several red marks next day.

This was Mama's end of Ireland so the choice of where we went and what we did was hers. First she ran me off my feet looking at things I didn't want to look at. We had to examine carefully the Houses of Parliament, and from there we moved on to Queen's University. I winced.

'Not there, Mama. Sam'll drag us there, when he comes.'

'Have you had a letter from him?'

'No. I think I must have passed out of his life when we boarded the train for Liverpool.'

Mama chuckled.

'Laura will probably tell him of your escapades on those horses.' She couldn't have said anything more depressing.

We saw the sights of Belfast in true tourist fashion. Mama, having made a number of tours, had the technique down to a fine art. On the third day she announced we were going to see the Mourne Mountains. My heart lifted a little. It wasn't that

I didn't like Belfast or Northern Ireland, it was just that I couldn't do things the way Mama did. She skidded through *seeing* things. I wanted to sit and *brood* about things. And I hated being prodded and told what to look at.

The Mourne Mountains, however, were different. We took a bus to Newcastle amid pouring rain and the mountains were not even visible.

'We'll have to find somewhere to go and sit,' I said.

'We're going to the *Slieve Donard*,' said Mama.

'Don't be silly,' I said scornfully. 'That's where the Governor-General goes, and dukes and admirals and things. Besides, we couldn't afford it.'

'We're going to the *Slieve Donard*,' Mama said. Then I remembered to notice that Mama hadn't worn her gaberdine raincoat this day. She wore her good tailored coat and carried fine doeskin gloves, and wore a neat little hat that could carry her head proudly anywhere. I looked at her suspiciously.

'Rain or no rain, Mama,' I said, 'I believe you meant to go to the *Slieve Donard* when we set out.'

'I did,' she said, and buttoned up her mouth as an indication she would say no more to explain her behaviour.

'I hope you've got a lot of money with you,' I said.

'I have,' she said.

As if Mama had ever had a lot of money in all her life! Well, she had carried us through this kind of situation before, doubtless she could do it again.

So to the *Slieve Donard* we went.

It was very beautiful, very comfortable and the view through the smaller drawing-room window gave us all that we could wish of the Mourne Mountains when periodically the rain clouds cleared away. The elderly ladies and gentlemen sitting about leafing through the *Sphere* and the *Tatler*, one felt were the fading scions of aristocratic families.

We lunched beautifully and were finally ushered out into the last of the misty rains as if we, too, were aristocratic.

'Now, Mama,' I said. 'Come clean. Why did you want to go to the *Slieve Donard*?'

'It was where Rory Montgomery made his famous horse deal that split the Montgomery family and sent at least three of them out of the country.'

So Mama had her sentimental moments too!

The day before Sam was due to arrive to give his lecture I

went into a state of open rebellion. I couldn't stand any more ruins or national monuments.

'You go your way, I'll go mine,' I said. 'You take a day tour somewhere, Mama. I'm going to Larne.'

'Why Larne? It's just a fishing town.'

I didn't tell Mama that in the bus depot I had seen an excursion to Larne advertised that went by way of the Glens of Antrim. Mama wouldn't like the glens, too much up hill and down dale. She would have said, 'Let's go and look at the countryside until they all come up out of those holes in the ground.'

'It will look so *odd*,' Mama said, 'you going one way and me going another.'

'Who to? There isn't anyone to see us.'

'Well, the bus people.'

'They see thousands of tourists all behaving the same way. We're not any different from any of them.'

This was an argument that carried no weight with Mama. We were a unique family with striking and enviable qualities. Not me or any bus company was going to shake her conviction of that.

To Larne I went, however. Mama went to Portadown and Armagh.

I sat back in my seat nearly at peace with myself and completely at peace with the world. There was no doubt about it, Greta Garbo and I had one quality in common. We liked to be alone. I could not lift my spirits above a certain level, however, for deep inside me I was bothering about Sam. His lack of corresponding talent hurt me and thoughts of Laura and what she would get up to were so searing I struggled to banish them from my mind.

How Sam had admired Laura! Why hadn't I told him about Laura in the days before she went back to Ireland and married Danny Montgomery? About the dance she'd led us all way back in Pepper Tree Bay, 'that damned country of heat and flies', as Danny called it?

What good would such recounting do but whet his interest? Was there any man, even a man of books, who would not look twice at a beautiful woman with an erratic past? There had been a definite gleam in Sam's eyes when he had looked at Laura when she came to the flat. Sam liked women who were poised and he loved them if they spoke well. The personality of the voice meant more to him than the personality of the

167

face. And Laura, with her touch of Irish accent, had a lovely voice.

The passengers disembarked from the bus and the driver told us we had an hour to go down into the glens.

'Keep to the paths and you won't get lost,' he said. 'If you do there's another bus through from Larne an hour later. It's a cold wait you'll be having and no tea for your troubles.'

True to my Greta Garbo mood I waited until all the other passengers had dispersed and then I chose a little wet, muddy by-path I hoped the others had missed. It led down, down, down between ferns and rotting trees, past mud cliffs over which the water continually dripped. The air grew cooler and was very still. Not a drift of wind moved a fern frond and there was stillness except for the dripping of water, the rustling of the stream and my own slipping footsteps.

I stood still. The silence was absolute except for dripping water. Down there in the glen it was a world of light and shade, of diamond-dancing pattern and deep secretive shadow. Presently when the circle of light above seemed a mile away I came to where the stream broke through the mat of ferns and fell down a tiny waterfall. I sat down beside it and gazed into the green depths of fern and bush of tree trunk and olive sliding water. I heard a bee, or was it some kind of fly, like the faint persistent note of the violins in a pastoral symphony. I leaned back against the dank cliff and pushed away the fern fronds that tickled my neck. I closed my eyes and listened to the bee and the water and the ancient silence of Ireland.

I had been sitting there quite a long time, with my eyes closed, when I heard the sound of someone coming down the path. The footsteps did not slide and slither or stumble as I had done. They came quietly and firmly as if the wet earth held no secrets from the walker. It seemed as if my head was heavy and hazy with a half-dream because it was quite a long time before I could look up. The footsteps were slower, as if their owner had seen me and was passing. It seemed as if my head was heavy and hazy, because it was quite a long time before I could look up. That is the way it is in dreams.

He was coming towards me now, his head tilted a little on one side, the smile on his mouth catching up with the smile in his eyes. His eyes were blue and easy and kind. His face was brown but his neck was white where it showed through his open shirt. He carried his short coat over his arm and there was a belt round the blue serge of his uniform trousers. His shirt was very white. His head was bare and his black hair was long and just a little unruly, as if it, too, was having a holiday. It was the policeman who stands on the corner near O'Connell Bridge.

'Ah! There you are,' he said softly, for all the world as if he had been looking for me.

'I didn't know you were here,' I said. 'How did you come?'

'In the bus. I was in the train from Dublin, too.'

'I didn't see you.'

'You didn't expect me to be there, did you? So of course you weren't looking for me.'

His sentences lilted upwards at the end. He sat down on the bank beside me but instead of leaning back as I had done he leaned forward a little so he could see me. He looked right into my face when he talked to me.

'Have you been looking for the fairies?' he asked.

'Are there any fairies?'

'Whist now! They're very sensitive about being disbelieved.'

'Have you ever seen the fairies?'

'You have to have a believing heart, Allanna.'

The sun, up above in the world, was leaning down to the west and it shone sideways into the grotto: behind the misty veil of falling water was a golden dancing curtain. In the tiny caves and valleys of the waterfall it was dark except where a diamond caught the light from the water. I felt a little hazy but very quiet and still inside me.

'I believe,' I said, looking up into his face. It was like saying The Creed.

'Then if you come across the waterfall with me. I will show you where the fairies live.'

I stood up and looked uncertainly at the falling water.

'Is it damp and slippery on the other side?' I asked. 'If I jump I might fall.'

'It's only a very small jump.'

'It's funny,' I said, taking his hand. 'It's like going under a ladder—some people won't do it. I have always been afraid to jump over a waterfall.'

'Kick off your shoes,' he said. 'If you go over the waterfall you will see where the fairies live. But you must not be afraid.'

He kicked off his own shoes and suddenly I noticed he didn't seem to have any socks on. His feet were bare and very white.

'The fairies?' I said. 'They have milk-white arms, and milk-

169

white limbs and they speak very softly. They are winsome and they lure one on.'

'If you come looking for the fairies, Allanna, you must expect to find one. Come!'

He put his hand under my elbow, and then the strangest thing happened. It was as if my body was buoyed up as it used to be when I went swimming in the river at Pepper Tree Bay. As children we used to do ballet dances in the water and were astonished and delighted at how beautifully and effortlessly we danced because the water buoyed us up. Now as I went over the waterfall my body was carried like a feather in the air. I pointed my bared toes like a dancer; and his toes were pointed too. When I touched the ground again I did not feel it. I might have been a feather coming to earth.

We were standing in the thick soft grass and the mist over the waterfall obscured the path where we had been sitting.

'Now lie down there,' he said. 'Turn over so you have your ear to the ground and can look into the tiny grottos, so!'

He lay down and leaned his head over the water and peered into the shadows on either side of the pool.

'Now if you watch, and listen, and lie very still, you will see the fairies.'

I lay very still. There was a sound of water and small rushing and a tinkle. Overhead amongst the ferns the bee droned quietly, finding the filters of sun between the leaf fronds.

When I was a child I had a favourite way of falling asleep. I would close the lids of my eyes so tight that I could see a silver haze like a curtain. Then I concentrated very hard and presently I could see shelves and shelves of toys and sweets. The shelves sloped upwards to some unseen ceiling so that the array of good things was illimitable. Everything was brightly coloured. It was only when I looked at one thing closely did its outlines blur and it become intangible and made of such stuff as dreams are made of.

It was a wonderful fantasy, one I could conjure up at will.

Now, deep in the glens of Antrim, I wanted to see the fairies and I knew that the belief I had expressed had to be supported by the powers of a believer's concentration. I did not close my eyes, but strained them into the inner recesses of the tiny caves. With all my being I concentrated on what my eyes must see, for clearly the fairies were not visible to all mortals.

The light danced between the water mists, the shadows became dark green curtains. There was a pattern in the movements there. Out of the silence there came to me the faint and myriad sounds of millions of little things of the earth. The silence was no more and the earth and the ferns and the cool, damp undergrowth was full of sound. I understood at once that I must *listen* to see the fairies. They are part of the sound as they are part of movement of light and shade. They are the rhythms of life, its echoes from profound and unsuspected depths. They are reverberations of that affinity between the human and the everlasting. They are the aspiring sweetnesses of music not known but only suspected in the undiscovered and imponderable depths of the soul. They are what Tchaikovsky heard when he composed *The Sleeping Princess*. What Wagner nearly heard when he sent his gods thundering across the roof of heaven.

In the fairy caves there were drifts of water-mist that were milk-white arms as intangible and as ethereal as smoke. It all came from:

> '*A land whose name is only heard*
> *In the strange singing of a bird.*'*

I understood why the mortals of Ireland feared the beguilement of the *little people*. To enter this world was to leave for ever the ways of man and man's ways with man.

I turned and looked into the face of the man lying on the ground near me. His face was my father's face, and Danny's face, and the face of the policeman who stood on the corner near O'Connell Bridge. The piercing blue of his eyes was the blue of men who live near that other world, half wooed from mortality and whose feet when bared and white and pointed are not on the earth, as we had not been on the earth when we went over the waterfall.

He smiled, and the beguilement in his smile was the sound and rhythm of the fairies.

'Shall we go now?' he asked.

We stood up and again he put his hand under my elbow and again we drifted back over the waterfall like feathers floating to earth. He sat down and put on his shoes.

'I must be going now,' he said. 'I have others to see.'

* Edith Sitwell, *The Sleeping Beauty*.

'Will I see you again?'

'I will be on the bus; and in Belfast; and on the train to Dublin . . .'

'On the train to Dublin?'

'Yes. I'll see you in Dublin.'

'But . . .'

He had picked up his coat and was walking down the path that led deeper into the glen. He turned and smiled and waved.

CHAPTER SEVENTEEN

Mama had been to Armagh and was full of happy recollections of a pleasant day.

'I sat beside a Canadian on the bus,' she said. 'She was just my cup of tea. We liked doing the same things, so we did them together. She was a much better travelling companion than you are, Theodora. Not so moody. And she liked *looking* at things.'

Looking at what things? Mama's feet were firmly planted on the earth and she liked the things she could touch as well as see.

In the morning we went to the post office to see if Sam had written to us there. There was no letter.

'Can't think what's come over him,' Mama said. She looked at me doubtfully. I shrugged.

'Then let's go to Queen's University. There will be news of him there surely. He's to lecture there tonight. Perhaps he's written to you care of the Registrar.'

I was resistant to going to Queen's.

'All the communications that would be with the Registrar,' I said aggrievedly, 'would be in connection with his lecture.'

'We have to know where it is, and when it is, if we're going to it.'

'We cound find out what time the boat comes in from Liverpool. He'll be on it.'

'That's it,' said Mama as if we had had a sudden flash of enlightenment. 'Of course, he would be expecting us to meet it.'

We made inquiries and found the boat was in before breakfast hours.

'Well, he must be somewhere here in Belfast,' said Mama.

'We must go at once to Queen's University. He's probably hunting all over for us.'

'Not for me,' I said. 'Why should he be looking in a University for *me*? That's his province.'

'Don't be difficult, Theodora.'

'Well, wouldn't you be?'

Mama was silent a while.

'Well,' she said gently, after a few minutes. 'You would marry a student, you know. They're all the same, absent-minded.'

He wouldn't be very absent-minded with Laura around, I thought. I said nothing of this to Mama. I didn't want her to think I was jealous. However, I wouldn't go to Queen's University. I was hurt because there was still no letter from Sam. I had written to him every second day, and I wasn't going to run after him now. So Mama went alone.

'I'll bring him back for lunch,' she said gaily. 'You watch and see.'

Somehow I knew she wouldn't find Sam. He would have been to the University by now and have gone off with some kindred spirit to bog down on the *emotional development of the sub-normal*, or *the advantages of giving it a classical education*, or some other such debatable subject.

Without knowing I was doing it I packed my bag. I was like two selves. One that was reasonable said, 'Dash it all, that's what he's come for. If he spends the day wandering round Belfast looking for me he'll miss the opportunity of meeting and talking with these people he's crossed the Irish Sea to be with.' The other self said, 'He ought to have bothered about me. He just takes me for granted. Only people like Laura can lure him out of himself for more than ten minutes at a time. He's only something inside myself that has always caused me chaos. A lecture is only one incident in his lifetime, while Ireland is a kind of cross-roads with me. I don't know whether I belong here spiritually, or back there with Sam. He ought to know what I'm going through. If he wants me he ought to fight for me. I would fight for him. He doesn't even bother enough to write a letter'.

My thoughts went around the bitter merry-go-round.

Mama came back without Sam. Her face had fallen and she looked as if she were trying not to be sorry for me.

'He came in all right,' she said. 'He has seen the Registrar and then went off with some Professor.'

'And there was no message.'

'Not exactly. He did tell the Registrar he was expecting you and me to come to his lecture tonight.'

Something inside my head went black and whizzy. I said nothing. 'I did leave a message to say where we were staying,' Mama said hopefully. 'They're bound to deliver it before long.'

'And we're to sit and wait here until such a time as his lordship deigns to turn up,' I said. 'Well, I'm not going to. You stay here, Mama, because you can't come with me. I'm going *alone*.'

'Where are you going?'

'I'm going to Dublin. I'll stay the night with Mr Hanrahan, if he'll have me, and tomorrow I'll go back to Magillicuddy.'

Mama tried to pretend this didn't sound like an ultimatum.

'Couldn't you wait for Sam, dear? After all, he must have the whole week-end to spare. He could go with you.'

'No. I'll never wait for Sam again,' I said, 'as long as I live. Besides, he'd be too busy to come to Magillicuddy. He always is. He only wants to go where his work takes him. And damn me.'

I caught the afternoon train for Dublin. Mama remained behind. There were no admonitions and no advice.

In the train I sat and stared unseeing over the landscape. I would not have believed it of myself that I would be so preoccupied with my inner self that I would not have the time or the inclination to look at Ireland. I had no misconceptions about what I was doing. There were two of 'me'. I had to live the life of one or the other. Until this year and hour of grace I had lived the one but I looked yearningly to the other. At any time in life I could have jumped over the Waterfall and become the other person. I could have done what Rory Montgomery did. I had a part of Rory Montgomery in me and it never gave me any peace.

The Vicar and Mesdames Anderson, Illington-Etc. and Bernard were far away and belonged to another world in which I had not even wanted to stake a claim. Sam was different. I had no illusions about what Sam would do. Or rather would not do. I knew that Sam would never come after me. Sam could never be pushed around. In his quiet way he was as firm as Gibraltar. I hadn't been able to push him around even in little things.

As a duet I did all the talking and Sam did all the getting.

Departing for Dublin was not a petulant gesture to make Sam take notice of me. I knew Sam too well. His logical mind would tell him that if I wanted to go to Dublin then I must have wanted to go, and that was that.

All this I thought about as the train trundled south. There was no going back and when I had got over my feelings of spiritual fatigue and emotional exhaustion I would begin to be happy. I was free. Free of Mama and my sisters, of Sam. Free of work and an orderly circumspect life when all I had asked of God was the place and the opportunity to be as mad as my ancestors speaking through my bloodstream had been before me.

In Dublin I went at once to Mr Hanrahan's house. When the butler took me into the library the old man rose waveringly from his deep leather arm-chair.

'Of course you may stay. Tamas will take your case upstairs while you tell me about Belfast.'

Instead I told him about Magillicuddy and my wish to stay there a while. He nodded and was silent. Presently he ordered tea and when it was brought in a beautiful silver tea service on a vast silver tray he bade me sit down behind the table and pour for him.

When I went upstairs to have a bath before dinner he escorted me to the foot of the staircase.

'Stay with me as long as you like, Theodora,' he said. 'I'm an old man but I could show you wonderful things about Dublin. There's the Dublin Horse Show now . . .'

I knew he was too old to show me anything but the way through the hall to the staircase.

'Remind me later on,' he said, waving his frail hand in the air. 'I must tell you about your father . . .'

His silken white hair was like a pale light at the foot of the stairs.

We sat at the dining-table that was lit by candles in a massive silver candelabra. Mr Hanrahan's head was in the shadow but his long hands had the light shining gently on them so that I could see the blue veins on their smooth snow whiteness. I thought of Joyce's poem—

'Whose soul is sere and paler

175

Than time's wan wave.

. . . .

Rosefrail and fair—yet frailest
A wonder wild
In gentle eyes thou veilest,
My blueveined child.'

In his sweet and great old age, Mr Hanrahan was gentle and
kind as the hands of a child.

In the morning Tamas gave me directions to the sights of
Dublin but there was only one sight I wanted to see. The
following day I would go to Magillicuddy but meantime I had
an appointment with my conscience at the corner near the
O'Connell Bridge.

Sam would have given his lecture by now. If he was the
kind of person that romance stories make of heroes he would
have taken the train south to Dublin. Sam, however, was not
that kind of hero. I didn't think he would even have been hurt
by my decision. He wouldn't have understood it, but he would
have accepted it.

As I came out at the foot of O'Connell Street I could
hear the rumbling of trains along the overhead bridge. Down
the side street was the way I had come from the station
yesterday. I stood with my back to it. I stood with my back to
everything it stood for, the solid circumspection of the North
Country. Mama's end of any country. Mama always drifted to
the north as automatically as I faced to the south.

A heavy shower of rain came down and I stood for a long
time in the shelter of some shops. The gutters ran little rivers;
drivers of horse-drawn vehicles huddled under their oilskin
coats and the water swept in sheets over the shining hoods of
motor-cars. Only the policeman stood unperturbed. His white-
gloved hand waved the traffic on. He was imperious and the
rain went over him as if it did not touch him. Once he took
his cap off and shook the water from it. He threw back his
head and brushed back his hair with his hand. He grinned
amiably at the passers-by.

When the rain stopped I walked to the edge of the pavement nearest the island and I stood watching him. Sometimes
he turned my way to command on the traffic, or occasionally
a pedestrian. He did not look at me any more than he looked
at everyone.

My heart was heavy. Perhaps if I stepped over this gutter waterfall and crossed over to the policeman, the man whose appearance most represented all things Irish, I would shake off the old life and the old chains for ever.

I took a step nearer the kerb.

'Magillicuddy!'

I couldn't believe my ears. Sam's voice? Impossible. Sam was immersed in a cloud of professors in Belfast.

I blinked my eyes.

'I've just got off the train. Where are you going?'

I turned round then. Sam had put his bag down and was shaking his hands to get the circulation back in his fingers. The rain had brought a touch of winter into summer and inside his gloves his fingers would be cold and white. He stood flicking his wrists and looking at me with the rather shrewd look in his eye that always startled me into realizing Sam was thinking more than one thought he was thinking.

'Where are you going?' he asked again.

'I was going to ask when the bus left for Kells tomorrow.'

Sam pushed his hat on the back of his head Australian fashion.

'Do you really want to go to Kells?' he asked gently.

'Did you give your lecture?' I asked coldly.

'Mm. It was a good one too. You missed something.'

'Why didn't you write to me?'

Sam sighed and dug his hand into his inside pocket. He brought out a pile of envelopes. He spread them out like a fan. There were perhaps six in all.

'Why didn't you tell me Magillicuddy was the name of a place and not a town?' he said. 'When I learned geography Magillicuddy was a town in Limerick. So I addressed them all to Limerick. They came back to me in London just before I left on Wednesday. There ought to be one or two more waiting for us when we get home.'

'Sam, you *know* Laura lives in County Meath.'

'I didn't, dear. You must just have taken it for granted I knew. You forgot to tell me where to write to you.'

'I couldn't have forgotten.'

'Darling, you forget hundreds of things. You forget where you put your shoes and your purse and your thimble and the breadknife. You never know where the scissors are.'

'I couldn't forget where the Montgomeries put Magillicuddy.'

'No, but you could forget to tell *me*.'

'You ought to *know*.'

'Where's Stainsacre Hall—the place my people came from?'

'Well, up in the north. Somewhere near Whitby,' I faltered. Where was Whitby, anyway?

'You see?' said Sam gently.

I took one last stand.

'How did you enjoy Laura's company?' I asked haughtily.

The twinkle appeared in Sam's eyes.

'To tell you the truth I ran away. Laura is a sight for a tired man's eyes, but she's too expensive for me. When she sent me a card that she would be passing through Dorking I folded up and made a dash for London.'

I gulped. I turned my head and looked back across the road to where the policeman stood, making a hand sign. The traffic obediently halted at his feet.

'So that's the policeman Mrs Monty told me about? Seems you and Mrs Monty lost your hearts to him.'

Sam looked speculatively across the wide space.

'A fine specimen of a man he is too! Shall I go over and speak to him and then you'll be able to see how much taller he is than I am?'

'He's very nice,' I said. Then I looked at Sam. After a long time I said: 'He's only just a policeman, after all!'

It was the middle of the morning and in the middle of a city but faint and far away I heard a cock crow thrice.

Rory Montgomery turned over in his grave.

'I don't have to be at Ardale until Tuesday. That gives us a long week-end. Where shall we go?' asked Sam.

I shrugged.

'There's all the south of Ireland.'

'Cork? Killarney? How about the Claddagh of Galway?'

'What do you know about the Claddagh?'

'Oh, I've been reading. Since I made a mistake about Magillicuddy it seemed necessary.'

'You don't want to go to Magillicuddy, Sam?'

'I don't think Magillicuddy would be very good for me, but don't tell Laura I said so.'

We grinned at one another. Sam stooped down and picked up his bag with one hand and took me by the arm with the other.

'Where's Mama?'

'It seems that you turned her down the other day and she found out for the first time what fun it is to travel without you. She wouldn't come south. She's going to make her own way to London.'

I knew very well, and Sam knew very well, that Mama had thought this a wiser time to leave us alone.

'How much money have you got, Sam?'

'Lots. They paid me for my work at Dorking and I got nine guineas for an article I wrote back there in Australia.'

'Riches! Let's go to the Gresham.'

'To the Gresham. Lead on, Magillicuddy!'

CHAPTER EIGHTEEN

September. Life at St Hilda's was like squirrels nesting. The weather was glorious but we were storing up our nuts for the winter. Heavy curtains were being brought out and aired; the coal was arriving and being stored in the caretaker's huge cellar; pots and bowls were being washed and painted in the colours of Joseph's coat ready for the sowing of the bulbs. Everything that could be washed was being washed and the carpenters were in caulking up the cracks in the great doors.

'We must make everything bright for the winter,' Miss Anderson said. She turned to me. 'Do you think you could finish those cardboard illustrations? Hung around the walls they will make the babies' room look like a new room.'

'I've only two more to do,' I said. 'I'll finish them by Friday.' I had not been able to finish them before the holidays because of new curtains that had had to be made.

Sam was entrenched at Ardale but I got a letter every day. I missed sending one every fourth day, just so I could keep the balance of attentions in my favour. Mama was keeping up a round of the shipping companies and the tourist agencies looking for a patient to take back to Australia. Gerry was having high jinks in Bloomsbury. Periodically she emerged from a blanket of Bohemianism to do some washing or sewing or repair work in the rooms in Streatham. Only Mama essayed a gentle inquiry about Reggie Arbuthnot.

'Oh, his ship's in Ceylon or somewhere,' Gerry said airily.

'Mama, I'm going to lunch with a couple of artists from the wrong end of The Boltons, do you think I can wear a red beanie cap, or am I too tall?'

'What do you mean the "wrong end"?' Mama asked severely.

'The right end is the rich and doubtful end and the wrong end is the Chelsea end. Everybody in Chelsea is good. Since they are amoral they can't ever be immoral.'

Mamma had never heard of the word 'amoral' so she didn't know what Gerry meant. She wasn't going to show her intellectual limitations, however, so she changed the subject.

'That case you're filling up with things is *my* case,' she said. 'I might get a call to take a patient home any minute and I don't want to have to chase my case round Bloomsbury *or* Chelsea.'

'It's not your case, Mama. If it was I wouldn't dream of taking it. It happens to be the case I brought my stuff ashore in when we arrived.'

'Nonsense. That's the case I took to Germany. You can see the German labels for yourself.'

'The fact that you took it doesn't say it is your case, Mama,' said Gerry patiently. 'I have no doubt you also took it to Scotland, and Wales, and the South of France. But it came to England with me. Just look at the Southampton label. You didn't come via Southampton, Mama. You came to the London docks.'

I sat patiently waiting until I could get a word in edgeways. Mama was thinking of something to say so I got my chance.

'When you've both finished,' I said, 'it is *my* case. Gerry borrowed it on the *Moreton Bay* and put her things in it instead of mine.'

'Nonsense,' said Mama.

'Rubbish,' said Gerry.

I picked up the case and turned its back towards them. There printed neatly under the hinges was my name. They both looked at it in silence.

'You ought to be ashamed of yourself, Gerry,' said Mama. 'You're always claiming other people's property as your own!'

'Well, I'm dashed,' said Gerry, looking at Mama with indignation.

'Quick,' I said, 'the kettle's boiling. Make the tea, someone. Hot, strong and Irish!'

Mama was successfully steered off both the subjects of Reggie Arbuthnot and Chelsea morals. Though Gerry was nonchalant I knew she was not heart-whole. Sometimes when she was being talkative and informative her wit had a savage edge to it as if her humour welled not from a glad heart but from a sore heart.

I spent a lot of time thinking about Reggie. There was something true-blue about his naval eyes and I couldn't quite fit the odd pieces of his behaviour together.

We had some months yet to go in Britain. Perhaps his ship would come home again and carry gold and all things bright and beautiful for Gerry!

Vicky and David were on their way back to Australia and the sea engulfed them in silence.

Way back in Australia Mary had been ill and Denney wrote doleful notes of her progress. Mama, now worried about Mary, renewed her efforts to find some way of getting back to Australia.

By the second week of September the autumn produced days that gave promise of the bitterness of winter to come. My rheumatism afflicted me again and it brought home the sharp necessity to live in a dry, warm climate. The damp mists of London were laying the ghosts of Ireland very effectively.

One day I made a dash home from school at lunch-time to get some books I needed and found Mama in a sea of open cases, piled clothes, and a cup of tea beside her.

'In the name of fortune, what?'

'I'm sailing on the *Themistocles* on the twenty-eighth.'

I did some rapid calculation after diving for the paper to discover the day's date.

'Fourteen days!' I said, aghast. 'What's happened. Mama? Have you got a patient?'

'Twenty of them,' said Mama, sipping her tea. 'Pour yourself a cup while it's hot. You'll need it.'

'Twenty patients! You and who else?'

'A man and a woman. Forgotten what their names are. Schoolteachers returning to Australia after exchange service in Birmingham.'

'What are the patients? Not lepers, for heaven's sake?'

'Not lepers.' Mama looked as if her patients might well be the next thing.

'Not lunatics? Mama, for heaven's sake, loosen up and talk.'

I had the teapot in one hand and a cup and saucer in the other.

'Children. Orphans. Going out to a farm school in Western Australia.'

'Children! Twenty of them! Mama, they'll drive you mad!'

'They couldn't be worse than you five girls were. You were worse than any twenty Pepper Tree Bay children all rolled into one bath-tub.'

'But you're fifty now. You can't do what you did when you were twenty, Mama.'

I didn't have it in me to deny the aspersions against the characters of myself and my sisters.

'I can, and I will,' said Mama haughtily. 'You don't seem to realize, Theodora, this post is one of high honour. Dozens —and when I say dozens I mean baker's dozens—of people applied for it. They selected me out of everybody. The persons who have to take charge of these children have to be of the highest integrity. They have to have had experience of children, be of stable character, have sufficient seniority to be able to handle stewardesses and their like. If two were school-teachers then the other had to be a nurse—so you see?'

I sat down on the edge of the bed with a bump.

'Listen, Mama,' I said. 'You don't have to go back now. You can wait another three months and come back with Sam and me. In three months the three of us can earn enough money to get us all back together . . . Gerry is coming back with us.'

'And what about Mary?'

'Mary will have got better or have died by the time the *Themistocles* docks in Fremantle.' I didn't feel as callous as I sounded. I just had confidence in the eternal quality of the Montgomeries.

Another dreadful thought assailed me.

'The *Themistocles* goes round South Africa, doesn't it? That means six weeks. Oh, Mama, you can't!'

'You'd better put the kettle on again. That tea won't be fit to drink.'

I put the kettle on.

'Anyhow, why pack now?' I demanded. 'You've got four-teen days, and besides, we haven't consulted Sam.'

'Since when has Sam been the head of the family? Marrying into it doesn't make him head of it.'

'All right, Mama. The first place is yours but there'll be

mutiny amongst the ratings if you go on with this idea.'

'It's not an idea . . . it's a fact. I'll have another cup of tea, too. Put three teaspoons of tea in that pot, Theodora, and don't drown it with water.'

'I've been making tea for twenty years . . .' I began.

'It's taking you a long time to learn.'

Sam was rung up, David and Vicky were cabled at sea, Denney was also cabled. It was of no avail. To Australia Mama was going, on the *Themistocles* on the twenty-eighth with twenty orphans, one male schoolteacher and one female teacher. Nobody except Mama and the teachers was over twelve years of age.

We could only wring our hands and groan. Mama went on placidly packing and making tea. When we realized her departure was inevitable Sam and I consulted one another at length on the phone and decided in the first place he would come to London the week-end of Mama's departure; and since his princely six pounds a week put him in the affluent class, we would give a party.

Who to ask?

The three people who had offered us hospitality, the Chairman of Lloyds, the Arbuthnots and the King, were out of the question. We would not have been able to receive them with adequate dignity in the rooms in Streatham Common. Mama explained that every time she accompanied a nurse from the Schools Medical Services it was a different nurse. Her superior officer resided in the same realms of unapproachable suzerainty as the Arbuthnots, the Chairman of Lloyds and the King. There remained Sam's friends and mine, Australian students scattered through Oxford, Cambridge and London. Would they come to a party for Mama?

We wrote and explained and invited. We didn't get a reply but everyone invited came.

We borrowed the communal kitchen table and set it up alongside our own table and covered both with a glorious Irish linen cloth Mama had bought as a last sortie into the realms of extravagance in Belfast. On this we put flowers, fruit, large dishes of curry—made only as the Montgomeries and the Indians can make it; and as many lemon meringue flans as we could find dishes in which to make them. There was also sufficient quantities of fruit salad and cream to fill a wash-basin. Mama believed in Pepper Tree Bay hospitality and if ten were invited then a repast must be prepared for forty.

First to arrive were the two medical students and one historian from Oxford. They had borrowed bicycles and informed us they would have to sleep in the bathroom or on the Common. They were broke. They also hoped there would be enough food for breakfast.

Then came the economist from the heights of Hampstead Heath. He knew how to manage his finances, that being his profession, and he made the journey in the dignity of the upper front seat of the London Transport buses.

It only cost the red-headed giant who was so big it made one proud to introduce him as an Australian threepence since he came from Clapham Common, being of London University. So he brought two bottles of cider with him. From Cambridge there hitch-hiked one scientist and from the East End there came the Canadian girl who still had difficulty in understanding or being understood in the various 'lingoes' required to meet the social demands of everyday life.

From Hendon came Sam's young cousin still with the freshness of schooldays on him and already claiming to be an airman since he had won a scholarship from Point Cook in Australia to join the RAF. He brought with him a young girl, a cousin of his but not of Sam's.

Sam and Gerry had brought large supplies of cider and a more modest supply of apple juice cordial—got up in a bottle with a label like the cider which bloomed with apples. From the first moment the guests were taken into the conspiracy that Mama's glass was to be filled with apple cordial but she was to be under the impression she was drinking cider, like everyone else. Cider, we had informed Mama, was just a pleasant cordial made of apple juice. Not a word was hinted about its alcoholic potential.

The glasses were filled and refilled and filled again with cider while Sam and the historian from Oxford kept a weather eye on what Mama was drinking.

'Look how happy you all are,' said Mama. 'I can't understand why some people think you can't have a party without *alcohol* to drink.'

Everyone remembered to nod a head in solemn agreement and not guffaw with laughter.

Each told anecdotes of his or her university and young George outdid them with tales of Hendon. Mama told anecdotes about her children.

We were in the midst of one of these when the door opened. There stood Laura.

She certainly was a sight for tired men's eyes. I was too surprised and entranced myself to remember to look and see how Sam was taking this. Somehow I felt proud, too. Laura was one of us, but she didn't look it. She looked beautiful and cool and svelte in a blue silk dress with a tiny black hat on the crown of her head. Her vivid expressive mouth parted to show her beautiful white teeth. Her black hair framed the pale oval of her face.

There was the sort of surprised silence that everyone who knows how to make an entry expects. In it Laura got her tributes.

'Glory be to God,' she said. 'Is it a party or a wake you're having?'

Sam gave me a wink. He filled a glass for Laura and offered it to her.

'Cider?' he said. The wink he had given me had indicated the bottle he held in his hand. It was Mama's apple cordial.

Laura took a sip, and Irish fashion spat it out.

'Glory be to God, what's that?'

'Cider,' said Mama.

'Cider be damned!' said Laura. And so the gaff was blown! Everyone made for the nearest cider bottle and hid it behind his person. If Mama was going on the Temperance waggon, then she was going to do it over a lot of dead bodies.

If the other people in the house thought there was a lot of noise they probably said:

'It's the wild Colonials.' Only in Laura would they have shown evidences of the banished grandsires' graces.

From the opposite ends of the room she and Gerry looked at one another with that feline expression that only two beautiful young women can have between them when one man is at stake. There was no mirror handy so I cannot tell how I looked at Laura. All the same I was proud of her.

It was a lovely party.

With those young men, though we did not know it there came Fame, Death and Glory. The shadeless trio sat unseen amongst us and did not whisper in any ear.

Death sat behind young George, Sam's cousin. He, in the not-so-far-distant future, was to become a Wing-Commander when he was twenty-three and die, not in glory, but in a bath of flames over Germany. The little girl who sat shyly with

185

him sometimes glanced over her shoulders. She was thin and delicate with tiny hands, and soft hair like a child's. The day was to come when she was ordered to face the sea off Banka Island and march into it while the Japanese machine-gunned her from behind.

The serious member of the party, the young bespectacled medical student from Oxford, was destined to precede the greatest army in the history of western civilization in a jeep carrying only himself, his staff, a white flag and as much of drugs and vitamins as they could carry into writhing Germany.

The red-headed giant from London University wore, invisible that night, the robes of a Deputy Chancellor of a University. The economist was the future Governor of a Bank. The scientist was to be one of a team that synthesized sulphaguanadine and atabrin and thus helped to defeat the Japanese in New Guinea. Every other man in that room was destined to be a Professor.

While Fame, Death, and Glory sat silent in our midst the medical student, the one without the spectacles, recited the chapter of *Lorna Doone* beginning with 'Spring came late that year,' from beginning to end. The historian told us that in America naval gents could get to being called Colonels if they rose high enough. Gerry told a story about a young lady in a West End store who 'modomed' her to irritation until at last Gerry leaned over the counter and asked in dulcet tones:

'Where do you live?'

Caught unaware, the young lady replied, 'Tooting, Modom.'

'I live in Bloomsbury. Let's talk in the Clapham Common dialect and I'll have gone more than half-way to meet you.'

This was greeted with a shriek of laughter.

'What did she do then?'

Gerry shrugged.

'I got sorry for her then and took her out to lunch. Seems like they have to talk that way . . . it's supposed to be a good selling technique.'

Gerry brooded into her glass of cider.

'I didn't seem to have an adequate excuse for the way *I* talk,' she said at length. 'That really puzzled her. Said she'd never heard anything like it out of the films.'

'Where did you both end up after that heart-to-heart?' Laura asked in an accent so charming everyone thought she should have kept out of the discussion.

'At the Voice Production School in Bloomsbury,' said Gerry.

'We both go to it now.'

Mama laughed till the tears were in her eyes.

'When we moved up from Pepper Tree Bay to Forty-Five we hadn't been in the house twenty-four hours and Gerry knew everyone in the street, their names, their histories and their ailments, right down to someone with an ingrowing toe-nail.'

Yes, I remembered that about Gerry. As a little girl she would walk up to anyone and ask their name. Whether they gave it or not she would introduce herself.

'I'm Geraldine Rory Montgomery and I've four sisters. There's Victoria Yvonne, Theodora Eileen, Mary Cathleen and Denney Shannon. My mother's name is Mrs Montgomery and my father's name is Joe.'

There was no such thing as anonymity with Gerry around.

Before the party was over everyone drank Mama's health and kissed her. Gerry slept on the floor, with cushions, in Mama's room. The others went home with the economist and the giant from Clapham Common.

There remained only Sunday and the last-minute packing. Then Monday and a doleful farewell to Mama at Euston. The party had depleted our finances and no one had enough money left to go all the way to Liverpool with Mama.

It's always the way with the Montgomeries that something goes wrong at the last minute and everything is spoiled.

Mama could not be reconciled to tipping. She would not leave a tip for the maid who did her room.

'But, Mama, you have to.' I said. 'It ekes out her wages.'

'Then they should pay decent wages.'

'But they don't; they're dependent on the tipping system. It might be regrettable but you can't alter it. You're one person against seven million Londoners. *You* can't alter them.'

'I don't intend to give into a wrong practice. Besides she is undeserving. She broke my bedside clock and didn't admit it. She broke the little balique vase I picked up in a second-hand shop and pretended it was the door slamming. She's never swept under the bed *once*.'

'I know. She's a rotten maid. I'll grant you she doesn't de-serve it. But you've got to do it all the same. We've got to go on living here and she'll take it out on us.'

'Nonsense,' said Mama. 'I'm not going to be bullied into giving that hussy one penny.'

'Mama, if you don't she'll go running through the house screeching for carbolic and caustic soda, the way she did when those Danish people went.'

'I won't be there to hear her,' said Mama complacently.

'But we will,' I said, exasperated.

She didn't leave the tip and we argued about it all the way to Euston.

'It's a *system*,' I reiterated. 'You can't alter a system in other people's country. When English people come out to Australia they think the basic wage an extortionate system. They have to pay high wages whether the work is well done or not . . . or go to court. They'd alter *that* if they could.'

We were still arguing when we put Mama in the train. Somehow we were heavy-hearted and angry with one another. Gerry said 'Shut up' so fiercely I walked down the platform rather than 'take-off'. Then the train whistle blew and I only had time to rush back to Mama's compartment and give her a miserable kiss.

'Oh, why did we quarrel?' I implored Sam.

'Blowed if I know,' he said. 'I sometimes think you and your mother like arguing, Theodora. It's a hobby with you.'

I said I had to make a visit to the waiting-room. I sat down on the wooden bench along with the ladies of the half-world and other miserables of womankind and wept my heart out.

It was Gerry who put a period to it. She came into the waiting-room.

'Blow your nose, and for the love of Mike powder it, if you don't want Sam running off with Laura.'

We put Sam on the train for Ardale and I returned alone to Streatham. All the way I was beset with the vision of Mama's gallant figure, in her navy-blue gaberdine raincoat with the blue felt hat and its absurd little feather stuck in the ribbon, leading the way up the gangway of the *Themistocles* like a female Pied Piper with her twenty children following after.

I hoped she hadn't forgotten her umbrella; and I put the tip in her room myself.

CHAPTER NINETEEN

The cardboard illustrations were finished. Green cords had been passed through the brass eyelet-holes on the top edge and they hung in gorgeous array around the babies' room at St Hilda's. There was Peter Rabbit and Cinderella; Little Boy Blue and Jack and Jill. All their companions of nursery rhymes depicted in the kind of primary colours that very young children understand.

I thought I'd done rather a good job of them. Each illustration was pasted on a large sheet of three-ply cardboard, then varnished and bound with bright green tape. The eyelet holes had been put in by a workman of Miss Anderson's acquaintance and she and Mrs Illington-Etc. had carried them backwards and forwards to school. In fact, it had been quite a sight to see Miss Anderson and Mrs Illington-Etc. crossing the park on the way to school when the cardboard sheets had been in the process of being eyeleted.

As each consignment was brought to school it was presented to me. Each member of the staff had one of these 'duty' projects to do in the course of the year, and these illustrations had been mine. The cardboard sheets I kept stacked behind the stock cupboard in my room, the only possible place in which to keep such big, flat objects.

The week following Mama's departure I had finished the last. With the co-operation of the babies' teacher I had cleared the walls of previous encrustations and hung my handiwork. It had been an arduous and messy job but now they were up I was rather pleased with them. When I invited Miss Anderson to come into the room and inspect them I felt like a small girl waiting for a pat on the head. This time, I thought, there'd be no faults found. I had finished them expertly, down to the last detail on the last illustration. If I had learned one thing under the direction of Miss Anderson it was attention to detail.

When she came into the room she stood just inside the door. Her face lit up with satisfaction.

'Splendid! Splendid!' she said. 'I must congratulate you. You have done them beautifully. And what a difference they make to the babies' room!'

She walked up to each picture in turn and examined it. She passed around the room like royalty at an art gallery and the little babies sat round-eyed and silent as much awed by her presence as delighted by their new acquisitions. When she had finished her inspection she returned to her place by the door and let her eye rove once around the walls. There was a faint puzzlement in her eyes.

'The other six, Mrs Richardson? Where did you hang the other six? Did you think there was not sufficient room here for all twenty-four?'

'Twenty-four?' I said, dismayed. 'There were only eighteen!'

Miss Anderson shook her head sorrowfully.

'That memory of yours again, my dear,' she sighed. 'I did hope they'd all be finished by this week too. There's so much to do before Christmas.'

'There were only eighteen, Miss Anderson. When you first brought them before they were eyeleted, I counted them and only selected eighteen illustrations from *Child Education*. All the pictures selected for the cardboards are used up.'

Miss Anderson looked at me with pursed lips. She shook her head very gently.

'I think you'd better look behind your cupboard, my dear. You'll find six more to do. I think you're going to be a very busy person for the rest of the week.'

I returned to my own room and looked behind the cupboard. I only did this out of deference to Miss Anderson. So I could say I *had* looked but this time I knew I was right. The whole procedure of doing the illustrations had been for eighteen, right from the start. I had selected eighteen pictures. I had cut off eighteen strips of green tape. I had taken eighteen greed cords from the stock cupboard upstairs with which to hang the pictures. This had all been done in the beginning so that once I started on the work I would have all the materials at hand. Besides, one couldn't ignore six extra pieces of that cardboard. They were so heavy and bulky that one couldn't carry six of them more than a few paces without changing one's hold, and the cupboard had had to stand an extra four inches out from the wall for weeks while they had been around.

I gave the children some work to do and sat down at the table to think. Miss Anderson was *never* wrong so there must be six more sheets somewhere. Six that I'd never seen. If I hadn't seen them before they had been taken away for eye-leting why hadn't I seen them since? Anyhow, *blow* having to do six more!

I looked behind every object in the room, which was silly, because the six cardboards were too big to hide themselves. I felt as if I was doing something about them, however.

I had barely commenced my work with the children when the knob of the door turned and Mrs Illington-Etc. came into the room. Whenever Mrs Illington-Etc. came into the room it was on some errand of Miss Anderson's. It meant Miss Anderson had gone into conference with her and now the second part of the duet was come to take up the theme.

'You know Miss Anderson is not well?' she asked me.

'No, I didn't know. I'm sorry. She seemed her usual self when she visited the babies' room . . .'

'Her heart is not at all good, you know. The doctor says she has a "tired heart". She should be spared worry and strain.'

I looked at Mrs Illington-Etc. steadily.

'I agree.' I said. By implication I was expected to feel guilty because Miss Anderson had 'worry and strain'. I'd done a good job on those illustrations. I wasn't going to be made to feel 'guilty' about anything in connection with them. I expect I jutted my jaw out a bit.

'There were twenty-four cardboard sheets, you know?' Mrs Illington-Etc. said. 'I carried them myself. So I know.'

'You mean you carried twenty-four cardboard sheets from this school to the man in Dulwich. And twenty-four back?'

'Not all at once, of course. You know quite well we took them three and four at a time.'

'But there were twenty-four?'

'Certainly there were.'

I looked Mrs Illington-Etc. straight in the eye.

'Then where are they now?'

Mrs Illington-Etc. took a step back. She looked from me to the table then hastily round the room.

'Very well, Mrs Richardson. I'll tell Miss Anderson I haven't been able to get any further forward with you.' She left the room.

I sat down at the table again. Was there going to be another of those long drawn-out psychological rows about the cardboards? Besides, I didn't see why Mrs Illington-Etc. should come on Miss Anderson's errands. Perhaps Miss Anderson did have a tired heart. I felt very depressed at the thought that Mrs Illington-Etc. had to fight Miss Anderson's battles for her. I had a sneaking feeling it wasn't Miss Anderson's weakness so much as Mrs Illington-Etc.'s dominance that brought the latter round the school on the former's errands. Perhaps it was a case of snatching of duties more than delegation of them.

I conceded one good point to Mrs Illington-Etc.: besides the fact she was an excellent, kindly and conscientious teacher, she was genuinely attached to Miss Anderson. When the Headmistress was tired or harassed, Mrs Illington-Etc. would cheerfully give her right hand to spare her associate. When she wasn't working for the children she was working for Miss Anderson . . . and it was from a sense of love and devotion. All the same, that didn't solve the mystery of the six cardboard sheets.

I felt myself becoming rapidly depressed. The only thing to do was to hunt the school. When the morning tea-break came I asked Miss Bernard if she had seen anything of the cardboards. She looked shocked and rapidly shrank into her shell. If there was going to be another fuss over lost property Miss Bernard wasn't going to be in it.

'Look in my room, by all means. They couldn't be there, you know. I'd have seen them.'

'That's exactly it. They couldn't be anywhere without being seen.'

The cardboard sheets were not in Miss Bernard's room, not in the babies' room and not in Miss Anderson's room, where the major store cupboards were kept. I felt as if I was braving a den of lions when I asked Mrs Illington-Etc. if I could look behind the cupboards in her room. She drew herself up and when she did this her bosom came out like a pouting pigeon.

'I would have looked myself if there had been any likelihood of them being there.'

'There could be a likelihood of them being there, you know. It was you who carried them back to school. You might have put them behind your cupboard waiting a more suitable opportunity to bring them to me.'

'Quite absurd. However, you may look, by all means.'

She accompanied me into the room and around it.

'You see?' she said, when the search had proved to be in vain.

'No, I don't see. That's the trouble,' I said bleakly.

I had to report failure to Miss Anderson. She stood by the fireplace drinking her tea. Her face was pale and her head shook a little as it did sometimes when she was feeling emphatic but not allowing her ladylike deportment to show it. Her eyes were full of angry reproof.

'I think you had better settle down and have a quiet think, Mrs Richardson. It won't be the first time you've forgotten what you've done with something, you know.'

'But I can't forget six cardboard sheets,' I said. 'They're too big.'

'They can't disappear into thin air, either.'

'Miss Anderson. I must reiterate,' I said desperately, 'there never were more than eighteen cardboards. I'm sure the mistake is in some other quarter. From the beginning I had only eighteen cardboard sheets in mind.'

'Strange things have happened to your mind before this. They could happen again.'

I stood looking at her in silence. There was flat disbelief in her eyes. Also what she had just said would have been insulting if it hadn't been for the matter of the key. I had a black moment of sheer despair and depression.

'Have you a suggestion where they might be, Miss Anderson? I'm perfectly willing to look anywhere you suggest.'

'Did you take them home to do in the holidays?'

'No,' I said. 'I couldn't forget taking those home. Mrs Illington-Wharton would know that. She has carried them and knows what it is.'

Miss Anderson half turned away to put her cup and saucer down.

'I'm afraid I could believe that you would forget anything,' she said drily.

'If I'd taken them home they'd be there and I'd see them.'

'I suggest you look when you go home. Miss Bernard, get Ronald Meekes to ring the bell, please.'

I turned away and went back to my own room. I felt sick. The whole thing was so absurd and I was going to be made to feel like some kind of pariah all over again. I could even feel like a thief except for the fact the cardboard sheets were useless except for the purpose of poster illustration. Miss Anderson didn't think I decorated my rooms in Streatham with nursery-rhyme illustrations, did she? The idea was impossible. Yet what did she think?

I rang Sam that night. I still hadn't told him about the key so he couldn't be expected to know the predicament in which I felt myself to be.

'What are you worrying about, dear? Everyone makes a mistake some time or other, and they've just mistaken the number of cardboard sheets. That's obvious.'

'There's two of them, Sam. They both handled them. They both say there were twenty-four.'

'Have you looked everywhere in the school?'

'Yes. They're not there.'

'Then what are you worrying about? They never were there. They can't disappear into thin air.'

'That's Miss Anderson's argument.'

'Where does she suggest they've gone?'

'Home with me.'

There was a long silence at the other end of the phone.

'Sam, what are you thinking?'

'I'll come down to London on Friday. I'll clear this thing up.'

I felt a lifting of spirits. On the way home from the phone box I had another idea. The caretaker—perhaps they were in his cubby-hole. I hadn't looked there although I had asked him twice if he had seen them while cleaning the rooms.

The next morning drew a blank with the caretaker's cubby-hole and since I was in Coventry once again there was no one to bother me with questions about the cardboard sheets. Since I returned to school empty-handed it was tacitly understood I did not have, or did not admit to having, the cardboard sheets at home.

When I rang Sam up again that evening he told me he would be down by two o'clock the next day, Friday.

'Find out the name of that man in Dulwich who put in the eyelets,' he said. 'Do it a bit subtly, don't go at it like a bull at the gate, or they'll know what I have in mind.'

'What have you in mind?'

'I'm going to see that man. Also find out the nearest London Transport lost property office dealing with stuff coming off that route. It will save me time when I get down.'

Oh, what a wonderful thing it was to have Sam! I suppose I could have done all these things myself, but somehow it was nice to be being taken care of.

I drew a blank with Miss Bernard about the man in Dulwich so I had to broach the subject with Mrs Illington-Wharton.

'Did you carry those cardboards from the tradesman in Dulwich back to Miss Anderson's flat and then later into London?' I asked her. Then I hurriedly added. 'Triple carryings would have impressed them on your mind, wouldn't it?'

'No, I didn't. He collected them from Miss Anderson and returned them there.'

'He did them very well, didn't he? What is his real trade?'

'He's a carpenter.'

'Is he an old-fashioned carpenter or a new-fashioned carpenter? What is his name?'

'I don't understand what you mean by old-fashioned, or new-fashioned. His name is Choppin.'

'Very suitable name, too,' I said, not trying to be funny but just trying to force the conversation out of periodic and pregnant silences.

'Were you thinking of employing him?' Mrs Illington-Etc. asked.

'Well, you never can tell. It's not very far from Streatham, is it? The only thing is we're returning to Australia soon, and tea chests at five shillings a time, expertly nailed up and bound, are cheaper than trunks. I thought I might get someone.'

'You'd need someone on your own doorstep for that.'

'Yes. I expect so.'

I'd got the name. One trick of the game to Theodora and Sam! Moreover, I hadn't really thought of the tea chests before and was delighted that I'd thought of it now. It gave us an excuse to call on Carpenter Choppin in the first place and in the second place was certainly a better idea than buying at least two extra trunks for the homeward journey.

This intelligence lifted my spirits throughout the day. I could hardly wait until half-past four and school-out to meet Sam in the little tea-shop on the edge of the park.

He was waiting for me when I got there.

'I got your message when I got home,' he said. 'I've checked the Lost Property Office and nothing has been handed in there. That, I'm afraid, is a blank. Did you find out about the man who made the eyelets?'

'His name is Choppin and he lives in Dulwich but not near enough Miss Anderson's flat for them to carry the cardboard sheets backwards and forwards to him.'

'If he provided service they wouldn't have to carry them. Well, I've got a detailed road map of Dulwich and now we must get there quick enough to look up a directory, or, better still, a telephone book.'

We dived into the telephone-box on the station. Sam found three Choppins in Dulwich and he wrote their addresses down. He looked up Miss Anderson's street.

'We'll try the nearest to her and then radiate out in circles. Our man might not be in the telephone book but he might be known in the village, and failing that we'll get hold of a directory. There's tomorrow, too.'

The first carpenter Choppin we found was the right one. We first made inquiries about tea chests and asked would he call at Streatham and nail and wire-bind them for us if we put in an order in good time.

He was a very old man, bent and white-haired. Very thoughtful, very deferential and he considered every word before he gave it utterance. He thought the work might be done. He would go into it. Had we the tea chests or did we want him to procure them?

'We can get them for five shillings at our grocer,' I said tentatively.

'I can deliver them to you for five shillings,' he said. I guessed by the gleam in his eye he could buy them a lot cheaper, being in the trade.

'Mr Choppin,' said Sam, 'my wife has been pasting poster illustrations on those cardboard sheets you eyeleted for Miss Anderson. That was a beautifully neat job. Is it done by hand or have you a tool?'

' 'Tis very simple, Sir. I do it with this, you see?' He showed us a machine for cardboard work. 'Makes the whole box, if you want it, Sir.'

'They are heavy things,' said Sam. 'Those boards you did for Miss Anderson. Did you carry them yourself, or have you a carrier?'

'I carried them myself,' he said, drawing himself up. 'It's a pleasure to do anything for Miss Anderson. She is a fine lady and very civil.'

'All eighteen of them?' I asked. I could hardly get the words out for my anxiety.

'Yes, certainly. All eighteen of 'em. Mark you I took 'em in two lots.'

'There were as many as eighteen—' said Sam.

'Eighteen there were, and no doubt about that, Sir. Too much for them ladies to be carrying to the tram, and I said so, taking leave of the right to say so. I've done a lot of work from time to time for Miss Anderson. Fixed up all them shelves in her flat I did.'

'Mr Choppin,' Sam said, looking at him very directly. 'There were eighteen cardboard sheets and not twenty-four?'

The old carpenter suddenly sensed danger.

'Now what would you be asking that question for, Sir?'

'I wanted to check a detail. Miss Anderson was under the impression she brought twenty-four cardboard sheets to be eyeleted and then delivered the twenty-four back to St Hilda's. You would have a record in your books, wouldn't you?'

I could see the man's hesitation.

'It's only a small point,' I said, trying to sound non-committal. 'We were having a discussion about it.'

'Would you look up your accounts and just settle the point for us, Mr Choppin?' asked Sam.

The old man was heavily suspicious. He obviously had a high regard for Miss Anderson, and he wasn't going to betray her, even on the smallest point, to a couple of wild Colonials.

'Don't keep accounts of them small jobs,' he said. 'Just do a little service now and again for a fine lady. Miss Anderson's a very fine lady. Treats everyone in the village very well.'

'I think so, too,' I said. 'I'm on her staff and I know. Everyone has the utmost respect for Miss Anderson. It would be a black mark against the person who didn't.'

His suspicion of us was not to be allayed, however.

'What was it you were wanting to know?' he asked slowly.

Sam fired straight.

'Were there twenty-four cardboard sheets or eighteen?'

'What was it Miss Anderson said there were?'

'Miss Anderson doesn't matter,' I put in hurriedly. 'I had a difference with her friend, the one who lives next door to her. Mrs Illington-Wharton. I said there were eighteen. That's all there is to it.'

'Well, eighteen there were,' said Mr Choppin. 'Now what was it you wanted about them tea chests?'

'If you can get them for us as reasonably as five shillings we'd like you to get them. They would need to be wired after they are packed,' said Sam. 'They'll contain books, and we can't afford to have them bursting out in the hold of the ship.'

'Right, Sir. You give me the dates and it will be done.'

We thanked him profusely and made to leave the shop.

'Mark you, Sir,' said the old man. 'I won't go against what Miss Anderson said. If she says there were twenty-four, then twenty-four there were.'

We were out on the pavement.

'Wouldn't it drive you mad?' I said to Sam.

'The facts of the matter are he's got a pretty high regard for Miss Anderson.'

'That's just it. That's why Mrs Illington-Etc. would have made the mistake. She would take what Miss Anderson said as gospel, carry the darned things up to London two and three at a time, and never count them.'

'There were only eighteen, that's certain. He made that clear enough. He also made it clear enough he'd stick to what Miss Anderson said, if asked.'

We were thoughtful all the way back to Streatham. While I was in the kitchen preparing some supper Sam put on his thinking cap.

'Where did those cardboard sheets come from originally?' he asked.

'From the Education stores.'

'They'd be ordinary schools' stock?'

'I think so.'

'With all the stocktaking you did before the holidays there must be some records in the school.'

'There are. There's a stock book. Miss Anderson keeps it in her middle drawer.'

'Then you'll have to get that stock book, I'm afraid. About when did they come into the school?'

'In the winter term. It would have been January or February.'

'Then you've got to get the stock book and look up January or February.'

'She'd never give it to me, Sam. It's inviolate.'

'You'll have to make up your mind, dear, whether you ask for the stock book or take it. I can't help you there unless you would like me to go along as an indignant husband and demand a show-down.'

'You can't do that in places like the London teaching ser-

198

vices. The discipline's like the army. What the Head says is final.'

We sat and drank tea and brooded on this.

'You know, Sam,' I said. 'We've satisfied ourselves we're right. Suppose we let it go at that. I've only a few more weeks to go.'

'You can't do that. By implication you've taken six pieces of St Hilda's property home. You're entitled by the laws of justice to clear up the matter. More important, if you leave St Hilda's under the cloud of their displeasure it won't be just you who will be criticized. It will be the entire Australian nation. They would dislike and distrust any Australians who came their way for the rest of their lives.'

'All right, I'll get the stock book. I don't just know how at the moment. I'll have to think about it. If Miss Bernard weren't such a cowdy custard she'd help me. She's too frightened.'

Sam decided to stay down from Ardale for the Monday.

On the Monday I went to school. When I went to sign the time-book, Miss Anderson was sitting at her desk, the long middle drawer slightly open and I could see the thick bulk of the stock book taking up the larger portion of the space. I could hardly see the time-book for looking at the back end of the stock book. As I signed on I tried to screw up courage to ask Miss Anderson to look up the matter for herself.

Her cold 'Good morning,' however, intimidated me. Even as I bent down, pen in hand, I heard Miss Bernard's footsteps coming up the stone stairs. The opportunity was lost.

Several times during the morning I made reconnoitres around the school to see if Miss Anderson was teaching. Just before the lunch hour I saw Miss Bernard crossing the playground, her coat on, and drawing on her gloves. I knew Miss Anderson had sent her on some errand and had taken over her class.

I gave the children some work to do and sped out through the door on to my own playground and ran up the stairs to Miss Anderson's room through the entrance used by the boys from the School Upstairs. I pulled the stock book out of the drawer and opened it on the table. I felt as guilty and as miserable as if I was in the act of stealing a hundred pounds.

The book was beautifully kept, as were all Miss Anderson's records, and it was only a matter of seconds before I had

199

found January and was running my finger down the items. There it was in the last week. Under several other items for January 27th was clearly written in Miss Anderson's beautiful flowing hand:

$1\frac{1}{2}$ *doz. Three-ply cardboard sheets.*

I closed the book, pushed it in the drawer and ran downstairs. A quarter of an hour to go and the children would be dismissed. I felt as if it would never pass.

When the last child had gone out and I had locked the school gates I walked with uncertain steps back to Miss Anderson's room. Mrs Illington-Etc. was in her own room preparing their two lunches. Miss Anderson was at her table looking at some correspondence. I knocked and went in when she said 'Come in.'

'Miss Anderson . . .'

She turned round. Her eyes still held their cold reproof.

'Well, what is it you want?'

She didn't ask me to sit down.

'I'm afraid I have something rather wretched to confess.'

'Not again? Is it the cardboard sheets you have found this time?'

'While you were teaching Miss Bernard's class a little while ago I looked at your stock book. I didn't like doing it that way but I knew you were as certain there had been twenty-four cardboard sheets as I had been I hadn't had the school key. I felt entitled to find out the truth.'

She was looking at me in cold silence.

'Very well. Go on.'

'If you look up the items of stock received on January 27th you will see only $1\frac{1}{2}$ dozen cardboard sheets were delivered to the school.'

She sat perfectly still for a moment, then slowly turned round and took the stock book out of the drawer.

'Sit down, Mrs Richardson,' she said. I sat on the edge of the chair and felt embarrassed. She opened at January and put her finger under the item.

'Would you go to Mrs Illington-Wharton, please, and ask her to bring to me the requisition sheets for January? Also the duplicate receipts for stock? Mrs Illington-Wharton keeps them. I would be glad if you would come back with her.'

I ran down the stairs. I met Miss Bernard on her way back

from her errand.

'What's up?' she whispered. 'What's amiss?'

'I'm just getting Mrs Illington-Etc. for the Head,' I said.

'About the cardboard sheets? Are they found?'

'They were never lost. Now if you don't want to be in at the death, bury yourself in your own room.'

This is precisely what Miss Bernard did.

Mrs Illington-Etc. suspected something was afoot, too, but we walked up the stairs in silence.

'Sit down, both of you, please,' said Miss Anderson. She took the requisition sheet from Mrs Illington-Etc. Her finger rested on the item of cardboard sheets. From my chair at the side of her table I could see the figure '2 doz.' written beside it. She then turned over the stock receipts until she came to the single item:

$1\frac{1}{2}$ *doz. three-ply cardboard sheets.*

Mrs Illington-Wharton had also seen what was on the papers. She leaned forward and then sat back rather heavily in her chair. Miss Anderson turned and looked at her.

'It is clear what happened. We measured up for twenty-four and I ordered twenty-four. They only sent us eighteen.'

Mrs Illington-Etc. said, 'Oh dear, dear!' several times and then lapsed into a staggered silence. Miss Anderson closed the requisition sheet and the receipts into the stock book and put it away in the drawer. She closed the drawer gently and sat looking at it in silence for a minute. Mrs Illington-Etc. said 'Oh dear, dear!' again. Then Miss Anderson straightened her shoulders and turned to me.

'Mrs Richardson, I owe you an apology. Will you accept it?'

I never felt worse in my life.

'I didn't want that, Miss Anderson,' I faltered. 'I only wanted to clear it up. I was so terribly wrong about the key.'

Mrs Illington-Etc. coughed.

'I would be glad if you would accept an apology from me, too.'

I looked at her but didn't feel so miserable at all.

'I only wanted it cleared up. There's—there's one more thing . . .'

'Yes?'

'I'm afraid we went to Mr Choppin.'

'Yes?'

'He said there were eighteen. But he was going to support you if you said there were twenty-four.'

'Who do you mean by "we"?'

'My husband. You see we were very unhappy about it. As I'm leaving soon we felt we had to find out what had happened to the other six.'

Mrs Illington-Etc. struggled to her feet and stood looming over us.

'Shall I go on with the lunch?' she asked. 'Shall I make Bovril or tea?'

'I must explain to Miss Bernard and the babies' teacher,' said Miss Anderson. 'Perhaps you will ask them to come here, Mrs Illington-Wharton?'

'No, please don't,' I cried, jumping up. 'I couldn't bear it. Please don't mention the subject again. I just didn't want to be wrong again, not about anything as big and unloseable as six cardboard sheets.'

I was embarrassed and made for the door.

'I hope you'll have lunch with us, Mrs Richardson?' Mrs Illington-Etc. asked eagerly. I had never known her eager before.

'Thank you,' I said. 'I'm having my lunch with my husband. He's waiting for me in the park.' With that I fled.

The postscript to the story took place next morning.

The Vicar never took prayers on Tuesday morning because he went on that day to another school. If the Curate didn't come in, then Miss Anderson took the prayers.

When we had had the usual hymn and the usual prayers we stood silent a moment waiting for the signal to raise our heads and unfold our hands.

'I have a special prayer this morning,' Miss Anderson said. I stole a glance sideways at her. She stood very erect, her face not bowed but turned upwards. She looked very good and even a little saintly standing thus. Farther along the room Mrs Illington-Etc. stood with her hands folded and her eyes screwed up. Miss Bernard's head was bowed so low her chin was nearly on her chest. The babies' teacher and her flock didn't come to prayers. They had their own in their own room.

The children stood meekly, their eyes closed and their tiny hands obediently clasped.

'Forgive those amongst us, O Lord, who are arrogant. It is just and meet that arrogance in us should be punished at Thy

Will. In our arrogance we make mistakes and are punished. Have mercy on us, O Lord, who have made mistakes. We humbly ask thy forgiveness, as we ask the forgiveness of those we have sinned against.'

I kept my eyes closed and my lips clamped together. I felt they were trembling. When, after a pause, Miss Anderson dropped her hands and said 'You may lift up your heads, children,' I felt she had really made the amend honourable in a way that was grand because of its simple humility.

CHAPTER TWENTY

'What's come over Miss Anderson?' asked the Vicar, 'she actually made me a cup of tea when I went into the school yesterday. As for the Illington-Etc. she was nearly eating out of my hand.'

I shook my head over the pile of envelopes I was addressing for him.

'I wouldn't know.'

He looked at me suspiciously.

'There's something odd about that school. There's something happening. What are you all up to?'

'Why, nothing. What could be wrong if they made you a cup of tea? That's something more right than wrong, surely.'

'I have worse to report,' said the Vicar, not looking up as he thumbed through a great pile of parish magazines.

'Worse?'

'I was in the church. They came in. Both of them. They don't usually come in except on Thursdays, and I didn't have time to run for it.'

He looked up now and his eyes were mischievous.

'I had my carpet slippers on, and they didn't even look at them. What's more they were very pleasant to me, just as if I didn't have 'em on.'

'Why don't you tell them about the bone in your foot, Father Reilly?'

'What do you know about the bone in my foot?'

'I noticed it the day you kicked off your shoes to put on your slippers. I had an uncle who had a bone protruding like that. The pain of it in a pair of shoes nearly killed him.'

The Vicar poked his long finger through his crown of hair. He shrugged and lifted both his hands in a questioning way.

'I'm always promising myself to have it carved off. I believe you can carve off bunions these days. Have you heard of that?'

'I guess you'll never have time to have it done. You have to go to bed for weeks. You might as well come clean, Father, and tell them why you wear carpet slippers. They'd be most sympathetic.'

'Ho, ho!' he said, looking at me in astonishment. 'What's this we've got in our midst? A peacemaker? I thought I was appointing a firebrand when I put you on that staff.'

'Why did you do it, Father?'

'Make a melting-pot . . . stir it all up . . . the good rises to the surface.'

'I consider that very mischievous of you, and definitely unfair to the staff.'

'In five years' time they'll look back and love every minute of it. Besides . . .'

'Yes, Father?'

'I had a brother went out to Australia many years ago. He was penniless and they gave him a job. He was ill and they put him in hospital and nursed him. When he died they gave his widow a pension. I felt I owed them something.'

I looked at him when he was leafing over his magazines again.

'Besides,' he added, 'you had a lean and hungry look.'

'I see. My countrymen threw their bread upon the waters, and after many days I came here to receive it back ten-fold.'

'Well, not exactly. There were the Anglican Sisters, you know. I set a lot of store by them.'

'I have a lot to thank them for, haven't I?'

When I told the Vicar I had really come to break the news that I would resign at the end of December he shook his head.

'That's another thing that's wrong with the school. Everyone's wanting to resign.'

'Me and who else?'

'Miss Anderson.'

'*No!* Oh, Father. Don't let her. She's a wonderful woman, really.'

'She's sixty and says she's getting to the stage when she makes mistakes. When people start making mistakes they ought to go, so she says.'

I looked at him in shocked silence.

'Don't look so worried, child. I didn't accept her resignation.'

'What—what did you say to her?'

'I said, "Well, I'm not sixty and I make mistakes every day, but the Lord forgives me." I pointed out that the Lord has more love for those He can pity, and it's just as well to bring down a little of the Lord's love on one's head now and again. I also pointed out she had a wild Colonial on her staff who made the most abominable mistakes, and she wasn't half-way to sixty.'

I smiled back at him as he glanced up at me.

'And she isn't going to resign?'

'Not this time.'

'I'm afraid I must resign, Father. We are going back to Australia.'

'Has that young man of yours got his doctorate yet?'

'We haven't heard. I nearly knock the postman down in my agitation every day. He still doesn't bring it.'

The news came a week or two later after Sam had returned from Ardale. We were sitting having our tea when the landlady came pounding up the stairs.

'There's a telephone call for Mr Richardson. Said it was important or else he wouldn't have rung.'

Who could it be? Not Gerry, because it was a 'he'. Reggie Arbuthnot home from the seas again? Young George, the Air Force cousin?

Sam went off down into the catacombs of the house where the landlady lived, and I made a fresh pot of tea.

Presently he came back looking sheepish.

'It was Professor Yeldon.'

'About the Ph.D.?'

'Yes, I've got it.'

'*Sam!*'

This time I felt released and I spilt the tea in my gesture to embrace him.

'Let's celebrate.'

'Certainly. At once!'

Sam also was released. He began to talk about the work; about long sessions he had had with Professor Yeldon. About men he had met and listened to at the University. About the rotten sandwiches they made in the refectory; about how much it cost him to have the thesis bound for presentation. About a mathematical formula he had thought to be wrong and how Professor Yeldon had been put out about it, and then when the results of his analysis had been assessed it was found the formula for that kind of work was indeed wrong, and his own adjustment of it would in future be used.

'Why, Sam,' I said, 'you'll be famous!'

He shook his head.

'Research work isn't getting famous,' he said, 'only the final few make that grade. The bulk of it is the closing up of the blind alleys, some of them infinitesimal, yet entailing years of work. Only when all the false leads and blind alleys are closed up can the final few make a straight path to discoveries.'

'Then you won't be famous?'

'I fear not. I fear I won't even be heard about. But I'll have made my contribution, small though it may be.'

'Nonsense,' I said, feeling I sounded like Mama.

We drank gallons of boiling tea and, alas, I smoked cigarettes again.

'Where shall we go to celebrate?'

'How much money have you got?'

'None.'

'I haven't either.'

'Let's hunt around.'

We turned out all the pockets of all the coats; all the handbags, and we looked in the jars in the mantelpiece and under the shelving paper in the cupboards. We searched every drawer. We found enough for my fare to school in the morning and one-and-sixpence. It consisted of two threepenny pieces and the rest in pennies and half-pennies.

'It's enough for the ninepenny pictures,' I said, 'if we walk down Streatham Hill.'

'Let's go. We can take some apples to eat.'

We had crossed the world for Sam to get his doctorate. Now he had won it. So we went to the ninepenny pictures at Streatham to celebrate. The same way we had celebrated my book. Somehow it seemed rather fitting.

I didn't tell the staff at St Hilda's. I had learned my lesson about thrusting knowledge on them. I would wait till they asked.

November darkened and deepened into December. I had

only two weeks to go. When I wasn't teaching I busied myself turning out the stock cupboard and restoring and even repainting some of the children's apparatus.

One lunch-hour Miss Anderson and Mrs Illington-Etc. made a rush trip to the West End to do some shopping. When I had finished my sandwiches I went into Miss Bernard's room.

'May I sit down for a while?' I asked. 'Have you a few minutes to spare?'

'Oh please do.'

She jumped up and fussed about putting a chair for me. Near the fire, but not too near.

'How's the rheumatism?'

'Bad,' I said. 'I couldn't sleep after about three o'clock.'

'Perhaps it's just as well you're going back to a warm climate.'

'Yes, it takes the sting out of leaving.'

'You're sorry to go? You like it here?'

'I love it and I'm sorry to go. But I'll come again. I've started planning it already. That reminds me, I must tell the Vicar something. He told me when I first came here that after two years I would understand why a soldier sits on a horse outside the Horse Guards in Whitehall.'

'Of course, my dear. It's most important. It's *tradition*.'

'I know. I understand it all now. I didn't at first.'

I looked at the quaint little middle-aged schoolteacher with her shocked face and smiled.

'You know, if you came to our country you wouldn't understand it at first, either.'

'Oh, my dear. But I'd never go.'

'Why wouldn't you?'

'Too far. It's really out of the world, isn't it?'

'Right out of the world. When you go through Suez it's like going through a gate. You pass out of one world into another.'

'Dear me!' said Miss Bernard. She took off her spectacles and wiped them. 'How brave of you to come here.'

'Before I go, I want you to tell me something. It's not just vulgar curiosity, it's because I love the Vicar. I'd like to take away my picture of him. I know he's good, and kind and immeasurably understanding. Why is it Miss Anderson and Mrs Illington-Wharton don't like him?'

'Oh, my dear! Really! You shouldn't ask me such questions. It wouldn't do at all for me to talk. It would be quite unforgiveable.'

I studied my hands, then I looked up.

'It would be nothing against any of them really,' I said. 'They're all good in their own way. Do please tell me, Miss Bernard.'

'Well, since you are going away, it couldn't matter very much, could it?'

'Not to anyone here.'

'Well, you see. It's mostly to do with their religion. They rather think St Hilda's neither one thing nor the other, if you understand what I mean.'

'It couldn't be just that, a difference in the practice of one's faith. That's all it amounts to, isn't it? Is it the carpet slippers, do you think?'

Miss Bernard assumed her shocked expression.

'My dear, he shouldn't really do that. Now should he? A man in his position.'

'Christ wore sandals. Besides, he has a bad bunion, the Vicar, I mean.'

'Oh, the poor man! Why ever didn't we know?'

'I think it amuses him to remain silent. I expect he thinks that God extends his charity to all people, whole or lame. He expects us to be charitable, too.'

'Yes, of course.'

Miss Bernard remained silent quite a while evidently debating with herself as to whether to go on with her story.

'You see,' she said, 'they don't think the Vicar should call himself "Father Reilly" and be a married man.'

'It's not against the laws of the Church of England.'

'No, not at all. Not at all. Most of them in the very High Church just don't do it. There is an occasional one, of course.'

'That's what they hold against the Vicar? That he's a married man?'

'Not altogether. It was the way it all happened.'

Miss Bernard suddenly became confused and got up and fussed with the fire. She put coal on and then took half of it off again. She was embarrassed and still only half willing to tell me the story.

She sat down at last and went on with it.

'You see, there was a young Sunday School teacher, very young, very impressionable. You know what I mean, I'm sure. Always going to church and being at the Vicarage, and carrying the Vicar's things for him. Looking after his vestments. My *dear*,' Miss Bernard lowered her voice to sepulchral depths. 'She was really quite in love with the Vicar. Everyone suspected it. It was talked about quite a lot.'

'I don't think there's anything wrong with being in love with a man, you know.'

'But it was the *Vicar*, my dear. People didn't expect him to marry. At least, Miss Anderson and Mrs Illington-Wharton didn't. They rather prefer a Vicar *unmarried*.'

'Did he marry her?'

'It didn't quite happen like that. A most frightful thing happened. It caused a stir in the Parish. There was a horrible man who lived across in Banwood Way. He wasn't quite right in the head, you know. Used to stand around and speak to the young people. They weren't really frightened of him because he'd been doing it for years. He wasn't a nice person at all. One night he laid in wait, and there was only the little Sunday School teacher going home . . .'

Miss Bernard was truly agitated with the recollection of what she was now telling me. She twisted her hands together and her eyes avoided me.

'My dear, he *molested* her.'

'What do you mean—molested?'

Miss Bernard looked at me then looked away quickly.

'You mean a fate that is worse than death?' I asked.

Miss Bernard nodded.

'Somebody heard her scream, of course, and ran out. They got there in time, I think. I *hope*. They thrashed the man, all the young men down the alleys came out. They thrashed him. They nearly killed him.'

'Go on. What happened to the Sunday School teacher?'

'Everything seemed to quieten down and then someone, one of these nasty young men who stand about on street corners, said something very unpleasant.'

Again there was that shocked and embarrassed expression in her eyes. I thought Miss Bernard would never go on. At last she drew in her breath.

'He said, "If it had been the Vicar now, she wouldn't have screamed".'

Miss Bernard looked as if she could take the horrible words back. She almost waited for me to blame her for ever giving them utterance.

'Go on,' I said quietly.

'Quite a lot of people heard about it. The nasty ones sniggered a bit. You know how they can if they've no breeding and no education? Then the Vicar heard about it.'

'What did he do?'

'He went straight to her home and proposed to her.'

'Oh!'

I felt tears spring into my eyes. I wiped them away with the back of my hand.

'Do you think he should have done it?' Miss Bernard asked.

'You might as well ask Sir Galahad why he sought the Holy Grail,' I said. 'Please *don't* tell me that's what Miss Anderson holds against him?'

'Well, not that exactly. It was generally agreed he had been very chivalrous. But you see,' again the long, dramatic pause, 'after they were married, they had two children.'

'Why not? They're both his, I suppose?'

'Yes, but don't you see? He's not leading the celibate life!'

'Good Heavens!'

How could I explain to this quaint little soul who probably had never even had her elbow brushed by a member of the opposite sex what marriage was?

'You see what I mean?' said Miss Bernard.

'Yes, I see what you mean. I'm so glad you told me. I think it was wonderful, it's one of the loveliest stories I've ever heard.'

Miss Bernard's eyes stopped looking embarrassed and uneasy. Her glance wavered out of the window and then back to my face. It was wistful.

'I really think so, too. I never had the courage to say so.'

CHAPTER TWENTY-ONE

The last days of December were murky with fog and the pain in my left leg became almost unbearable. The ghost of misty damp Ireland was laid for ever. Mr Choppin came with the tea chests and they were filled with books, wired up and despatched to the docks. Sam went north for our last week-end in England so that he could see the home of his people outside Whitby. On Monday, the ship would sail and on Sunday I was alone. I had said farewell to St Hilda's and nearly said a tearful one when I left the Vicar.

'I'm sorry I never came to Confession,' I said.

'But you did,' he said. 'About once a week, if I remember rightly.'

'You mean when I came to the Vicarage?'

'Of course. What is confession but the opening of the heart? And you never went away that I didn't send my blessing after you, my child.'

'I won't ever forget you, Father,' I said. 'Nor St Hilda's.'

'What will you remember about St Hilda's?' he asked, with a twinkle in his eye.

'I couldn't catalogue all the things. I learned more about real education there than in all my preceding years. I learned that it is the child that matters and not a mere page of arithmetic.'

'Did you learn about Christian charity?'

'Yes, Father, and about chivalry, too!'

As I turned to the door he beckoned me back. He bent his head on one side like a conspirator.

'You didn't tell me if you saw any fairies in Ireland.'

'Only one, Father. He was a leprechaun.'

'As long as you can tell the difference between a good fairy and a bad fairy you'll be all right.'

He put his hand over his mouth and whispered out of the corner.

'Don't tell the fairies I said so, will you? They're very sensitive about being misunderstood.'

Here it was Sunday. Damp, foggy, drearily cold, and I was alone. I sorted out in my mind all the wonderful things I would like to see for the last time.

I chose Whitehall, Westminster Abbey and St Paul's. I had my lunch in the Piccadilly Corner House and took an affectionate farewell of the Guard sitting astride his lovely horse in Whitehall.

'Be here when I come back,' I said. 'Without you there'll be no England.'

On Monday Sam and Gerry converged on London, the former from Whitby and the latter from High Wycombe.

'How are the Arbuthnots?' I asked.

'Alive and breathing,' said Gerry.

'And Reggie?'

She shrugged her shoulders and turned away.

'Somewhere at sea.'

211

'Maybe there'll be another Third Officer on the *Jarvis Bay*.'

'I've lost interest in ship's officers,' said Gerry. Her words sounded hollow and did not ring true.

'I'd like to screw Reggie Arbuthnot's neck,' I said to Sam.

'She'll get over it,' said Sam, 'everybody does, you know.'

'Think of all those wasted lessons in voice production. She'll have to spend the voyage back learning to speak Australian again.'

The first day in the Channel I took three salt baths in spite of being swayingly sick. My leg felt better. In the Bay of Biscay I took three more salt baths each day. I'd got my sea legs and the pain was nearly gone. In the Mediterranean it went for ever.

The sea became calm, was blue and the sun shone. Gerry, looking older but better looking, was taking her modicum of fun with the men passengers and the ship's officers. Often, however, she was alone. She would spend hours leaning over the ship's rails gazing down into the slide of deep blue water below.

'I wish she'd snap out of it,' I said to Sam.

'She seems to me to be having a very good time. Sun-tan suits her, too.'

'But it's not *Gerry*. She's different. That flamboyant wit of hers, the way she used to be the centre of every party, it's all gone.'

'She's grown up. That's all.'

'She's got a broken heart.'

'Mildly cracked. perhaps.'

'That's what you think.'

Malta, Port Said, Suez. The Red Sea for once was kind with a pleasant head breeze. Then Aden, hot and cheap with the bum-boats crowding the stern of the ship and the black boys diving for pennies. I bought a quill box for a shilling when the vendor wanted two shillings for it.

'When you come back, Mrs Macintosh, you pay me other shilling?'

'It might be ten years.'

'I'll remember you, lady.'

I had a feeling he would.

'If ever we come this way again, Sam,' I said. 'Remember the one-eyed man. I owe him a shilling.'

The ship was Aberdeen and Commonwealth Line, so the

boatees called everyone by a Scottish name.

Six days through dry monsoon to Colombo!

At Colombo Gerry left us.

We came into harbour just after sunrise and the morning lay with a glimmer of pearl-shell over the harbour and the yellow palm-fringed shores. It was warm, with a hint of the day's heat yet to come.

The steward had brought us early morning tea and we were up and dressed to see the ship glide into harbour. All around us lay ships with a future of glory hanging, an unseen aura, over them. Our feet were on the decks of the *Jarvis Bay*. Beside me, and taking precedence because she was a Royal Mail boat, was the *Rajputana*. *Renown* and *Hood* lay off the coast. All now was still and peaceful and very lovely in the first hour of a tropical day.

A flotilla of bum-boats was waiting like a fringe of seaweed a hundred yards away. When the clearance flag went up they would assail us with their gaudy wares and high, thin, musical cries.

I stood looking over the side and talking to the Purser. Now and again he leaned out and looked up to the signal flags on our own ship. He pointed them out to me.

'That's the Customs, the next is the Doctor's flag. There goes the Mail. Now you watch that brown motor-boat come in. Expecting any letters?'

'There'd better be,' I said. 'With a family the size of mine you'd expect at least one letter per port.'

'What ho!'

The Purser was looking up at the signals.

'Naval Intelligence. See that flag go up?'

'What do we want with Naval Intelligence?'

He shrugged.

'Who knows? Look, here it comes.'

A small grey cutter shot out from the shore and cleaved its way towards us. It carried the blue ensign and I could see an officer in tropical whites standing in the stern sheets, balancing himself as if standing at ease, legs slightly apart. I remembered when we had been going to England seeing Reggie Arbuthnot rejoining the ship from one of those boats. He had looked so clean-cut, naval and handsome. I remembered a woman saying:

'Makes you proud to be British, doesn't it?'

213

The First Officer ran down the steps from the bridge and stood waiting at the top of the newly-lowered gangway.

I watched the cutter nearing the ship and I couldn't drag my eyes away from the man standing alone on it. He was so like Reggie Arbuthnot. Could history be repeating itself? My heart began to pound and I'm certain my eyes began to bulge. It was Reggie Arbuthnot! His face was turned up scanning the decks. How bronzed he was!

'That man,' I said to the Purser. 'He was the Third Officer on the *Moreton Bay* going to England two years ago.'

The Purser grinned.

'Probably on a special assignment. You might have been carrying a load of spies. Do they have spies in Australia?'

I wasn't listening to him. I leaned so far over the deck I nearly fell over.

The sailor from the cutter caught the gangway with his boathook and the craft came alongside. Reggie was still looking up, scanning the decks. He saw me and saluted.

He sprang on to the gangway and came up the steps to the deck. At the top the First Officer and he returned salutes. They exchanged a few words and the First Officer returned to the bridge. Reggie walked quickly towards me. He caught my arm. 'Where's Gerry?' he said.

'What do you want with her, Reggie?'

His uniform was naval and he had the rings of a Lieutenant-Commander, two and a half.

He grinned at me.

'I just want Gerry. Where is she?'

'I suppose she's below.'

At that moment Gerry, very tall and slim in her white linen dress, came round the corner by the Officer's quarters. Reggie almost plunged forward. He caught her by both arms. I don't know what he said, but the next minute he had pushed her into the companionway leading to the First Officer's cabin. They disappeared. The Purser stood looking at me quizzically.

'Funny sort of spies Intelligence is looking for today,' he said with a grin.

'Could be, could be,' I said, 'that that cutter is Gerry's ship come home.'

I ran into the lounge in search of Sam. Probably he was going the same way round the ship as I was, for it was ages before I found him. Then it was by bumping into him on the smoke-room stairs.

214

Sam looked astonished at my haste.

'Where've you been?'

'Sam, Reggie's here. The mystery's all solved. He's a naval officer. He's in Naval Intelligence. I suppose he couldn't say so before. He's with Gerry, they're in the First's cabin.'

'Hey, wait a minute. Not so fast. Reggie's here? How did he get here? Go on from there.'

'Oh, Sam. Don't be so *dull*. He's here. He came on a boat, of course. Do you think it's only a passing visit?'

'We can only wait and see. Where did you say they were?'

'In the First's cabin.'

'Is the First with them?'

'Of course not. He's on the bridge.'

'Then we'll have to wait till they come out.'

'Darling, give me a cigarette, quick.'

'Not before breakfast.'

He resolutely put away the packet he had automatically taken out.

We walked round and round the decks. It seemed as if breakfast would never come, and as if Reggie and Gerry would never emerge.

At last the gong clanged through the ship. I tugged at Sam's arm.

'Don't be in such a hurry. You'll get indigestion to begin with, and secondly breakfast won't bring Gerry and Reggie any sooner,' he said.

I could hardly eat my breakfast, but I realized that sitting at the table and toying with iced cantaloupe and hot coffee was something better to do than pounding round the deck trying not to look in the officers' companionway every time we passed it.

Sam ate his full breakfast with routine precision.

'Sam,' I said. 'You've got the patience of God. Why can't I have some of it?'

'A matter of glands and temperament, my dear.'

When at last we left the dining saloon we found Reggie on the deck talking to the First and Second Officers.

'Where's Gerry?' I asked.

Reggie was laughing at me.

'I haven't thrown her overboard,' he said. 'As a matter of fact she's gone to her cabin to get some clothes.'

I left Sam with him and fled down below.

Gerry had two suitcases out and was throwing clothes all

over the cabin. Her hair was nearly standing on end and she
had cigarette butts sticking out from ash trays all over the
place.

'For Heaven's sake, you'll burn the place down. Gerry,
what are you doing? What did he say? Where are you going?'

Gerry sat on the edge of her littered bunk and burst into
tears.

'I'm going to get married, and I can't find anything. Oh
Theodora, where are my clothes?'

'Making bonfires for burning down ships by the look of
those cigarettes. Here, give me one quick. Move over. Now
begin at the beginning.'

'I can't, I haven't time. I've got to pack, and I can't find *anything.*'

'All right,' I said more calmly. 'You're going to get married,
but I guess you've got all day, haven't you?'

Gerry was calmer.

'Yes, I suppose so. We can't get married until his superior
officer confirms it, probably tomorrow or the week after. But
I'm going ashore with him now. He's got a friend, somewhere
up in Kandy. I'm to go there.'

'Where's he been all this time?'

'He's Naval Intelligence. He couldn't tell me because he's
been a lot on passenger ships in the Near and Far East. But
it's all right now. He's got leave.'

'That accounts for Lloyds,' I said thoughtfully.

'What about Lloyds?'

'Well, I kind of thought I saw him there, milling round
amongst all those ships' captains and admirals and things. I
wondered why he didn't come over. I suppose he was *spying*
on them.'

'Don't use that horrible word. Intelligence is the proper
word to use.'

'If there's a war on the enemy won't discriminate.'

'Well, there's not a war on,' snapped Gerry. 'Now get off
my blue evening dress.'

'*My* blue evening dress.'

'Possession is nine points of the law and you've never worn
it. Where are my cosmetics and my underclothes?'

Sam put his law-giving head in the door.

'Happy day, Gerry,' he said. 'Reggie's just asked my permission. As head of the family . . .'

'Fiddlesticks,' I said. 'You wouldn't talk that way if Mama

216

was around. And how are we going to tell Mama? Send a cable?'

We all thought about that.

'I think we'd better tell her,' said Sam. 'Only nine more days.'

'And it won't cost so much,' said Gerry. 'Sam look at this mess. How am I going to pack anything?'

'Simply,' said Sam's calming voice, 'put away this big case first. It takes up too much room.' He suited the action to the word. 'Now in this case pack your immediate needs. A change of everything, cosmetics, slippers. Don't forget your tooth-brush.'

Reggie's head appeared over Sam's shoulder.

'Gerry, have you had any breakfast?'

'No,' she wailed, 'I haven't eaten for years.'

'How would you like to breakfast with the Captain and the Pilot not to mention the Medical Officer of the Port of Ceylon.'

'I'm coming ... wait a minute till I find my lipstick. Theodora, you pack for me. And darling, don't forget the blue dress.'

She went out like a flurry of cyclones.

'Now,' said Sam, rapidly restoring the cabin to law and order, 'we'll pack one case first and send it ashore with her. The rest can follow before we sail tonight.'

I sat down on the bunk again.

'Thank God for you, Sam. You're so *calming*. I sometimes think if it wasn't for you we'd one day fizzle up and go off.'

'I wish you wouldn't talk in superlatives and positives. Sometimes I think you'll fizzle up anyway.'

Thus it was, on a brilliant summer morning, we came home to Pepper Tree Bay without Gerry.

Down on the wharf below us stood Mama, no worse for her long hard way home; Vicky, looking, as always, like a million dollars; Mary, slim and a little pale but better from her illness. Denney, of course, was directing operations amongst the Press unit.

From the height of the deck we could not tell them about Gerry, so while they looked up, their eager Irish-Australian faces full of curiosity and puzzlement, we looked out over their heads, beyond the Customs sheds, the grey, paintless roofs of Fremantle, to the curve of the river where it coiled round the yellow sands of Pepper Tree Bay.

'On Saturday,' I said to Sam, 'we'll go sailing.'

'In nothing less than a twenty-footer,' agreed Sam.

'And on Sunday we're going to lie and sunbake on the beach.'

'All day,' said Sam.

I looked wistfully down at the row of Montgomery faces.

'I wondered if they remembered to bring some peaches and some money to tip the stewards. We haven't anything, have we?'

'Don't mention tipping to your mother. Not till after they've given us the peaches,' said Sam.

"Rarely has a writer of our times delved so deeply into the secret places of a woman's heart."—*Taylor Caldwell*

DENISE ROBINS

LAURENCE, MY LOVE. Vere's homecoming is brightened by meeting a handsome suave neighbor—until her mother hints darkly that because of a secret past she can never know happiness. . . .

GYPSY LOVER. Was she beloved—or a pawn in a game of revenge? The Michael she loved was in reality Miska the Gypsy, and his bitterest enemy was her fiancé. It was possible that his love for her might very well be hatred. . . .

THE UNTRODDEN SNOW. A young girl's discovery that she was adopted sends her on a flight to Switzerland, where she finds love—and the mother who abandoned her!

LOVE AND DESIRE AND HATE. Fran suspected she was losing the man she loved to another woman—but if she fought back, she might destroy them all. . . .

YOU HAVE CHOSEN. When Toni came into a small inheritance, her roommate Helena offered to strike a bargain: for half the money, Helena would sell Toni her fiancé!

THOSE WHO LOVE. Convinced that he was a dying man, Noel persuaded Peta to marry him, hoping to repay her kindness with the money he would leave her after his death. But then Noel recovered. . . .

BRIEF ECSTASY. Hidden beneath a heavy wedding veil, Rosemary took Mercedes' place and married Pablo in her stead. It was to save Mercedes from a forced marriage, but Rosemary was now in the same predicament—Pablo refused to let her go. . . .

To order by mail, send 80¢ for each book (includes handling and postage) to Beagle Books, Dept. CS, 36 West 20 Street, New York, NY 10011.

Romance in the tradition of Lucy Walker

IRIS BROMIGE

AN APRIL GIRL. Philippa and Rupert's love was a fragile thing, needing encouragement to grow. But something in Philippa's past held her back—and Lucille Pallys was quick to take advantage of it.

THE QUIET HILLS. Christine and Rachel were friends—very good friends, so they thought—until handsome and charming Neil came between them. But was he after Rachel's money, as Christine accused—or did Christine want him for herself?

THE MASTER OF HERONSBRIDGE. Hoping to prove her independence, Charlotte left her wealthy parents to work for the Staverton family. But soon she was intimately involved in their traditions, their rivalries—and their romances.

ONLY OUR LOVE. Linda was sure her hated relatives were deliberately disgracing her, but she wasn't sure if her beloved Angus would see it that way.

THE TANGLED WOOD. Alison thought she had a chance for a new life—but an inherited feud with her nearest neighbors threatened her newly found confidence and her hopes for love.

THE STEPDAUGHTER. Bridget was no kin to the wealthy and tightly knit Rainwood family, and so she never felt completely accepted—especially when they began to spread rumors about the man she loved—the man who'd married her cousin.

THE YOUNG ROMANTIC. It seemed as though Robin knew all about what she did before she even had time to tell him herself. Something—or someone—was undermining their engagement—and she was totally helpless.

THE ENCHANTED GARDEN. Julian's garden had always been Fiona's refuge when her world became too harsh. She loved him dearly, but to him she was just a child—and Fiona thought the only way to bring him to his senses was to leave him.

THE CHALLENGE OF SPRING. When Tony died, Delia took refuge in her grandparent's peaceful country home, hoping to fill the void. But soon she realized she was in love with their neighbor, Gavin Dilney—a love whose destiny hinged on someone else's despair.

"A woman can hardly read it without a jolt of recognition . . ."
—*Savannah Morning News*

GENTLEMEN PREFER SLAVES
Lucille Kallen

A MAN'S HOME IS HIS CASTLE, AND HIS WIFE IS THE JANITOR

Somewhere behind the dishes, the laundry, and the economy-size dustcloth, lurks Ruth Bernard, Genuine Person. Not wanting to be washed down the drain of domestic drudgery, Ruth launches a campaign to go to work. All she has to do is find a housekeeper, not feel guilty about leaving her kids, and pacify her husband. The last obstacle is like a slave in the Old South trying to have an intelligent debate on civil rights with the owner of the plantation. . . .

"If you feel like giving up bed and board, plunging back into the glamor of a career, try it first vicariously with this provocative novel . . . all along the way you'll have a revelatory time."   —*Charlotte Observer*

"One of the most hectic laugh marathons yet. Author Kallen is the most humorous new writer this reviewer has read in several years. She writes with a pen dipped in friendly acid . . . devastatingly hilarious."
—*Worcester Sunday Telegram*

"You must have been living in my closet when you wrote that book. It was my life, any day of it . . ."
—Mrs. B. S.
Hyannis, Mass.

JANE DUNCAN

"My Friends . . ." are the men and women who shape Janet Sandison's life, from her girlhood in Scotland to work, love and marriage in England and the colorful West Indies. In this delightful series of novels, Jane Duncan creates a world of vivid characters, warm humor, and searching emotional understanding—and a plucky, perceptive heroine who is very much her own woman.

MY FRIEND ROSE . . . had classic beauty, a problem child, a cold husband, and a taste for illicit romance. And she had Janet to confide in, or order around, and, eventually, to suspect. . . .

MY FRIEND MURIEL . . . was clumsy, plain, pathetic; but she did have one talent—getting Janet in trouble. All the same, it was through Muriel that Janet met the devastating Alexander. . . .

MY FRIEND MADAME ZORA. Was she a true psychic or a pathetic fake? Either way, she had a decisive effect on Janet, her husband, and the home they loved.

MY FRIEND MY FATHER. Jean Grey becomes housekeeper for the Sandison family after Janet's mother dies—but Janet and Jean can barely tolerate each other. And so it comes as a terrible shock to Janet that the father she worships is going to marry the woman she hates. . . .

MY FRIENDS FROM CAIRNTON. Four oddly assorted women from Janet's past descend on the West Indies with a variety of views on life, love, and society—and Janet suddenly becomes the center of their squabbles—and accusations of adultery!

MY FRIEND MONICA . . . is the glamorous, wealthy, and sophisticated Lady Monica, who maneuvers herself into Janet's house, and when Janet is paralyzed in an accident, attempts to steal her husband.

MY FRIENDS THE MACLEANS . . . are established members of the Paradise Estate's hierarchy, and Janet has nothing but admiration for them—until their son Roddy pleads for Janet's help in escaping his parents!

MY FRIEND SANDY. Janet innocently becomes involved in several island scandals when she repels the amorous advances of a "friend!"

To order send $1.00 (includes handling and postage) to Beagle Books, Dept. CS, 36 West 20th Street, New York, NY 10011.

BEAGLE GOTHICS

*Novels of romantic suspense . . . each with an eerie twist
and a dark hint of the supernatural . . .*

The Craghold Legacy, *Edwina Noone*
   Destiny took her to the sinister old hotel in the hills—
   and to death. . . .

The Craghold Curse, *Edwina Noone*
   She fled one horror only to find another more ghastly
   waiting for her. . . .

The Craghold Creatures, *Edwina Noone*
   She searched for perfection and found a house that was
   perfectly evil!

Bell, Book and Candleflame, *Isabel Stewart Way*
   Was her dark heritage really the terror it seemed?

The Humming Top, *Dorothy Spicer*
   The toy, cherished since childhood, was the focus of her
   strange ability to see into the past . . . and future.

The Shape of Fear, *Lyda Belknap Long*
   Her holiday in an art colony turned to nightmare and a
   strange battle with dark forces.

House of the Deadly Nightshade, *Lyda Belknap Long*
   Foul and perverted rites performed by her ancestors
   threatened to claim her soul—as well as her body. . . .

Doomway, *Evelyn Bond*
   The letter came from the man who loved her . . . and
   who had been dead for a year!

The Girl from Nowhere, *Evelyn Bond*
   She spoke a prehistoric language while in a trance, and
   her strange ability threatened to destroy them all!

The Devil's Footprints, *Evelyn Bond*
   She had ignored the prophecy of doom—until one
   woman died—and now she knew she was next. . . .

Shadows on the Water, *Dorothy Fletcher*
   Her cousin was slowly dying in Venice—would she follow her down that same dark path to death?

The Scorpion of Chateau Laverria, *Mary Mann Fletcher*
   Her best friend had disappeared into the bizarre castle—
   and now she followed the same paths. . . .

The Second House, *Jan Alexander*
   She came to *La Deuxieme* to masquerade as a man's
   wife—then had to play the role of his widow. . . .

Historical romances by

HEBE ELSNA

Saxon's Folly. The eccentric nobleman adopted her, raised her—and then found he'd produced a young woman who baffled him! *A Regency romance.*

The Love Match. Caroline was determined to marry Lord William Lamb—even though his powerful and elegant mother despised her. *A Regency romance.*

The China Princess. Aminta's uncanny resemblance to a royal princess was the start of a dangerous game of intrigue and romance. *A Regency romance.*

The Brimming Cup. Two sisters, poor but beautiful, manage to enter into court society, becoming the center of admiration and envy, of love and hate. . . . *A Regency Romance.*

The Heir Of Garlands. As a child, Ormonde was pledged to marry her cousin Lance. But seven years after Lance is presumed lost at sea, a man claiming to be her cousin demands to be acknowledged as heir to the vast estates —and as Ormonde's betrothed! *A Regency romance.*

Gallant Lady. Barbara and her young cousin escape from France at the height of the Revolution. Instead of finding safety, she uncovers a plot to kill her cousin. And can she really trust the dashing Englishman who is aiding her?

The Queen's Ward. A fragile and delicate fifteen-year-old, Morag is summoned to the court of Elizabeth I, where her cousin Amy Robsart recently died under mysterious circumstances—and where Morag is ordered to marry by royal command. . . .

The Wise Virgin. She relied on wisdom and wit to avoid becoming one of Henry VIII's many wives. But how long could she repel the lecherous advances of a king?

To order by mail, send $1.00 for each book to Dept. CS, Beagle Books, 36 West 20 Street, New York, NY 10011.